Burn

ALSO BY PATRICK NESS

And the Ocean Was Our Sky

Release

The Rest of Us Just Live Here

More Than This

The Crane Wife

A Monster Calls

Monsters of Men

The Ask and the Answer

The Knife of Never Letting Go

Topics About Which I Know Nothing

The Crash of Hennington

Burn

PATRICK
NESS

WALKER
BOOKS

First published 2020 by Walker Books Ltd
87 Vauxhall Walk, London SE11 5HJ

This edition published 2021

2 4 6 8 10 9 7 5 3 1

Text © 2020 Patrick Ness
Cover illustration © 2020 Alejandro Colucci

"Burn Up"
Lyrics by Siouxsie Sioux
© Copyright 1998 BMG Rights Management (UK) Limited,
a BMG Company & Domino Publishing Company Limited.
All Rights Reserved. International Copyright Secured.
Used by Permission of Hal Leonard Europe Limited.

This book has been typeset in Sabon by User Design, Illustration and Typesetting

Printed and bound by CPI Group (UK) Ltd, Croydon CR0 4YY

British Library Cataloguing in Publication Data:
a catalogue record for this book is available from the British Library

ISBN 978-1-4063-9397-2

www.walker.co.uk

For Kim Curran,
golden soul

King Salamander, that's his name
A desert maker, that's his game
The benign Cremator, branding iron in his hand
Eager and willing to torch the land
—Siouxsie Sioux

Burn, baby, burn
—The Trammps

Part 1

1

On a cold Sunday evening in early 1957 – the very day, in fact, that Dwight David Eisenhower took the oath of office for the second time as President of the United States of America – Sarah Dewhurst waited with her father in the parking lot of the Chevron gas station for the dragon he'd hired to help on the farm.

"He's late," Sarah said, quietly.

"It," said her father, spitting on the oiled dirt, hitting the cracks of a frozen puddle. "Don't call it by its name. Don't tell it *yours*. It. Not he."

This didn't address the question of the dragon's lateness. Or maybe it did, in her father's sternness, in the spitting.

"It's freezing out here," she said.

"It's winter."

"Can I wait in the truck?"

"You're the one who was so eager to come with me."

"I didn't know he'd be late. *It* would be late."

"You can't trust them."

Then why are you hiring one? Sarah thought, though knew better than to say. She even knew the answer: they couldn't afford to pay men to clear the two south fields. Those fields had to be planted, and if they were, then there was a chance – a small one, but a chance – that they wouldn't lose the farm to the bank. If a dragon spent a month or so burning the trees, carrying out the ash and remnants, then maybe by the end of February, Gareth Dewhurst could be turning the charcoal over with a pair of cheaply hired horses and the plough that was thirty years out of date. Then perhaps by April, the new fields would be ready for planting. And perhaps *that* would be enough to hold off the creditors until harvest.

Such had been the overwhelming, exhausting thought of both Sarah and her father in the two years since the death of her mother, as the farm slid slowly beyond the ability of two people to run and further and further into debt. The worry was so strong it had shoved their grief to one side so they could work every hour her father was awake and every hour Sarah was not at school.

Sarah heard her father breathe out, long, through his nose. It was always his preamble to softening.

"You can drive home," he said, quietly, back over his shoulder.

"What about Deputy Kelby?" she asked, her stomach tensing as it always did at the thought of Deputy Kelby.

"Do you really think I'd be meeting a hired claw if I didn't know Kelby was off-duty tonight? You can drive."

She was five feet behind him but still hid her smile. "Thanks, Dad," she said. At nearly sixteen, she was a few months shy of being granted a licence by the great state of Washington, but a lot of things got overlooked for the sake of farming. Unless it was Deputy Kelby doing the looking. Unless you were Sarah Dewhurst being looked at, with her skin so much darker than her father's, so much lighter than her dearly departed mother's. Deputy Kelby had thoughts on these issues. Deputy Kelby would be only too happy to find Sarah Dewhurst, daughter of Gareth and Darlene Dewhurst, illegally behind the wheel of a farm truck, and what might he do then?

Sarah pulled her coat tighter around her, tying the belt. It was her mother's coat and she was already outgrowing it, but not by enough to find the money for a new one. It strained across her shoulders, but at least it kept her warm enough. Almost.

As Sarah put her hands back in her pockets, she heard wings.

They were an hour from midnight – the Chevron was closed, only security lights on – and the sky was bitter cold and sloppy with stars, including a spill of the Milky Way across the middle. This part of the country was famous for its rain, though more accurately for its endless grey days. This night, though, January 20, 1957, was clear. The three-quarter moon was low in the sky, bright but a supporting player to the specks of white.

Specks of white that now had a shadow cast across them.

"It won't hypnotize you," her father said. "That's an old wives' tale. It's just an animal. Big and dangerous, but an animal."

"An animal that can talk," she said.

13

"An animal without a soul is still an animal, no matter how many words it's learned to lie with."

Men didn't trust dragons, even though there had been peace between the two for hundreds of years. Her father's prejudice wasn't uncommon among people his age, though Sarah wondered how much sprung from the way the articulate, mysterious creatures so comprehensively ignored men these days, save for the few willing to hire themselves out as labour. In Sarah's generation, though, it was hard to find a teenager who didn't also want to be one.

This particular dragon was flying in from the north, which Sarah liked to think meant it had come from the great dragon Wastes of western Canada, one of the few natural landscapes left in the world where dragons still flew wild, still held their own societies, still kept their own secrets. She knew this was fanciful. Canada was nearly two hundred miles away, the Wastes a farther two hundred beyond that. Besides which, the Canadian dragons had withdrawn official communication with men a decade before Sarah's father was born. Who knew what they got up to in the Wastes these past fifty years? The individuals who still hired themselves out as labour gave no answers, if they even knew. This one was probably only coming from another farm, another place of grubby, poorly paid hire.

It flew over them.

He, thought Sarah. *He flew over them.* The only reason she didn't think *she* was because her father had slipped when he first mentioned the hiring. "It's not illegal," he'd said, which Sarah knew, "but there'll be trouble no matter what. We keep quiet until he's already working and no one can stop him."

14

Sarah was unsure what had happened in the intervening week to move so firmly from *he* to *it*.

Beyond the light of the gas station, the dragon remained a silhouette as it circled, but even so, Sarah was surprised by its size. Fifty feet from wing tip to wing tip, possibly sixty.

The dragon was small.

"Dad?" she said.

"Hush, now."

They watched it fly over them once more, then take off again into the sky. This meeting place wasn't so surprising, nor was the hour. Enough light and civilization to make the man feel safe, enough darkness and lack of other humans to make the dragon feel the same, what with everything her father had rightfully said about potential trouble. Even so, this dragon was clearly more cautious than most of its kind.

When it finally landed, she saw why. She also saw why it was so small.

"He's blue," she said, breaking several of the rules her father had set down.

"I won't tell you to *hush* again," he said, not turning around, for his eyes were only on the dragon now.

The dragon *was* blue. Or *a* blue, Sarah corrected herself, and of course, not actual blue but the blue of horses and cats, a dark silvery grey that tinged into blue in the right light. What he was not was the burnt blackish red of the Canadian dragons she'd occasionally seen working farms or flying over the mountains in the distance, making their trips to who knew where for who knew what purpose.

But a blue. A blue was Russian, at least originally, in heritage. They were very rare; Sarah had only seen them in books and was more than a little surprised she hadn't heard any local rumours of this one. A Russian dragon was also troubling for other reasons, what with Khrushchev, the Premier of the Soviet Union, threatening to annihilate them pretty much every week these days. Dragons didn't get involved in human politics, but having this dragon on their farm wasn't going to make the Dewhursts any new friends either.

It had landed just outside the ring of light from the gas station sign, the ring of light Sarah and her father stood well inside. The ground hadn't shaken when the dragon settled – a ginger step to the dirt from the air as it stopped its glide – but it did shake as the dragon came forward now, its head and long neck angling down low, the claws at the end of its wings hooking into the ground at each step, those great wings flaring on either side, making itself look bigger, more threatening.

When it finally came into the light, she saw it only had one eye. The other was scarred over, indeed seemed to have rope-like stitching holding it shut. The surviving eye led the rest of its body towards them until the dragon stopped and inhaled two big gusts of breath. Sarah knew it would do this. Their noses were sharper than a bloodhound's. It was rumoured they could smell more than just odour, that they could smell your fear or if you were lying, but this was probably the same old wives' tale about them being able to hypnotize you.

Probably.

"You are the man?" it said. The words rumbled from so deep in its chest that Sarah almost felt rather than heard them.

"Who else would I be?" her father replied, and Sarah was

16

surprised to hear a buried note of fear there. The dragon's eye narrowed in suspicion. It clearly didn't understand her father's answer, something her father saw as well. "I am the man," he said.

The dragon looked him up and down, then cast its eye over Sarah.

"You will not speak to her," her father said. "I only brought her as a witness, since that's what you require."

This was news to Sarah. A witness? Her father had made it seem like coming along was her own irritating idea.

The dragon kept its head low but arched its neck, looking for all the world like a snake about to strike. It brought its nose close to her father, so close it could have eaten him in a single snap.

Though that rarely happened any more.

"Payment," it rumbled. A word, not a question.

"After," her father said.

"Now," said the dragon, spreading its wings.

"Or what? You'll burn me?"

Another low rumble from the dragon's chest, and Sarah panicked for a moment, wondering if her father had gone too far. This dragon had lost an eye. Perhaps it didn't feel bound by the–

Then she realized it was laughing.

"Why does the dragon no longer kill man?" the dragon asked, a smile curling the ends of its mouth.

It was her father's turn to be confused. "What?"

But the dragon answered its own question. *"Society,"* it said, and even in the non-human (and for that matter, non-*Russian*) accent, even in its lack of a soul, Sarah could hear the amused bitterness with which it spoke the single word. "Half," the dragon said, negotiating now.

"After," her father said.

"Half now."

"One quarter now. Three quarters after."

The dragon considered, and for a brief moment its eye was on Sarah again. *It can't hypnotize you,* she reminded herself. *He can't do that.*

"Acceptable," the dragon rumbled, and sat back on its haunches, awaiting the quarter payment. Gareth Dewhurst turned to his daughter and gave a small nod. They had expected this, and Sarah went to the truck, opened the passenger door, and reached into the glove compartment. She pulled out the small shiny fingerling of gold her father had formed by melting down his cheaply made wedding ring. It was all they had. They had nothing left to pay the dragon with at the end of his labour, but her father had refused all of Sarah's attempts at solving that worry. "It'll be taken care of," was all he said. She assumed this meant melting down her mother's silver-service heirloom set, hoping the dragon would take the lesser metal, knowing it probably would.

But what if it refused? What if it took badly to being cheated? Though on the other hand, what choice did it have in the end? Even deputies who weren't Kelby wouldn't care all that much about a dragon being underpaid. Still, it didn't sit well in Sarah's stomach. Not much did. It was where she kept all her anxiety. And there was a lot these days.

She brought the small sliver of gold over to her father. He nodded at her, at her bravery, she thought, as he took it from her. He held it up for the dragon to sniff, which it duly did, in an intake so strong it was as if it was trying to pull the gold from her father's outstretched fingers.

"Meagre," the dragon said.

"It's what was agreed," her father said.

"What was agreed was meagre." But the dragon reached forward an open claw, and her father dropped the gold into it.

"Our deal has been witnessed," her father said now. "Quarter payment has been made. The agreement is sealed."

After a moment, the dragon nodded.

"You know where the farm is?"

The dragon nodded again.

"You'll sleep in the fields you're clearing," her father said. "You'll begin work in the morning."

The dragon didn't nod at this, merely smiled again, as if pondering how it had allowed itself to be so commanded.

"What?" her father said. "What is it?"

Another laughing rumble in the dragon's chest, and it said, again, *"Society."*

It took off into the air so suddenly Sarah and her father were nearly blown off their feet. Just like that, it was a shadow in the sky once more.

"It knows where the farm is?" she asked.

"It had to assess the work," her father said, heading back to the truck.

"Where was I?" she said, following him. "You said you got it through Mr Inagawa's broker—"

"You don't need to know everything." He got behind the wheel and slammed his door shut.

She opened the passenger side door but didn't get in. "You said I could drive."

He let out that long breath through his nose again. "So I did."

A moment later, they were on the road. Sarah shifted through the gears easily, even with the truck's notoriously sticky clutch, even through the hills and turns that marked this part of the county. She avoided potholes, she signalled even though they hadn't seen another car for miles, and she didn't pump the accelerator the way she knew drove her father crazy. He had absolutely nothing to complain about. He complained anyway.

"Not so fast," he said, as they trundled off the last stretch of paved street in Frome, Washington, the little hamlet their farm was in distant orbit of. "You never know when a deer could jump out at you."

"There's a dragon in the sky," she said, looking up at the stars through the windshield. "The deer will be hiding."

"If they know what's good for them," her father said, but at least he stopped talking about her driving. The road was black save for her headlights. No street lights, no lights from nearby houses as there weren't any, just heavy forest closing in like the night itself. They drove in silence for a few moments, Sarah thinking about having to rise in six short hours to tend to the chickens and hogs before heading to school.

Then she remembered. "What was that about a witness? What was I a witness to?"

"Dragons think men lie," her father said, offering an explanation but no apology, "and require at least one other to witness every legal agreement."

"Couldn't the witness just lie, too?"

"Of course, and of course it happens, but at the very least, the guilt spreads. Two men are compromised, not just one." He shrugged. "Dragon philosophy."

"*We* lied."

He glanced over at her.

"We did," she said. "We don't have any gold to pay it with at the end."

"I told you not to worry about that."

"How can I? Dragons are dangerous. We lied to it. The guilt is spread between both of us."

"There's no guilt on you, Sarah." His tone was such that no further questions were allowed, not least how much guilt he was carrying. "Besides, it's more about compromising *them*. Their sense of what a word means. Their adherence to whatever they regard as principles."

She couldn't help herself: "That sounds a lot like what creatures with souls do."

"Sarah," her father warned.

The truck flew off the road.

At first, Sarah thought she'd somehow swerved into a ditch as the front of the truck dropped, slamming her into the steering wheel and sliding her father all the way off his seat into the dashboard. He called out, but more in surprise than pain, catching himself with his hand. Sarah slammed on the brakes, but nothing happened. They kept rocking forward as if they would turn a complete somersault–

Until they were rocked back, both of them helplessly thrown into their seats as the rear of the truck now dipped.

"What the hell?" her father said, alarmed.

The truck rocked forward again, and Sarah looked out at the road.

Pulling away beneath them.

"He picked us up," her father said, stretching around to look out the back window.

Sarah glanced, too, though she was too afraid to let go of the steering wheel to glance for long. The rear claws of the dragon had grabbed the truck on either side, like an eagle that had just caught a salmon. Sarah looked forward again, at the road and trees that were now rushing past beneath them as the dragon's great wings beat, carrying them, she hoped, to their farm.

"He picked us *up*," her father said again, barely controlling his anger, not seeming to notice the change back to *he*.

"Is he going to drop us?" Sarah asked.

She could see that her father didn't know the answer. They were in the dragon's claws. They had absolutely no say in what would happen next.

2

He hit the ground hard, catching his wrist, and spent a moment not moving, purely out of hope he hadn't broken it. He breathed, and the pain settled down into an ache, not the livid sharpness of a break. He'd had those before, had the crooked collarbone to prove it. He gingerly rolled over and flexed the wrist. It hurt, but it would work.

With a grunt, he got to his feet. His bag had landed some twenty metres away and was only located after an increasingly frantic search. If he lost it, things would be much, much harder. Well, just say it: if he lost it, things would be impossible.

And that would be the end of everything.

There it was, though, deep in a fern that left dead spores stuck to his heavy winter coat as he dug it out. He unzipped the bag, checked the contents, closed it again. The important thing was there, but so were the rations of food and water that would allow him to make this journey interacting with as few people as possible.

Some interaction would be unavoidable. This didn't frighten him.

He was prepared.

It was after midnight, but he had a long walk ahead and was keen to start. A clear sky and bright moon lit the way. He was at the edge of a forest, as expected, near a road that followed a river. He would mostly keep to the latter, but at this late hour, the road would work best to get the miles begun.

First, though, he knelt to pray. "Protect my path, Mitera Thea," he said. "Keep me from distraction. Keep me from everything but the fulfilment of my goal."

He did not pray for safe return. He did not expect one.

Prayers done, he stepped gently from the grass to the road, as if it might rise to bite him or give way underneath his rough shoe. Neither happened, and he turned south. He began to walk.

It was cold, but again, he was prepared. The coat over a woollen top, the thick woollen trousers, gloves, and a cap that came down over his ears and nearly swallowed his face. It was a face others would trust, bright and surprisingly young, still a teenager, with blue eyes that neither threatened nor dazzled, a smile that was modest and appealing and wholly lacking in danger.

The last part was completely misleading.

He kept on through the night, the bag over his shoulders, enjoying the clouds of steam from his breath with an innocence that was perhaps younger than his apparent age. He passed a few houses, pulled far back from the road and isolated from one another, but he didn't see a single car. In fact, it took until sunrise, when he was almost ready for his first rest, to hear the distant churn of an engine.

An enormous yellow Oldsmobile turned onto the road well ahead of him. Hiding was simple; he disappeared into the thicker forest on the non-river side of the road and waited. He sat against a tree, facing away from the road, listening to the car's engine grow louder. He was unafraid. They would likely not have seen him, and even if they had, what more was he than a normal young man out walking? He dug into his bag for a small bite of hard tack biscuit while he waited for the car to be on its way.

He had the second bite halfway to his mouth before he realized the engine had stopped changing in pitch and volume. He listened. Yes. The engine was still running, but the car was no longer moving. He took a slow, slow peek around the trunk of the tree, back towards the road.

The car had stopped exactly where he'd entered the woods. It was enormous, all curved corners and obvious weight, like a bull ready to charge. It sat there in the frozen morning, on a deserted forest road, as if waiting for him. Through the trees he couldn't quite tell how many people were inside or what they might be doing. There was a small click and the car seemed to settle. He guessed that this was as it shifted from drive to park.

He returned the biscuit to his bag and with a flick of his wrists, slid into his palms the razor-sharp blades hidden in his sleeves.

The woods were quiet at sunrise. Even without snow, the frost was thick. No insect yet buzzed, no morning bird sang. The only sound was the engine and his breath.

His eyes widened. His *breath*. Great steaming clouds of it, giving him away as surely as if he'd lit a fire. But then, he thought, why should this be a hiding place? Why should this be anything more than the curiosity of a random driver wondering why a man walked off the road into the woods? On the face of it, nothing unusual was happening.

He heard first one, then another car door open. Open but not close, the engine still running. The risk of another peek was staggeringly high, but how could he not? He held his breath, slunk down the tree until he was almost lying flat, then slowly, slowly, slowly, peered around the lower trunk.

The first gunshot took out the side flap of his hat and the middle of his left ear. The bullet reached him before the sound did and for a dizzying few seconds, he had trouble linking cause and effect, thinking he'd merely been stung by an out-of-season bee. The second gunshot tore away a fistful of tree terrifyingly close to his face. He dodged behind the trunk again as the shots kept coming, striking the trees around him, a shower of splinters raining across his body.

His ear hurt now, and when he touched it, his hand came away with an amount of blood that made him focus. He had no gun himself. There had been reasons, good ones, why he was only armed with knives and blades, plus it had been thought the level of counter-aggression he might face was too low to need his own gun.

Too late to complain, he supposed.

The firing stopped, and for a moment, the only sounds were the engine again and one angry, distant crow expressing its displeasure at being woken.

"There's no way out of this, Malcolm," a man's voice called from the road.

Malcolm. One of the names he had been given to use from a list of a dozen, to cycle through should they be needed. It was a very early one, which probably meant something about who these men were, but he didn't know what that was.

"Throw down your weapons," the man continued. "Believe it or not, Malcolm, we want you out of this alive."

"You shot me in the ear," he called back.

"Throw down your weapons," the man said again.

"I don't have a gun."

"Now that, I don't believe."

"Then we have a problem."

"Not *we*, Malcolm," the man said. "I don't have any problem at all."

Malcolm – he embraced the name for the moment – pulled his bag onto his chest, hoping it contained a surprise or two, knowing it didn't. He heard a branch snap over to his right, almost certainly another man coming around to flank him. Another man with another gun.

The bag held nothing he didn't expect. The only thing different about it from two minutes ago was the bloody hand-print he'd added to the cloth.

"This cannot be," he whispered. "This cannot be the end, so soon after the start." He looked up into the rising grey of the morning. He put his hand back to his throbbing ear and whispered again, a plea, a prayer, a wish: "Mitera Thea, protect me."

He held his breath and listened again. The walker to his right had either stopped or gotten better at disguising his steps. The man on the road was quiet now, was perhaps advancing, too.

There was a new sound. One the men wouldn't have heard yet. But Malcolm did, because he had been listening for it.

"I surrender," he called out.

A pause. "You do?" the man on the road said.

"If you give me a moment," Malcolm said, "I'll lay down my weapons and step away from them. No one needs to get hurt."

"I agree with you, Malcolm," the man said, "but how do I know you'll keep your word?"

"I can only guess you know where I come from? What I Believe?"

"We have an idea, yes."

"Then you know I cannot, *will* not, lie to you. Even though you shot me, I'll still surrender to you." He turned his head so his voice would carry back better to the first man. "It's a matter of principle."

Malcolm could almost hear the man thinking.

The second man, clearly sensing the same thing, shouted, "It's a trick!" to the first man, his voice contemptuous. "You know what these people are like. They're fanatics. And the intel says—"

"Yes, I know what these people are like," the first man said. "Which is why I know what they mean by that word. Principle."

"As if there aren't ways around principles," said the second. "As if you and I don't know how every principle *and* its opposite can be justified."

"Are you philosophers?" Malcolm asked, genuinely curious.

For answer, a bullet struck the tree trunk above his head. "Philosophical question," said the second man. "Was that a warning or was that a miss?"

"The philosophical part would be wondering if those were the same thing."

"They're not."

"And there you are," Malcolm said. "Your philosophy."

"Will you *shut up*, Godwin?" the first man snapped.

Godwin shut up.

"I'm going to count to ten, Malcolm," the first man said. "At ten, you'd better be standing where both of us can see you with your hands up. Understood?"

Malcolm closed his eyes and whispered a prayer of thanks, before saying, "Understood."

"I mean it. One false move, and the philosophical questions will end. And that is a matter of *my* principle. Now... One."

Malcolm breathed, pulling his senses away from his throbbing ear.

"Two."

He exhaled through his mouth, watched the enormous cloud of steam that erupted from it.

"Three."

Malcolm sat all the way up.

"Four."

He pushed himself to his feet. He could see Godwin now, a stout man altogether different than Malcolm had expected.

"Five."

"Quit staring at me and get a move on," Godwin said.

"Six."

"I'm sorry for this," Malcolm said.

"Seven."

"Sorry for what?" Godwin said, and exploded in a wash of fire and blood that Malcolm stepped back behind the tree to avoid, not incidentally stepping out of the line of sight of the first man's gun. He still caught a wave of blood across the side of his face, Godwin's mixing with his own and spattering Malcolm's bag. Flames clawed at the tree trunk, scorching it but not catching.

The bag, of course, was fireproof.

"What the hell was that?" the first man shouted. "You said you'd surrender."

"I *am* surrendering." Malcolm pressed himself back into the tree trunk for what he knew was coming. "I can, however, be overruled."

The screaming began a second later and ended two seconds after that, so at least the man did not suffer long. Malcolm waited until the roaring stopped, until the great lunging of wings quieted in the sky and all that was left was the tick of cooling metal and the pop of boiling rubber.

"Thank you," he breathed, in unfeigned amazement. "Thank you."

He gathered his bag, Godwin's blood already drying. He didn't look at the blackened circle of forest where Godwin had died, just headed quickly for the road.

The Oldsmobile was now a philosophical question all on its own: was it still a car if most of it had ceased to exist and what was left fit into a shallow puddle? Was there a spirit to the Oldsmobile that could be said to still live if Malcolm remembered it?

He crossed the road ten metres down from it lest the heat in the tarmac melt his shoes. He entered the trees that led to the riverside, hoisted his bag onto his back, and continued his walk, not looking back.

He would rest later.

For now, there were a good hundred and eighty miles to go to the American border.

3

"Where did your father find a blue?" Jason Inagawa asked Sarah as they walked the dirt road back from school.

"From the broker *your* father recommended," Sarah replied, surprised.

The sun was out, but it was still near freezing. They kept their steps quick to stay warm; the school bus never seemed to make it out to the farms of the school's only mixed-race girl and one of its very few Asians. Funny that.

"Yeah, but he never mentioned a *blue*," Jason said. "I've never even heard of a blue around here before."

"Me neither. But my dad said he was going to give your father a piece of his mind after what the dragon did."

The dragon had not killed them. Of course. Dragons never did any more. No one quite knew how long dragons lived – the rumours of immortality were surely just that – but a dragon valued its life enough not to break treaties hundreds of years old with a species that had proven especially adept at weapons

33

of mass destruction. The periodic and costly dragon/human wars across the millennia had finally ended in the 1700s. Dragons had moved to their various Wastes around the world at more or less their own request, and a peace had endured long enough for humans to turn their aggression against themselves. World Wars I and II – from which the dragons had completely abstained – were the two most obvious examples, among countless smaller ones. Even just this week, the Soviet Union had captured an American pilot spying on them. Eisenhower had threatened retaliation if the spy wasn't returned, but retaliation these days meant bombs big enough to vaporize entire cities. Sarah knew kids at school who prayed every night that they'd wake up in the morning. Truly, despite their ability to squash, swallow, or melt any human with barely an effort, dragons were quite far down the list of human worries these days.

This hadn't made Sarah and her father's flight home in their truck any less harrowing.

"If you *ever* pull a stunt like that again!" he had shouted, after the dragon had safely dropped them in their drive.

"You will do what?" the dragon rumbled. "Pay me even less?" It sounded amused and certainly didn't look at all troubled by Gareth Dewhurst's ranting.

"I mean it, *claw*," her father said. "The authorities around here don't take kindly to dragons."

"The authorities cannot fly," the dragon said, taking off, leaving her father mid-sentence and circling to the first field where it already knew it would work. Sarah watched it curl up at the edge of the trees. She had no way of knowing for sure, but some part of her felt certain that it had fallen promptly to sleep.

"I'm going to give Hisao Inagawa a piece of my mind," her father had said, stomping into the house.

"People are always giving my father a piece of their mind," Jason Inagawa said now. "You ever notice that?"

"They did to my mom, too," Sarah said, feeling the usual quickening in her chest at speaking about her mother. "Especially when she caught Mr Hainault cheating her at Frome Grocery."

Jason left a respectful silence after this, as he had since she became motherless like him, a rarity in a time when it had mostly been fathers lost to war. It had brought them closer, but they'd been friends (and sometimes more than friends) since they were little kids who noticed they looked different from everybody else. They were only three weeks apart in age, both had even been born on their farms, though Jason's first memories were all from "Camp Harmony", the name given to the internment camp over at the Fairgrounds in Puyallup where all the Japanese families from Washington and Alaska had been forced to move. Even that had only been temporary: not-even-yet-walking Jason Inagawa and his mother and father – both born in Tacoma, both US citizens, both viewed as potential "enemy collaborators" by the government for no other reason than their heritage – had been sent on to a permanent camp in Minidoka, Idaho, where, two years into their three-year forced stay, Jason's mother had died of pneumonia.

People talking about the Inagawas used the phrase "at least" a lot. *At least* Hisao had managed to get his own farm back; not everyone had been so lucky. *At least* no one bothered them too much any more in this part of the country where there were *at least* a few other Japanese families around.

35

Sarah was careful to never say *at least* around Jason if she could help it. They also never went to the Puyallup Fair, which ran every September, no matter how many times people at school said it was great.

"Did the dragon tell you his name?" Jason asked now.

"I'm not even supposed to tell him mine. I'm not even supposed to call him *him*."

Jason kicked a rock across the road as they walked. "The red we hired when I was a kid we called Grumpy. She didn't seem to mind."

"Like from *Snow White*? Ours would definitely mind."

"You could call him Doc. Or Sneezy. That's a good name for a dragon."

"Or Lippy," Sarah said. "He sure does know how to talk back."

"They're supposed to be scholars, blues. Super-smart, but tricky."

Sarah scanned the horizon. "We should be able to see him now."

They were coming around the last small hill that blocked the view of Sarah's family farm – Jason's was down the road another half-mile. The two fields that needed clearing were farthest off the road, edging onto the base of another hill with a radio tower on top that began the vast forest which reached all the way to Mount Rainier.

"There," Sarah said.

The dragon rose from the field amid faint columns of white smoke, carefully controlling a stream of flame. He had to, lest he start a forest fire, but dragons could control their greatest weapon with terrifying ease.

"It's small," Jason said.

"Blues are smaller," Sarah said, feeling oddly defensive about her dragon. Though, she supposed, it was in no way *her* dragon. "He's still plenty big."

"And agile..." The dragon spun, perhaps a little ostentatiously, before aiming quick white-hot blasts at three of the thicker trees in the field. They were more or less vaporized in equally quick puffs of white smoke.

"He's showing off," Sarah said.

"He's going to attract attention," Jason said, and the words were almost prophecy, for who should come driving down the road behind them but Deputy Kelby himself.

"Nuts," Jason muttered under his breath as the police car pulled to a stop next to them.

"Shouldn't you two be at your chores?" the Deputy said through his window, kept open despite the cold so he had a place to spit his chewing tobacco.

"We're on our way home from school," Sarah said.

He smiled at her, his teeth smeared with black dregs of tobacco slime. He spat it "accidentally" too close to their feet. "You're on your way home from school what now?"

"We're on our way home from school, *sir*," Sarah said.

"Heard your daddy hired a claw. A Russki, no less."

Sarah and Jason turned to see the dragon now tearing up burnt stumps with its back legs and tossing them almost jauntily into a pile. "That's some good detective work, Deputy," Jason said.

Kelby's face hardened fast as a snakebite. "You giving me lip, boy?"

Sarah stepped in, trying to head off trouble. "Nothing

against the law in hiring a dragon and they aren't involved in governments–"

"Nothing against the *law*," said Deputy Kelby, "about marrying outside your own kind." He spat again. "Don't mean people gotta like it." He looked back out to the dragon. "Don't mean people gotta put up with it."

"Well, yeah, actually," Jason said, "it kind of does."

"*Jason*," Sarah hissed.

"What did you say to me?" Deputy Kelby was all eyes on Jason now.

"If there's no law against it," Jason said, "then that actually does mean people have to put up with it. That's how laws work."

Deputy Kelby took a moment, then he put on his Deputy hat with a deliberateness that spoke of no good whatsoever. "Was it law," he said, "when your country bombed mine at Pearl Harbor?"

"*This* is my country," Jason said. "This one, right here, where we're standing."

"Was it law," Kelby said, getting out of his car, one hand on his gun, the other on the billy club in his belt, "that killed my daddy in Guadalcanal?"

"Was it law that dropped nuclear bombs on Hiroshima and Nagasaki?" Jason said, his gaze level with the Deputy's.

"Jason," Sarah said again, sickened at how quickly this situation had gone south. It was getting worse, too. Kelby unbuckled the billy club.

"Human girl," a voice rumbled from the sky. The dragon was suddenly overhead, flying so close Deputy Kelby ducked. It turned a curve, then landed in the road, resting one long, hooked foreclaw on the hood of the Deputy's car, for seemingly no good reason whatsoever.

"Your father wants you home," the dragon said, turning his good eye to take in all three of them.

"Get your filthy claw off my vehicle," Deputy Kelby snapped, now unlatching the leather strap of his gun.

"I merely bring a message," the dragon said.

"I ain't seen you round these parts," Kelby said. "And I don't like making the acquaintances of new dragons."

"How interesting. The sentiment also applies to dragons about officers."

Kelby drew his gun, but kept it pointed at the road.

"I said get your claw off my vehicle."

The dragon seemed to smile again. *How does he do that?* Sarah wondered. There was the slight curl of a lip, obviously, but when a dragon smiled, it made you really realize how much of a smile was in the eyes. Or eye, in this case.

An eye it turned to Jason and Sarah. "Good mammals know when to return home," the dragon said, as it lifted its claw, leaving not so much as a scratch in the Deputy's paint. Sarah didn't need a second hint. She pushed Jason down the road in front of her, passing the dragon, who returned his attention to Deputy Kelby.

"A Russian dragon," the Deputy said. "In my town. With the way the world is today. You a Communist, claw?"

"I am a dragon," the dragon said simply.

"You a threat to my country?"

"I do not know. Are you a threat to mine?" the dragon said, and again, even though Sarah couldn't see his face now that she and Jason were heading fast to their respective farms, she could have sworn the dragon was still smiling.

* * *

Once she was sure Jason was as good as back to his own farm, Sarah cut through a line of trucks to make it to her own. Spectators from local farms, checking to see if the rumour was true that Gareth Dewhurst, of all people, had hired a blue. It was. The dragon was already back from whatever business it had exchanged with Deputy Kelby; she could see it in the field, burning trees and digging up stumps.

"Your daddy lost his mind?" one of them, Mr McKeegan, said, but in a friendly way.

"Does that seem likely to you, Mr McKeegan?"

"No," Mr McKeegan chuckled. "I don't suppose it does."

"This is going to cause trouble," another one, Mr Svoboda, said. He wasn't friendly at all.

"That seems possible," Sarah said politely, looking back to where Deputy Kelby was pulling in at the end of their long drive. A general groan went up among the farmers, each of whom started heading back to their trucks. Kelby was not a popular man.

Sarah was already in her bedroom by the time Deputy Kelby finally made it to the house. "What can I do for you, Deputy?" she heard her father say outside, loud and annoyed as he came from the barn, his voice not happy at all.

She didn't try to eavesdrop. No time. Kelby was a jerk, but he was right, there were chores to do, always, every moment on a farm. She'd have to face her father if he finished before she did. She changed out of her old school clothes into dungarees and rubber boots that made her look like a temperamental boy, but it wasn't like she had many options.

She went out the back of the house, grabbing the buckets she needed for the hogs and the chickens, filling them with feed from the granary, then heading over to the pens. The hogs were waiting for her. Three of them, all sows, Eleanor, Bess, and Mamie. They snuffled as she approached, greeting her in that way of hogs that sounded absolutely nothing like "oink".

"Here you go, girls," Sarah said, emptying feed into the trough. None of them were pregnant now. They'd sold the last batch of piglets to the butcher in the summer and were wondering how they were going to pay Mr Svoboda to bring his boar around in a few months to get them pregnant again. Maybe that's why he'd been so cross. She scratched each of them between the ears as they ate, which she knew they liked. "They're just pigs," her father always said. "Pigs who recognize me," she never quite replied.

Chickens next. They didn't recognize anyone, not even each other. She tried to love them, but honestly, she'd met smarter celery. "Get *back*," she shouted, shooing them from the pen door. She eyed the rooster, who always thought she was a threat that needed attacking. She hadn't bothered naming him, but the chickens were all Martha. All of them, collectively. The Marthas. It was just easier.

"That stupid man," she heard her father say as he came around the house. She knew he'd seen her because that's not what he would have said if he thought she couldn't hear him. "Did he bother you?"

She kept scattering chicken feed. If she stopped, even for one second, the rooster would start kicking her boots. "He tried."

"You stay away from him."

She gasped at the injustice. "How am I supposed to walk home? Over the mountains?"

"None of your sass."

"That's what he said to Jason."

Her father's temper changed. "He go after Jason?"

"It was going to be bad, too, until you told the dragon to come fetch me."

"Fetch you?" Her father looked surprised. "I didn't tell it anything."

Sarah stopped scattering feed. "Then why...?"

They both looked out towards the far fields. The dragon was currently pulling a large boulder into the air, then flinging it with almost contemptuous ease into the larger forest. They actually felt the thud when it hit the ground.

"He probably shouldn't be doing that," her father muttered, and she noticed the dragon was back to a *he*. "The *dragon* said I'd sent him?"

"Yes, sir." She gently booted away the rooster attacking her heels. "It's a good thing, too. We were fixing to get into real trouble."

"Huh," her father said, his all-purpose sound that could mean anything from "Fancy that" to "You're mistaken and I'm too embarrassed to correct you." Here, Sarah thought, it just meant her father was presented with something he didn't understand. She didn't understand it either. Why would a dragon care about *her*?

"Maybe he just hates sheriffs and wanted to cause trouble?" she suggested.

"That's probably it," her father said, but as he walked back towards the fields where the dragon was working, she didn't think he sounded convinced.

She waited until her father was asleep before she snuck out. She already knew which creaky stairs to avoid and how to close the back door so it wouldn't slam. Farm girls got responsibility young, which meant they had to learn how to break the rules that much earlier.

The dragon had told her father nothing that afternoon, refused to even acknowledge that he'd spoken to the Deputy, which seemed ridiculous since Kelby had railed on about it to her father for the entire time it took her to feed the hogs.

"He can't do anything," her father said at dinner. "I haven't broken the law."

"We should be careful, though," Sarah had said. "Don't give him any reason."

"If you think Deputy Kelby needs a reason, then there's more about the world I need to teach you."

That had made Sarah think of her mother, who had also felt the need to teach Sarah a lot about a world where things might not be easy for her. Sarah felt that any world that needed this many lessons must have something deeply wrong with it.

As for the dragon, he – for it seemed they were firmly in he territory now – had simply pretended her father wasn't asking any questions at all. "I am finished for the day," he'd rumbled as the sun set, curling up again in the still woodsy part of the field.

The woodsy part Sarah was heading to right now.

It had been a worryingly dry winter, though still bitterly cold. Another clear night, too, when they were usually deep into a fourth month of grey by this time of the year. But there were the stars. There was the moon. There was her crystal breath, white in the dark.

She had known no other home than this farm. Nothing on it scared or surprised her. The path she took was so sure under her feet, she wouldn't have been able to describe it as anything like a decision. This was her home, her movement across it as much as the ground itself.

The great anomaly of the dragon wasn't hard to track.

The first field he had been working still smouldered slightly, very faint in the moonlight. The smell was better evidence. Ash, certainly, but also a kind of odorous heat, charcoal, and beyond all that the faint chemical tang of the fire dragons generated in the organ just above their lungs. A tang so specific and un-human that a little voice in Sarah's head began to murmur her father's belief they had no soul. How could such a creature even really exist? How could they not just be a magical fancy? If they hadn't always been there, no one would have believed in them. That didn't stop every teenager she knew from wanting to be one, though, engaging in endless debates about the merits of the five types (red, blue, green, white, and desert), which continental Waste was the best, and what it would be like to fly. Sarah knew her choices, but would never have admitted them to anyone.

The dragon was curled around a small copse of trees in the far end of the field, seemingly asleep. She had no idea how to tell if a dragon was awake or not. For that matter, she had no idea if approaching a sleeping one was the height of stupidity. Had it eaten today? *What* had it eaten? It was near the forest. Had it found a deer or a beaver? Would it be very, very hungry if she turned up in the dark of night?

But no, that was foolishness. Childishness, even, something Sarah Dewhurst would never believe of herself. She simply had to speak to it, hungry or not, and there was no way she could do that with her father not safely asleep, back in his own bed.

"Hello," she called quietly. The dragon's head was turned back in the trees, so all she could really see was one great wing, covering himself as he slept. His great body rose and fell in breaths much slower than her own.

"Look," she said, "I don't know if you can hear me but..."

But what? What did she want to say to him?

"Thank you."

Maybe it was as simple as that. Kelby was known for administering beatings, and he no doubt felt he could have given one to Jason or even Sarah without much fear of reprisal or punishment. Then again, perhaps he wouldn't have beaten her. Her father was a white man, and his word would carry more in court than Hisao Inagawa's. Such was the broken world in which her father was judged for hiring a dragon.

"Thank you," she said again.

Did the dragon's breathing change? It was hard to tell. She was getting colder, too. She turned to go, vaguely disappointed both in the dragon and herself. She'd wanted to ask it why. Was it just hatred of officers? Did he do it just to deprive Kelby of joy? Maybe.

But still.

She found herself stopping. She found herself turning. She found herself saying, simply, "My name is Sarah," breaking the rule her father had set down so firmly.

Still no response. She turned and left again, but hadn't

gotten more than three steps before she heard, low, in the dark and the night, "I know your name, Sarah Dewhurst."

She turned back immediately. The dragon uncurled slowly from the trees, his great neck swinging around to her. She was suddenly more afraid than she'd expected to be.

"Kazimir," the dragon said.

"What?"

"My name."

"Cashmere?"

"Kaz-i-mir," the dragon enunciated. "It means 'Famed For Destruction'."

"Kazimir," Sarah repeated, then asked, "how did you know mine?"

But as with her father, Kazimir simply acted as if the universe had never spoken such a question. He re-curled his neck into the trees and, for all intents and purposes, fell back to sleep.

After a moment, still shivering, Sarah walked back to the only house she had ever known.

The dragon was not asleep, however. He had positioned his head so he could watch the girl pick her way deftly along the path back to the farmhouse. He didn't stop watching her until his one keen eye – so much sharper in darkness than a pitiful human one – saw her re-enter the house.

She was brave, much braver than most humans, to come out here on her own, at night, to speak to a dragon she did not know. He could already see the yearning in her, the *reach* so many humans had when they wished for more, a reach that was almost a magic on its own, if they only knew it.

Good, she would need all that in the days to come. There was so very, very much she didn't know. But she would learn, thought Kazimir. Yes, she would learn.

And oh, what a glory that might yet be.

4

"A red," said Agent Woolf, and Agent Dernovich could already feel his heartburn flaring.

"We're in western Canada, Agent Woolf," he said, a grump in his voice. "What sort of dragon would you *expect* it to be?"

She ignored him. She did that a lot, especially when dragons were the topic of conversation, and with Agent Woolf, there weren't many other topics. He watched as she bent over the uneven puddle of hardened steel that had, at some point this morning, been a fully operating car.

"We can't dally, Woolf. Even you must realize how this changes things."

"You can tell by the smell, mainly." She blinked at him with eyes that always felt like they were pinning him down to an opinion he was forced to make up on the spot. "The reds alone leave a trace of sulphur behind."

"Tell me something useful," Agent Dernovich said, "or don't tell me anything at all."

The FBI were allowed in Canada – the Cold War demanded cooperation, and Americans were always happy to take a mile when Canadians offered an inch – but Agents Woolf and Dernovich almost certainly weren't allowed *here*. Their mole on the local police force could only promise to keep the site secret for an hour, maybe two, before their Canadian counterparts – the Special Branch of the Royal Canadian Mounted Police – showed up.

Canada had an international reputation for politeness. The RCMP Special Branch did not.

Then Agent Woolf *did* say something that made this stolen hour worth all the future trouble it might cause. "This isn't dragon blood."

She was down the road from the wreckage – if "wreckage" was even the right word for such complete obliteration – kneeling directly onto the cold tarmac. The knees of Agent Woolf's cheap, Bureau-issued stockings were always full of runs and tears because she always raised her Bureau-issued skirt above them to kneel, which, to Dernovich, made absolutely no sense – the fabric of the skirt could probably stop your lazier bullets – but which he'd given up trying to explain as anything other than the typical behaviour of Agent Veronica Woolf.

That name, first of all. Veronica Woolf sounded like a *femme fatale* in a detective movie. Or the girl from college you could never introduce to your mother. It didn't even sound *real*, much less accurate for the dowdy, distracted, frequently-with-mustard-stuck-in-her-hair agent he'd been partnered with for the last eight months.

Female agents weren't common, but they weren't such unique ducks either. Paul Dernovich had even worked with one who'd done a sterling job gathering intelligence in Cuba. But Woolf was one of the Bureau's Dragon Specialists, who were already weirdos to begin with. They almost never went out into the field, and Dernovich thought Woolf was a pretty good example why.

Still, she did know her stuff.

"We've got another ten minutes at most," he said, looking at his watch.

"Human," she said, pointing to a rusty stain on the tarmac.

"How can you possibly tell–?"

"There are more drops and a stride between them," she interrupted, another thing she did. "A human stride."

Agent Dernovich looked at what she'd found. She was probably right, he had to admit, if only to himself.

"One of the agents who was here?" he suggested. "We could have an injured man out there–"

"Oh, no," she said, rising, "they're quite dead." She pointed to a faint white ring at the side of the metal puddle. "Vaporized fat," she said, as if discussing an order with the butcher. "Plus–" she reached down and picked up what looked like a coin from the tarmac– "remnants of a metal filling."

"Oh, Christ."

"I saw the same ring in the forest for the other one."

"Well, then, at the very least, there aren't any FBI bodies to have to explain–"

"But this," she interrupted again, gesturing back to the blood trail, "came after, or the blast would have evaporated it." She walked along the tarmac a few steps across the road. "As I thought." Dernovich went over to her.

More spots on the road, smaller, fainter, but there, if you knew where to look, disappearing off the edge of the road.

"Someone escaped," he said.

"They only did if the dragon wanted them to."

"And why would they want that? If they so casually broke hundreds of years of canon law about not killing humans?"

His irritation was not just about the murders – though they altered every single thing in what had seemed like a complete nothing of an investigation up until now – but the *thoroughness* of the killings. Faint rings of fat and nauseating metal fillings aside, these men, colleagues both, colleagues who had clearly jumped the gun on information they hadn't seen fit to show anyone else so who knew exactly how they'd ended up here, had been obliterated, *disintegrated*. By creatures who had stayed out of human affairs for all of Agent Dernovich's lifetime.

Even as late as an hour ago, Dernovich had assumed this case – and his pairing with Woolf – had been some kind of punishment from Cutler, their new boss, stitching an agent fresh from success in Havana onto a case with few leads and even fewer possibilities for real trouble just to show that, as new boss, he could. Ninety-five per cent of the Bureau was currently scouring the country for Communist infiltrators, and here was Paul Dernovich, in Canada, chasing stupidly vague rumours that had been circling around what was a widely despised but, at least in Paul's lifetime, completely harmless cult. "You're from the area," Cutler had said, which was only sort of true. "I need you there." It felt like an insult, because it *was* an insult, to a man who came *this*close to getting the job instead of Cutler.

52

But now, this. This absurd possibility that the whispers of danger were more than true, they were actually *terrifying*. If dragons were changing their behaviour now, if they were breaking the highest law of human/dragon coexistence and the beasts of unfathomable power decided they no longer needed to coexist with the *other* beasts of unfathomable power, if that had suddenly changed perhaps on this very morning...

Well, then, Agent Dernovich could only wonder if any of them would actually make it to the end of 1957. The dread was so strong he had, for the moment, forgotten their primary mission. Agent Woolf had not.

"I think we've found him," she said, a small twitch on her upper lip marking the happiest Agent Dernovich had ever seen her. "I think we've finally found him." She blinked. "Or her."

Malcolm's ear was becoming a problem. The small first-aid parcel in his bag had a single thin bandage that failed within an hour of him tucking it under what remained of his hat.

He would not die of the wound, but it was annoying. He washed his hands in the river for the fourth time in an hour, watching his coppery blood flake away into the current. All this stopping. He wasn't getting far enough from the incident with the car. People would be concerned. They would have questions. Insistent ones.

They would be looking.

So, the dilemma was thus: he was not moving fast enough, but to move fast enough, he would have to find a ride – he was only supposed to do this in extreme circumstances, which, he felt, this would obviously count – but in a car, not many people would forget someone bleeding from a hole where part of his left ear once was.

He knelt again to pray. "Help me, Mitera Thea," he whispered into clenched hands still cold from the icy bite of the river. "I beg your indulgence a second time. What should your servant do?"

The only answer was the ever-trickling sound of the river.

"So be it," he said, standing. "Thank you."

He would keep walking. He would ignore his ear. It would stop bleeding or it wouldn't. Whatever else happened, he had to trust he would be taken care of.

And so he was, for the rest of the day, at least. The river path wasn't arduous, sometimes veering back to the road he'd left, leading him under occasional bridges. As the sun crossed low in the winter sky, he grew hungry and his mind returned to the biscuit he had started ... was it only this morning? It was. A biscuit that had marked the deaths of two men. Men who had wanted him dead.

"You will be hunted," the Mitera Thea had told him. "I will help you if I can, but you must not be caught. At any price."

At any price, he thought, remembering again the melted car. Remembering the way the first man had just *exploded.* He breathed deep and tried not to think of it. The Mitera Thea knew best. He prayed to her, after all, even though she wasn't a dragon or any kind of god. She had always looked out for him, and that was enough. She had chosen him for this mission, trained him, and though he might go a year without seeing her as she went out into the world to spread the Believer message, she was still the closest thing he'd ever had to a mother.

"Thank you," he prayed again to her, almost without knowing he'd spoken the words. He stopped under a bridge, digging out the biscuit to finish it. As he swallowed the last of it, waiting for a truck to pass, he stood–

And woke a moment later, his face in the mud where it had been the only thing that stopped his faint. Now his nose was bleeding, too. He sat up, slowly, still woozy. He took off his ragged hat and put a hand to the sticky mess of his ear. How could it be bleeding this much? Enough to make him light-headed?

He washed his face in the river, gasping at the coldness of the water, splashing it on his ear. Fresh blood spouted from it.

"This is ridiculous," he whispered. "It's an ear–"

Then he remembered. The enforcers of law in Canada and the United States sometimes coated their bullets in anticoagulant. Not for when they shot men. For when they shot dragons. Dragonskin was unbelievably hardy, and if it didn't deflect the shot altogether, the wound would close so quickly you could almost see it happening. The anticoagulant was a development from the last ten years of the West's Cold War with the Soviet Union, even though neither of them were actually fighting dragons. Who had thought ostensible peacetime would be even more beneficial to weapons research than actual war?

It did mean one thing: the men today had been prepared to shoot someone other than just him, and now he was going to bleed to death from an *ear* wound on the first day of his mission. There was nothing for it. He would need a proper bandage, one that would at least hold the wound shut until the anticoagulant was out of his system.

He would have to find a store.

"But it would be helpful," Agent Woolf said, as they drove. "There was a memo on international, interdepartmental cooperation–"

"You actually read the memos?" Agent Dernovich asked.

"You don't?"

He glanced over to her. Her look of disgust was, apparently, quite real. He sighed to himself again. "Identifying ourselves and our mission to RCMP Security Services only after two of our agents are killed on Canadian soil might not go down well." He watched another car in the oncoming lane. A large Oldsmobile, two men in the front seat, each wearing the same hat Dernovich currently wore. "Speak of the Canadian devil," he murmured, "and he drives right by."

Agent Woolf turned to watch them as they drove past.

"Draw a little more attention to yourself, why don't you?" he snapped.

"If you made them as agents," she said, unbothered, "they surely made us."

He glanced in the rear-view mirror. They didn't seem to be turning around. But Agent Woolf was right. Again. Dammit. He sighed once more.

"Can you please stop that?" she asked. "Once one notices you doing it, one can't un-notice it, no matter how hard one might try."

Agent Dernovich sighed again, louder this time. "You hungry? I missed breakfast."

"I had a hard-boiled egg at the hotel."

"I'm going to take that as a yes." Crossing a bridge, he saw a diner on the left, across the street from a small drugstore. It was as good as any. Besides, if the RCMP *did* decide to turn back and ask them a few questions, it was better to look like he and Woolf had been expecting them all along.

A bell jingled as Malcolm opened the door of what seemed to be an appropriate business near the bridge. Betty's Drugstore, the sign read. *Please guide my words,* he prayed, in his head. *And please prevent me from having to kill Betty.*

"Help you?" said a woman's voice, before the jingling even stopped. He couldn't see her behind the shelves.

"Bandages?" he called back.

"Well, now, let's see what we've got..." He heard footsteps coming up the aisle. He panicked slightly, having to fight off the urge to run back out the door–

But the woman who appeared around a shelf of suppositories was small, roly-poly, with glasses shaped like cat's eyes. "Oh!" she said, looking right at his ear. "What on earth happened?"

Malcolm put his hand over it protectively. He had no idea what to answer. *I was shot* probably wasn't going to lead to an easy conversation.

He saw her eyes move from his ear to his wrist. His sleeve had fallen a little, exposing the skin there. Exposing the ink. The woman's face grew suddenly serious. Malcolm tensed, rapidly going through his options. He could physically overpower her, he thought, but would it *have* to end with–

"Was it those bullies again?" she asked. "At the high school?"

57

Malcolm barely knew what this meant. "Yes?" he ventured.

She tutted, took his arm, and led him to a shelf full of bandages. "I thought all that had stopped after that poor kid from Valemount drowned. I mean, I know you people aren't exactly *popular*, but violence tells you nothing about the victim and a whole lot about the victim*izer*, don't you think?" She took a box off the shelf, opened it, and lifted a ball of cotton up towards his ear.

"I can do it," he said.

"You got eyes on the side of your head?" She swabbed away the blood, then took out a large bandage, peeled back a sticky part, and stuck it firmly over the wound and down the back of his ear. "That's a lot of bleeding," she said, as she worked. "I'm Betty, by the way."

"Malcolm," Malcolm said, surprising himself. "You smell like flowers."

"It's my perfume," she said, a little embarrassed. "It's called Primitif." She walked towards the back of the store, clearly expecting Malcolm to follow. He did. "A bit fancy for rural British Columbia, but a woman's got to have her treats, don't you think?"

She went to the register at the back counter, making it ring with a few taps. "Thirty-five cents for the box, young man," she said, and smiled at him.

He thought to the money he'd been given. There was something close to five thousand dollars each in Canadian and American in his bag.

"I have thirty-five cents," he said.

* * *

"They do make a good corned beef hash up here," Agent Dernovich said, tucking into his.

"For lunch, though?" Agent Woolf replied, picking with some distaste through an admittedly dry-looking chicken supreme.

"I said I didn't have breakfast." He took another bite. "Besides, when in Canada..."

"What?"

"What?"

"When in Canada what?"

He blinked at her. "Do as the Canadians do."

She blinked back. "And they eat corned beef hash for lunch, do they?"

"It's on the menu, Agent Woolf."

"So are pancakes. I don't think I'd have *those* for lunch."

"Just–"

He stopped because his eye was caught by a young man coming out the door of – he read the sign – Betty's Drugstore. The young man's clothes were poor, or perhaps just very old-fashioned, or perhaps this part of Canada still had school uniforms designed with the word "prairie" in mind. Nothing particularly out of the ordinary, though nothing particularly *in* the ordinary either. If Agent Woolf had asked him straight out why this one boy out of everyone they'd seen on this trip had caught his attention, he wouldn't exactly have been able to spell it out but–

"Those are the public clothes of a Believer," Agent Woolf said.

Yes, Agent Dernovich thought, that was it.

Woolf watched the boy, too, as he trudged down the street,

bag on his shoulder, hand going once, twice, three times to the side of his head facing away from the agents.

Agent Dernovich frowned. "*Believers*. I've never seen so many otherwise rational people take such complete leave of their senses. Lost idiots."

"I used to be one," Agent Woolf said, calmly drinking her coffee, seeming to take no offence whatsoever.

Dernovich damn near sputtered. "You what?"

She pulled up her sleeve about two inches. Sure enough, a dense set of tattoos started there that Agent Dernovich knew would cover all the skin she wouldn't be expected to show the world. That it reached her wrists showed how deep her commitment had gone, at least at one point in a previous life Dernovich was now angry with himself for having had insufficient curiosity about.

Believers. A small cult that had sprung up two hundred years ago in BC and Alberta to worship dragons. It was insular and so surprisingly anti-human – despite being exclusively human in membership – it had never, unlike many North American sects, made the transition into a wider religion. They worshipped in churches they called Cells, observed a disgusting policy of free love and communal family-rearing, and were always led by someone called the Mitera Thea, "Mother Goddess" in Greek – a language neither of dragons nor western Canada – who was a kind of Pope to them, an infallible representative of a living deity. They even *prayed* to her, rather than any dragon god or goddess, because they considered themselves unworthy of direct contact. She controlled every aspect of their daily lives. When she died, the fools didn't free themselves, they just elected another.

They had been terrorists for a while, though mostly towards the end of the last century, burning down buildings deemed to be owned by the enemies of dragons, tearing down the border fences of the Canadian Wastes (even though the dragons themselves seemed to prefer the Wastes and obviously cared not for fences), and once – this was the bit that had sent the FBI to Canada, when the verb had resurfaced in their intel – assassinating the US Ambassador to Dragons as being insufficiently respectful in the 1890s. But that was decades ago, before Dernovich was born, before the dragons had withdrawn from communications even. Believers were a historical footnote that, by virtue of decades of quiet, had somehow persisted into an irrelevance to most people.

The great joke of it all was that – even when Believers were committing crimes on their behalf – the dragons seemed to ignore them as much as they ignored everyone else these days, which was to say, almost completely. What kind of person would worship a god who clearly lived in the world, but who just as clearly didn't care whether you lived or died?

They'd been watched idly by governments, usually by very bored agents nearing retirement, but filed away as a dead case. Until those now-somewhat-less-bored agents started reporting strange plans being made, hints of a prophecy the Believers thought was real, possibly even aided by a dragon or two. Maybe. The details were maddeningly thin and often contradictory. Through an improbably lucky car-search at the US border, they'd gotten copies of the runes that supposedly told this prophecy, but Agent Woolf went over them every damn day and could barely make sense of them either. Dragon runes were a spectacularly inexact language that changed with each breed, and so obscure they could mean anything or nothing. Except this time, the Believers clearly saw a something that had made them act. The dragons weren't talking, and worse, by virtue that most of the core Believers actually lived in the Wastes, they were technically under the purview of the dragons. You couldn't just barge in and start arresting people to get more information, as much as you wanted to.

Dernovich had considered it all a wild goose chase, even with the word "assassin" showing up now and then. Until Chase and Godwin – who were cold-interviewing members of the non-Waste Cells willing to talk to them (a perishingly small number) – had clearly found something they acted upon without deciding to tell the Bureau. Dernovich thought they were probably hoping to get in good with the new boss by making an arrest, but had instead turned up melted with their car this morning. Now he had to face the extraordinarily unpleasant possibility that the Believers not only did have a serious plan but seemingly the wherewithal to commence it with gusto. It was enough to make him lose his appetite.

"You're Canadian, then?" he asked Agent Woolf, setting down his fork.

"Montana," she said. "There are some isolated chapters in the wooded north of our own country, Agent, not just here."

"How long?"

"Until I was nearly thirty."

Dernovich wouldn't have guessed she was much older than thirty *now*. He was on the verge of asking when she answered. "Thirty-four," she said. "But I was on my way out of it for many years before then."

"The journey out isn't years long," he said. "You just *leave*."

"Spoken like someone with opinions on the subject but no actual experience."

His face got hot. "Not the way you want to be speaking to a senior agent, Woolf."

She shrugged, as if it was nothing. "I was merely being factual. That's our job, isn't it?"

"Our *job* is to ascertain if there *is* an assassin–"

"There is. We know the runes they're reading from."

"Find him–"

"Or her. It's likely to be–"

"And stop him."

She finally seemed a little piqued. "Shall we just arrest every Believer we see? Like this boy?"

"Of course not," Dernovich said, so firmly that it shut off all the ambiguity he'd felt when he'd first seen the boy. And "boy" was right. He couldn't be more than seventeen, disappearing into the trees that lined the river, probably to smoke, or whatever Believer teens did to rebel. Not a chance he was the one they were looking for, and they needed to find that person, as soon as possible. It had all suddenly gotten very serious.

Obscured as it was by the shock of finding out Woolf had once been a Believer, Agent Dernovich would only remember this mistake when it was far too late.

Malcolm walked along the riverbank. He had not had to kill anyone, which, despite all he'd been taught, was a relief that nearly made him dizzy again. All in all, a success.

"Thank you," he remembered to whisper as he walked.

His ear felt better, too, and the day, though still bitterly cold, was shaping up to remain clear. He had no doubts. His fears had lessened. The FBI agents who were hunting him, had they but known, had *he* but known, were receding behind him.

The border would only grow closer.

So would his target.

And when Malcolm – or whatever he was calling himself by that point – crossed the border, walked a farther two hundred miles and *found* that target.

Well, then. What a day that would be.

He picked up his step and moved on.

5

Sarah looked up Kazimir's name in the decaying encyclopedias in her school library. "Someone famous for his prowess in battle," the book said, confirming Kazimir's own explanation, but it also meant "destroyer of peace" as well as, in that way that language was so often unhelpful, "*bringer* of peace".

"How did he know your name, though?" Jason asked as she put the J–K volume back on the dusty, dusty shelf.

"Maybe he heard my dad say it?" They both knew how unlikely this was, given how careful Gareth Dewhurst was around a dragon. Around anyone.

"They're inscrutable. Always have been."

"And you're a vocabularian," she said back. "Always have been."

"It's a really ace name," Jason continued. "I'd probably get picked on less if I was named Kazimir."

"You don't really think that."

"I don't, no."

In truth, neither of them was so much picked on at school as effectively invisible. Even Kelby's anti-Japanese feelings now felt out of date, what with all the newspaper headlines screaming about the Soviets.

"Did you see today's?" asked Miss Archer, coming over to them. She was their kind, young librarian who preferred the word "bachelorette" over "spinster".

"Are they going to nuke us into oblivion?" Jason asked, as he gathered his things to go. He had his part-time job tonight, Sarah knew, at Al's, Frome's one and only diner, run by Albert, whose real name was Noriyuki, but Sarah only knew that because Jason had told her.

"They wouldn't," Sarah said, meaning the Soviets, though who knew, really? She scanned the paper. It was full of photographs of the USSR testing new launch equipment, deep inside the boundaries of that mysterious, closed country. The Soviets still had the US spy they'd caught, maybe he was even the one who took these pictures.

"They've got *something* planned," Miss Archer said. "Most likely the space race. Everyone wants to be the first ones in orbit or on the moon."

"And they can bomb us from there," Jason said.

"Not necessarily," Sarah said. "Space could be hopeful, couldn't it? A place where maybe it doesn't matter if you're American or Russian."

"Or dragon," Jason added.

"You think they want to go into space?"

"Who knows *what* they want?" Miss Archer said, but her friendly smile also contained a pointed invitation to gossip aimed directly at Sarah.

"Does *everyone* know?" Sarah asked.

"Frome isn't that big," Miss Archer said.

"Unfortunately," Jason said.

"Is it going to be a problem that our dragon is blue?"

"Is he actually Russian?" Miss Archer asked. "Does he speak to you? What's his accent like?"

"He sounds like a *dragon*. They don't really have countries, do they? Except the Wastes? Even if we call them Russian or Canadian. Besides, it seems like he's been here long enough to just be American."

"That argument didn't work for my parents," Jason said.

Sarah frowned. "Do you really think there could be trouble?"

"I *always* think there could be trouble," Miss Archer said. "That way I'm never surprised."

"That's probably less of a comfort than you think," Sarah said.

"But you know how people are," Sarah said to her father over dinner. It was little more than simmering stew and cornmeal, but at least it was warm. "If they think he's actually Russian–"

"Stop concerning yourself with that dragon," her father said, not looking up from the *Tacoma News Tribune and Herald*, the same one she'd seen at school.

"I just don't want people giving you trouble because we hired–"

"You don't need to concern yourself with my trouble either. I will handle the claw."

"They don't like that," she said. "When you call them that."

67

He glanced at her over the corner of his paper. "Well, they don't. It's not a nice word."

"What do you think they call us?"

"He's only said *human* or *mammal*."

"And that doesn't strike you as insulting?"

"I'm just saying–"

"They don't need you to defend them." His voice was harder now, stern. "They weigh seventy tons. They can fly and breathe fire. They are, in fact, *dragons*, Sarah. Soulless animals. They don't have feelings to hurt any more than a wolf who would eat you for his breakfast." He made an annoyed flick of the newspaper and went back to reading it. "Just because the devil gave them the gift of speech doesn't mean you're talking to anything more than a mostly undomesticated predator."

"The devil?"

"It's just a saying."

"An old one. An ugly one."

"Sarah–"

"People called Mom names, too. And you for marrying her."

There was a silence behind the newspaper, a stillness that did nothing for Sarah's anxiety. She didn't know why she was poking so much. The oddity of her father hiring a creature he so clearly mistrusted was hard to square, especially from a man she knew to be difficult but not hateful. He'd nursed her mother without complaint through the tumour that had devoured her stomach less than two months after first diagnosis, bringing an end to a marriage that had been happy but had never, not once, been easy.

68

Washington wasn't the South or their neighbour Idaho, where marriage between whites and blacks was still illegal. It wasn't even Oregon, which hadn't repealed its laws against interracial marriage until just six years ago. Washington had done it in 1868, the sixth of the forty-eight states to do so (so early, in fact, it hadn't even been a state yet). This was a forward-looking place. But that hadn't stopped the looks. The messages left in their mailbox that a younger Sarah occasionally found. Hadn't stopped the surprising resistance Sarah herself had occasionally even faced at the beauty salon her mother had taken her to in Tacoma to "properly learn how to manage that hair of yours". The roomful of laughing women, their skin matching the dark of Sarah's mother, coming to an uncomfortable silence once Darlene and Sarah arrived. It picked up again, almost immediately, but that pause was there.

Come to think of it, maybe her father's anger wasn't so surprising after all. Maybe it was the natural outlet for a man who'd married for a love that cost him and then was taken–

"If you think what people called me and your mother is anything like the same as what I call a dragon," he said now, too quietly for comfort, "then I don't know what to say to you, daughter."

He went to bed shortly thereafter, directing not another word at her, as if he really *didn't* know what to say. She lay awake long after she knew him to be asleep. She was troubled, to be sure, but that wasn't why she'd resisted sleeping.

Tonight was the night Jason closed up the diner for Al, and for half an hour or forty-five minutes, the diner was the one place on earth where she and Jason could ever be properly alone.

69

* * *

Deputy Emmett Kelby was a stupid man. He knew it, which was bad enough, but he knew everyone else knew it, too. He'd never make it past Deputy, that much was clear. Even if Sheriff Lopez moved on – and don't think *that* last name didn't bother Kelby on a daily basis – and the entire rest of the Pierce County Sheriff Department were somehow razed to the ground, he'd somehow *still* be Deputy Kelby until the day he died.

But though he may have been stupid – and, it can't be overemphasized, he *was* – he was very, very cunning. He knew exactly how much he could get away with and exactly how those limits changed with the person who was its unfortunate recipient. He knew which neighbourhoods he could drive through in Frome to harass residents who would never call his boss to report him. He knew which ones he could stop for a busted tail light – that was, of course, working perfectly until Deputy Kelby put his baton through it – and who'd never officially complain, even when he did it again a month after they'd had it fixed.

He was the thing the world had suffered from most in her four billion years of existence: a stupid man with power. When the lights of the universe went out one day, standing over the plug, having pulled it despite all warnings, would be a man like Deputy Kelby, defiant in refusing to believe the advice of anything but his own sheer dumbness.

Like many stupid but cunning men with power, he also never forgot a slight.

That dragon. That blue dragon. That *Russian* dragon had slighted him. He would find a way to make it pay. But that wasn't today. Today was for one Jason Inagawa. Hadn't we just fought a war and *won*? And here was someone like Jason – there he was now, look at him, bussing crates of return bottles out of the back of the diner – at a job that should rightfully have gone to a proper *American* teenager.

Deputy Kelby pulled a drag on his cigarette so hard and long he burnt his lip. Cursing, he flung it out the window he'd cracked on this stake-out. Because yes, he was staking out Jason Inagawa, who wouldn't forget the rest of *this* night in a hurry. Nosiree, when the last lights went out and Jason Inagawa started the long walk home, something was going to happen which would make sure he never forgot the name Emmett John Kel–

He sat up straight in his seat. Were his eyes deceiving him or was that Sarah Dewhurst sidling out of the shadows and knocking on the back door of Al's, not seeing Kelby's cruiser in the dark? And here was Jason Inagawa opening the door for her, greeting her only with a nod as she followed him inside.

Deputy Kelby smiled. It was a stupid smile. It was a cunning smile.

This was going to be even more fun than he thought.

"Stop," Jason said.

"What's wrong?" she asked, pulling away from the kiss.

"I'm sorry," he said. "I'm being a real sad sack tonight."

She moved over next to him. "A little bit. But so what?" She looked around Al's cold and dingy office. "This is a sad sack kind of place."

"I just…" he said. "I'm angry."

71

"At me?"

"No, just angry. But I realized today that I feel it all the time." He turned to her. "All the time."

She didn't answer him, but of course she knew what he meant. Every day in a town with people who didn't look like you, in a *life* that didn't look like you, it eventually just wore you out. Like even today, she got strange looks in all her classes, and Velma Doone accused her straight out of having a dad who was spying for the Russians. What would he spy on in Frome? On a *farm*? That Velma Doone was a stupid person who would never transcend her name was beside the point. She knew what Jason meant. But what could they possibly do about it?

"Is it Kelby?" she asked anyway.

"I guess. I mean, he's just the top of a long list."

"My mom always said that dragons weren't just out there in the world. That if you cut some people open, they'd have dragon right below the surface. An angry one, trying to get out."

Jason leaned all the way forward, almost until his forehead touched his knees. "My father wants to send me away."

Sarah sat up. "He what?"

"He's found some prep school in Minnesota run by a Japanese guy. Says it's the best way to get me into the right college."

"When would this be?"

"Summer and then all of senior year."

They sat in silence. There wasn't a chance Sarah was going to be able to afford college. Her grades were good enough to get in somewhere, but probably not good enough to get the scholarships she'd need to even come close to paying for it. But Hisao Inagawa wanted his son to not just succeed but thrive and, Sarah and Jason guessed, *conquer* the exact types of people who forced his mother to die in an internment camp. Even working at this diner while still having all the chores of any teenager living on a farm was practice to get Jason working harder than everyone else.

Sarah knew – had always known – that she didn't fit into his future. But then, she had sort of given up on the future when her mother died. You just got days, it seemed to her, where stuff happened or it didn't, where planning just showed you what a fool you were to think you had any say over what your life would be. If Jason left in the summer, well, it was going to happen whatever her ache about it might be.

She could already feel that ache beginning.

"Don't you ever want to go on a real date?" Jason said now, clearly feeling it, too.

"Of course," she said. "Why wouldn't I?"

He looked at her, surprised. "I thought you wanted to keep this secret."

"I thought *you* wanted to keep this secret."

He was shocked for a moment, then laughed. "How stupid are we?"

"I don't think my dad would complain. He likes your dad."

"No one likes my dad. They tolerate him."

"My dad respects him."

"Does he?"

Sarah shrugged. "He never talks bad about him."

"Which for this town is something like respect, I guess."

73

"I always thought it was *your* dad who'd have a problem."

"He would. A big one."

"Well, there you go. That's why we keep it a secret."

"But why should my dad having a problem be something that stops us?"

"Because we're young. Because he runs your house. Because he's got the power to send you to prep school."

"You haven't said you'll miss me."

"You haven't said you'll miss *me*."

He sighed slow and long. She was surprised to see he was holding back tears. She moved into the space under his arm. The smell of him now wasn't exactly *nice* – it was sweat and hamburger grease and whatever it was beneath that was Jason's own individual smell – but she liked it. It was a place to rest. Safely.

Plus, he could kiss her – as he did now – with a softness that made her toes wriggle.

"Don't you feel like there's two reasons to keep a secret?" she said. "Because on the one hand, it would get you into trouble. But on the other, if it's secret, it's valuable. It belongs to you and not anyone else."

"So you want to keep this a secret still?"

"Want? I *want* a world where my mother is alive and where we're not going to lose our farm and where nuclear war isn't a daily threat and where no one will hold us down because of the colour of our skin or because we're so poor we had to hire a dragon. That's what I *want*."

He sniffed. "Point taken."

She moved out from under his arm, missed it, but started buttoning up her coat anyway. "Plus, dating is one thing, but neither of our fathers would have anything positive to say about us meeting like *this*."

"My father would kill me."

"Oh, *you*," she said, a bitterness in her voice that surprised her. "I'd be ruined. The town harlot. You'd just be–"

"Regularly beaten up by local police officers?"

She looked at him. At his short hair, cut brutally up the sides, at the lanky arms, at the few hairs that sprouted where a moustache might theoretically be. He was right. *She* was right. And there was nothing either of them could do about it.

"Secret because it's valuable," he said.

She let her silence be a yes, then she said, "We should get going."

She opened the back door of the office, the one that led into the small alley behind Al's where the dumpsters were, where there was only a distant street light to cast any illumination.

It was still enough to see Deputy Kelby waiting there for her, his police baton out, and a smile on his face that would haunt Sarah Dewhurst for the rest of her life.

"Slut," he said. His first word. A word that told her everything she needed to know about how this was going to go.

"Sarah–" Jason said, following her out, stopping when he saw Kelby.

"Everyone knows your kind are whores," Kelby said, with a calm delight that was more unnerving than his stupid rage could ever have been. He glanced over to Jason. "But doing it with the Yellow Peril? That's gotta be the lowest of the low."

"And you'd know, would you?" Jason said.

This time, Sarah didn't even try to warn him. There was nothing going to happen now that could possibly be made worse.

"Slut," Kelby said again, still with the smile. "Your daddy is gonna *love* this."

"Stop talking to her like that," Jason said.

"And who's going to make me?" Kelby stepped forward, tossing the police baton up in the air with a spin, catching it like he was playing a game.

"We weren't doing anything wrong," Sarah said, her voice shaky.

"Then why were you hiding it?" Kelby sneered.

"Why do you do this?" she whispered as he approached, backing her up. "Why are you like this?"

"I don't have to have a reason," he said, "not for a filthy whore like you."

"Don't call her that," Jason said, stepping between them. Kelby's baton lashed out so fast Jason didn't even have a chance to duck. It hit him on the throat, and he fell to his knees, coughing as if to choke.

"Stop it!" Sarah yelled.

Kelby turned back to her. "Or you'll what?" He advanced on her again, until she felt the dumpster at her back. He came uncomfortably close. "Hey," he said, whispering now, "maybe we can come to some understanding. Maybe you could give me a little of what you give him."

He moved even closer. She could smell his rank body odour, see the way his hungry, weaselly eyes darted in the street light. He moved the baton down to the hem of her skirt and started to raise it.

"No," she said.

He didn't listen.

"No." But he kept pushing up the fabric. In her terror, she said something, too quiet for him to hear.

"What did you say?" he whispered.

"I said, everyone hates you."

He stopped. She was trembling now, her voice, too, but somehow her eyes were steady when they met his. "Everyone in this town hates you. Don't you see their eyes roll when they say your name? How stupid they think you are? Even the most hateful people here think you're an idiot."

The word was too much. The sentence was too much. The entire *paragraph* was too much. Sarah knew it, could see it on Kelby's face. She had stepped off a cliff and had only to wonder how far it was until she broke all her bones on the ground below.

"Sarah," Jason coughed, getting to his feet, but too late.

Deputy Kelby stepped back, unbuckled his gun and took it out. "You're under arrest, girl."

"For what?" Sarah said, but she knew. No one who looked like her could ever talk like that to someone who looked like *him*.

"Assaulting a police officer," Kelby said.

"She didn't assault you," Jason rasped.

"Really?" Kelby said. "Then how come I had to fight back?"

Without warning, he swung the gun, hitting her jaw, knocking her to the dirt of the alley. The shock was more overwhelming than the pain, which was distant and not immediate. It was as if her head had fallen off somehow, her blood jumping right out of her skin, her whole body reacting against this this *this*—

Above her, she could hear grunts and thuds, flesh against flesh, fist against bone. Jason had gone for Deputy Kelby. She'd been wrong. There were *lots* of ways this situation could get worse. She had no idea who was getting the best or worst of the fight, but there was no outcome that would be good for Jason or for her.

She tried rolling over, a hand to her jaw, wondering if it was broken, still trying to speak. "Jason—"

They still grappled.

"Jason, just let him go—"

The gun went off.

She froze. Jason and Deputy Kelby seemed to hold each other in a kind of shock.

"Jason?" she said. "Jason!"

Jason lurched back a step from Kelby. Even in the dim light, she could see the shine of blood across the white shirt Jason wore for the diner. White no longer.

"No," she said, still struggling to rise, still struggling to *talk*, a loosened tooth falling to her tongue so she had to spit it out. "Jason—"

Deputy Kelby fell to one knee. He dropped the gun, as the hand that was holding it didn't seem to work any longer. Jason took another step back, eyes wide, as Sarah saw the small wet circle on the front of Kelby's uniform. It seemed so minor a wound, so modest against his stomach.

"Oh, no," she heard Jason whisper.

Kelby looked up at him, his face stunned. He opened his mouth to speak but spat out only blood. He turned slightly,

78

and Sarah saw the exit wound. A crater had opened on his upper back.

She expected him to fall forward, every bit of logic said he would, but incredibly, he started to stand again. He was struggling to his *feet*. Jason looked as terrified as Sarah felt. They watched as Kelby, still trying to speak, hoisted himself upright, spat out more blood, but still didn't fall.

He reached out for Jason and died.

She could actually see it. Deputy Kelby's eyes were still open, but something vanished. His soul? Did he have one? It didn't matter. He died.

Before his body fell to the ground, Kazimir was there, stepping out of the air at the end of the alley, snaking his head down the passage between Al's diner and the tall fence behind. He grabbed the falling body of Deputy Emmett Kelby in his mouth, bit him in half, then swallowed both parts in two great gulps. He took another bite out of the dirt where Kelby had bled, scooping it up like a shovel and spitting it into the field behind the diner.

In less than thirty seconds, no trace of Kelby remained, aside from the gun on the ground and the blood on Jason's white shirt.

"You are more reckless than I expected, Sarah Dewhurst," Kazimir said, looking at her with his one eye.

There again was the smile.

6

Malcolm was falling behind. Clouds had settled in as he walked south and were threatening snow. They were to be expected, of course, this was Canadian winter, but he had daily goals to meet, set for him before he departed. He had missed the very first one because of the two men and the wound to his ear. He'd missed the second even though he'd been rushing to catch up. And if snow started he was going to miss the third.

Delay had been built into the schedule, one couldn't foresee everything, but there was a deadline he had to make. A particular place on a particular day at a particular time.

Or everything was lost.

"But that will not happen," he said to himself, as happily as he could. "My path is blessed. My path is guarded."

Your path will be guarded, the Mitera Thea had told him, before she'd left the last time to prepare other Cells for the success he would bring, reminding him – as if he needed it – that he was expected to bring success. *Because your duty is sacred. You go to defend everything we believe in. You go to stop a war.*

But I will have to kill to stop it, you say, Malcolm had replied, as he had many times over many years.

Your worry is why you were chosen, my son. An eager assassin has no moral purpose. But you know what you do. You know why you do it. The young are always the truest Believers, which also is your best disguise and why you, among all, were chosen. No one will know who you are. No one will see you coming. Not until your fist strikes knowing exactly why it does so: to save the Exalted we worship. Besides, what is a human life compared to a dragon's? We are insignificant. We are as rats. They ignore us because we have failed them, but you, my son, you and I shall capture their attention again through this great, great act.

And we will stop a war?

No, my son, you will stop a war.

"My path is guarded," he said again now, watching the clouds. "My path is blessed."

If it did snow, he had instructions on the options he might take. Hotels were out because they required a record of his presence – no matter what name he might give, they'd still have something to attach to the memory of his face – but no one required him to freeze to death.

Make a solitary camp, if he could, with a fire. That was first choice. He had a small tent in his bag, and even if there had been those who'd questioned his skills and suitability for this journey, there was never any question about whether a Believer could make a fire. It was like asking ice to make water. But where? Civilization had started to creep in, and there were any number of houses who would see a stray column of smoke and worry about an odd stray fire, even in a wintry forest.

It had to be a campground. Fires were normal; even if others used them, Malcolm could blend in. He knew the locations of several along his route, both official and itinerant. One wasn't too far, and the first snowflakes of what promised to be many more eased his decision.

He turned off the road, waiting for a tractor to pass so he could climb a fence and cross a long-harvested field without being seen. On the other side, he ducked through some trees, crossed a creek, and found himself behind a sign indicating the campground, right where he expected.

He carried no map except the memorized one in his head. It was reassuring to know it matched reality. He looked into the clearing that made up a poor but clean camping area. There was already a fire going, in what seemed to be a concrete communal hearth. Malcolm could see only one tent, planted close to the fire, with a young man in front of it, warming himself on the flames.

One man. Malcolm could handle one man if he had to, and who said he would have to? The long and short of it was that it had been two days since he'd left the drugstore, two days since he'd spoken to anyone except in prayer, and Malcolm ... well, he was ashamed to admit it as that, too, was one of the questions about his suitability for this, but out here, with no one to judge him, he could admit it to himself. He was lonely.

The campfire seemed safe enough.

So Malcolm stepped out of the trees and met Nelson, and the fate of billions was changed.

* * *

"One more day," Agent Dernovich begged into the phone, and it *was* begging.

"You've found nothing, Agent Dernovich," said Cutler, crackling across a long-distance line from Washington DC.

"We found evidence of murderous dragon activity–"

"You've found nothing *since*." Cutler's voice was a granite cliff. Waves could crash on it for thousands of years before he'd change his mind. "Which is rather more to the point."

"Our guy *must* be nearing the border–"

"You know you should be looking for a woman. Believer cults are heavily matriarchal."

Dernovich glanced over to Agent Woolf, who was writing god only knew what in painfully tiny lettering in her notebook. She was hard to think of as a matriarch.

"I have a hunch it's a he," Dernovich said now.

"A hunch is worth exactly jack in this office. We have a very dangerous set of murders-by-dragon to solve before it becomes an international incident, Agent. Unless you've got facts..."

Agent Dernovich didn't have facts, but he did think he had more than a hunch. The trail – if it had ever been one – had vanished. Drops of blood in a forest turned out to be a better metaphor for something hopelessly lost than needles and haystacks–

But that boy. That Believer coming out of the drugstore who had vanished into the riverbank. Dernovich had followed up on him, after it had gnawed on his brain all night in that horrible hotel room where he could hear Woolf snoring through the walls. The boy wasn't a student at either of the local schools. The pharmacist had never seen him before either, but she did say he gave his name as Malcolm.

She also said it looked like he might have been shot.

"We're still looking for that boy," Dernovich said to Cutler.

"That boy you watched walk away and did nothing about? That *teenage* boy we've had an APB on for the last thirty-six hours who'd stick out like a sore thumb in what the Canadians think of as a populated area."

"He would have been trained to be inconspicuous–"

"They would not send a boy for this job!" Cutler shouted. "It was the women who did all the dirty work in the past. You and I both know they would send someone who looked like Woolf. Or either of my ex-wives."

Dernovich glanced again at Woolf, now taking a sip from her root beer in the booth of what felt like the thousandth diner they'd eaten at this week. What Cutler said made a lot of sense. In fact, it made so much obvious sense that Dernovich was increasingly certain that Cutler was one hundred per cent wrong.

"One more day," he said, as calmly as possible. "I'll get you proof."

"One more day," Cutler relented, "but you won't."

He hung up. Dernovich idly put his finger in the coin return to see if any money had come back, then headed to the booth. Woolf didn't greet him or ask how it went with Cutler; she just said, "I've been thinking we should check a certain kind of campground."

"They've all been searched," he said, sitting down,

gesturing to the waitress for more coffee. "He's not there. No one's seen him."

She looked at him askance. "He's a moving target, Agent Dernovich. We aren't watching all the campgrounds simultaneously. We haven't even been honest about why the RCMP should be looking for him."

This was true. He and Woolf were still there not-quite-officially. Their home office had had to come up with a cover story about a suspected Communist sympathizer, which Dernovich was pretty sure no Canadian would ever believe. Woolf had gotten nowhere with calls to local Believer Cells, but then she was a known apostate, so that wasn't surprising. Not one of them even acknowledged knowing about the existence of a boy.

"Which is odd," she said now. "If they were going to try and throw us off, they'd have pretended to know him. Create too many trails rather than denying there's one at all. That's how Believers work."

"But that's not what they did."

"*How* they refused my inquiries suggests they thought I was a time-waster, that they actually didn't know about the boy."

"And so?"

She took a thoughtful breath. "Do you have children, Agent Dernovich?"

He coughed in his coffee. "We've been working together all this time, and you don't know the answer to that question?"

"You didn't know I was a former Believer."

Touché, he thought. "All right. No, I don't. I never met the right woman. I'm from a small town east of the mountains in

86

Washington state. No one there wanted to do all the travelling I do, and no one in the east coast offices wanted to settle in a tiny mountain town. Plus, you know, the work."

"The work *is* extensive," she said, in what for her probably counted as warmth.

"It's the biggest regret of my life not having children. I lost three brothers in the War. I wanted a family more than anything but ... not to be." He felt the familiar despair in his chest at these thoughts, which made him even more annoyed that he'd revealed them all to Woolf. "Why do you want to know?" he asked, with considerably less grace.

"Believers raise their children communally," she said.

"I know."

"This is often mistaken for neglect, but that isn't the truth. They're protected fiercely, as it's believed dragons do their broods."

"So?"

"So how and why is a young Believer on his own in the winter in western Canada with no local Cell knowing who he is? There aren't *that* many of them. If I were to walk into a Cell here, chances are I'd probably know at least two people personally."

"So where did this boy come from?"

"And where might he be going, seemingly without the assistance of any other Cell?"

He looked down as she unfolded a road map. She'd circled five potential campgrounds, all of them within driving distance.

"What other leads do we have?" she said.

He knew she was right, of course.

* * *

Before he even asked Malcolm's name, Nelson offered him food. It wasn't much – some salted pork – but he held it out to Malcolm by way of greeting as Malcolm stepped into the circle of the campfire.

"Thank you," Malcolm said. He took a bit of travel bread from his bag and added it to the mix. Nelson nodded gratefully. As he'd neared the campfire, Malcolm had guessed Nelson's age at early twenties. Now that they sat eating, he saw that Nelson was younger, perhaps only a year or two older than Malcolm himself, if that.

"Nelson Arriaga," Nelson said.

"Malcolm."

"No last name?"

Malcolm mentally grabbed one at random from the list he'd memorized. "McCormack."

"Scottish?"

Malcolm shrugged. "Just Canadian."

Nelson laughed at that. "My grandparents came here from Guatemala. I can tell you for sure that no one will *ever* call us 'just Canadian'."

Malcolm smiled back, though to be honest, he didn't quite understand.

They ate their small meal, and after, Nelson took out a rolled cigarette. He didn't offer one to Malcolm, who wouldn't have taken it anyway. To be honest, Malcolm didn't quite know what to do now. The fire was warm, the food had been good, but the snow had picked up, little tablets of it drifting into their food as they ate. Malcolm needed to get back on the road, but it was just that little bit hard to get going right this minute.

"Where are you headed?" Nelson asked, and for a startled moment, Malcolm genuinely believed his mind had been read.

"South," he said, vaguely.

"The border." Not a question, merely the obvious assertion. "You crossing it?"

Malcolm went to one of the stories he'd been given. "I'm going to my aunt and uncle's farm," he said. "To work."

Nelson raised an eyebrow. "In January?"

"Always work needing to be done on a farm."

"Yeah, I guess that's true," Nelson said, concentrating on his cigarette. "I'm heading that way. I could give you a ride."

Malcolm perked up. "Ride?"

"Yes, 'Malcolm McCormack'–" saying the name in a way that clearly didn't quite believe it– "I have a truck."

Nelson nodded past his tent and, sure enough, a truck sat parked, not in the campground's lot but in some trees on the other side, as if he had hidden it.

Here was a tantalizing possibility. Rides were a last resort, but it was day three and he was behind. There were only fourteen days to go. What if the snow slowed him down more? What if the men who shot him had colleagues who were still searching? What if–?

"You a Believer?" Nelson asked, nodding at Malcolm's exposed wrist.

Malcolm pulled down the sleeve to cover the tattoos.

"It's okay," Nelson said. "Everyone says you people are crazy, but I'm not prejudiced." He exhaled smoke through his nose. "As long as no one gets hurt, what people do is their own business." He looked into Malcolm's eyes again. "You get me?"

"Maybe I do," Malcolm, who didn't, said.

Nelson flicked the end of his cigarette into the campfire and got up for a stretch. "Were you thrown out?" he asked, not looking at him. "By your parents, I mean."

"I never knew my parents," Malcolm said. "The Believers took me in as an orphan."

"*Someone* there must have been your parent. Canada doesn't let churches adopt whole people." Nelson sat back down next to him, a little closer this time. Malcolm didn't mind. It increased the warmth. "Kind of stops slavery, I think."

Malcolm thought of the Mitera Thea. "There was a woman who took me in."

"So she's your parent. Even if the ones you're related to are dead, you still got a mother."

"Yes."

Nelson was silent. It took Malcolm a second to realize what he was supposed to say next. "Were *you* thrown out?"

Nelson nodded. "By my own mother, too. The one who gave birth to me."

"Why?"

Nelson stayed silent but met Malcolm's eyes again. Nelson's were brown, but light and striking. His skin was darker than Malcolm's and a lock of black hair stuck out from beneath the woolly cap. Malcolm had a strange moment of wanting to brush it back under the wool, had his hand halfway up, in fact, before stopping himself, mainly because Nelson hadn't moved.

In an instant, Malcolm grasped it, all of it. He'd been told about this, that it might happen to a young man travelling alone.

He'd been instructed what to do.

To his surprise, Malcolm found himself wondering if those instructions might be put off another moment or two.

"It's snowing harder."

"I can *see* that, Agent Woolf."

"He'll be looking for shelter."

"He wasn't looking for shelter at the last three places."

"My point is that he may have been driven into one of the next two by the weather."

It was starting to annoy him how often she was right. "So do you still believe?" he asked her, as they drove through the thickening snow.

"I'm no longer a Believer, Agent Dernovich," she said, and for the first time, he heard a little annoyance in her voice. *At last,* he thought.

"Yes," he said, "but that's different than whether you still believe or not. People leave churches. Doesn't mean they leave their faith behind."

In an incredible happening, Agent Woolf *laughed.* "I think," she said, a rich, surprising humour in her voice, "you may not really know what Believers believe."

He bridled. "I'm one of the leading Believer experts in North America, Agent–"

"Yes, but the real truth of it? How much do they believe is literally real versus how much is symbolic?"

He sighed, just to annoy her. "It's understood that key elements of the faith are allegorical–"

"But you want to know if I literally believe dragons are

91

angelic representatives of an afterlife on earth? If the purpose of a man or a woman is to serve that divine representative and not push them onto reservations? If we were vomited from the stomach of a great dragon Goddess–"

"I just want to know who you pray to," he said, a little too hard. "If we meet a dragon, do I need to watch my back?"

"You always need to watch your back when you meet a dragon, Agent Dernovich," she said. "Surely whoever you pray to would agree with that." She nodded out at the road. "It's the next turn."

"That looks messy," Nelson said, as Malcolm took off his hat. The bandage on his ear was on the point of falling off, and it was time for a new one.

"It's not so bad," Malcolm said.

"You want me to do that?" Nelson asked as Malcolm fumbled with the new bandage.

He felt bashful, but said, "Would you? It's hard when you can't see."

Nelson positioned himself in front of Malcolm. He took off a last bit of bandage stuck to Malcolm's ear, and Malcolm could smell the tobacco on his fingers.

Nelson whistled in admiration at the wound. "What the hell happened to you, Malcolm McCormack?"

Malcolm tried to remember what he'd told the pharmacist, but the closeness of Nelson had made his mind go quite blank. "I fell," he said, weakly, noticing the faint stubble across Nelson's chin.

"Baloney, you fell," Nelson said, but not in a taunting way.

"I got shot," Malcolm said, unexpectedly.

Nelson sat back. "Yeah, that sounds a bit more like it." He unrolled the new bandage and started pressing it into place. Malcolm winced. "I don't have any painkillers."

"My faith doesn't believe in them."

"And that makes the pain go away, does it?" But he didn't push, just took some adhesive tape and gently set the bandage in place. He finished, once more meeting Malcolm's eyes. "Who would shoot Malcolm McCormack the Believer?"

Nelson reached out to brush a snowflake from Malcolm's cheek. Malcolm smelled the tobacco again along with the warm, worn smell of another person. He tipped his nose up involuntarily to follow Nelson's hand as it left his face. There was a silence, and Nelson's look was more serious now.

"Is this the time that you kiss me?" Malcolm asked, genuinely curious.

"Is it *what*, you dipstick?" But Nelson was still smiling. "Kiss you? You want me to kiss you?"

"Have I misunderstood–?"

"You just come right out and say it?"

"I'm sorry, I–"

"You got a woody down there, too?"

Malcolm blinked. "A what?"

Nelson laughed out loud. "Are you for real?"

"I'm not sure. We've got a slightly different approach to reality."

"Do you now?"

Malcolm nodded. "Some of us believe this is all a dream. That reality, whatever it is, never had dragons in it, that this world existed for thousands and thousands of years with just men, until one day, we entered a dream where dragons were with us. Had *always* been with us."

Nelson's eyebrow twitched up in a way that Malcolm found oddly stirring. "That sounds like more of an argument why you *shouldn't* be a Believer."

"It's more of an argument about why we should never wake up."

Nelson laughed again, but his confusion was plain. As was a surprising amount of pain. "A world where you never wake up? Sounds like paradise."

"What do you mean–?"

He stopped because Nelson's face had frozen in a glance over Malcolm's shoulder. Malcolm turned.

A black Oldsmobile was pulling up in the campground parking lot.

"Did you get the licence plate?" Agent Dernovich asked, out of breath, near the fire the two boys had run from.

"Just that the first numbers were forty-seven," Agent Woolf said, already scribbling in her notebook.

"It was him, though, wasn't it?"

Woolf eyed him. "Maybe."

"Oh, come on." Agent Dernovich stood now, still out of breath, hand on his side. It hadn't even been much of a dash after they saw the boys take off. He really needed to cut down on the apple pie and ice cream. "Who else could it have been?"

"We wouldn't expect our target to have made friends."

"Friends? Why did they have to be friends? He could have forced the other one to take him. Or they could have–"

"Agent Dernovich," she said, in a way that stopped him. He saw her bend down by the tent the boys had abandoned, though he'd had a first glance while Agent Woolf – not winded at all – had chased after them as they peeled away, fast as criminals, in a truck that neither agent had seen parked there, disappearing before there was any chance of getting back to the Oldsmobile. He hadn't seen anything in the few belongings left in the tent that indicated that the second boy, whoever he might be, was any sort of Believer.

But that's not what Woolf was picking up from the snow. With the tip of her notebook pencil, she had hooked a snow hat. She spun it around to show Dernovich a side that was bloody and torn.

"At last," Dernovich said. "Proof."

"Proof that it's the boy we're after. Not proof that he's our target."

"Oh, for Pete's sake, Woolf!" he said, finally shouting, letting all the frustration out at once. "We have who knows how little time to stop *someone* from fulfilling a so-called prophecy that just *might* start an all-out war between men and dragons, and you, of all people, however former a Believer you might be, know damn well that that is a war we do not want. It's goddamn proof enough." He stopped, took in a deep breath, losing steam. "Because it's all the proof we've got."

"I know full well what we're facing," she said, her face stern. "I know better than you."

"Then you won't complain when I ask you to find a pay phone and tell the Canadians we've got an assassin on the loose, now, will you? Let that cat out of the bag. Go! I'm going to keep searching through this stuff."

She didn't even say yes as she hurried back to their Oldsmobile. He blinked away the snow as he watched her. So close. *So* close. But the way the boy (and the other boy, whatever poor unfortunate *that* kid turned out to be) had run. It couldn't be anyone else.

They'd found him. And Cutler could go sit on a pole if he doubted them again.

"I lost my tent," Nelson said, driving.

"I'm sorry."

"I had a sleeping roll in there."

"I'm sorry."

"You're just lucky most of my stuff is still in here."

Malcolm looked in the small cavity behind the seats of Nelson's truck. The entirety of Nelson's belongings barely even matched Malcolm's, carried in the bag he'd run with, though now minus a hat.

"I'm sorry," he said again.

"Why'd you run?" Nelson demanded.

Why did you? Malcolm wondered. Nelson had followed him without a pause, had raced away in the truck like the road was on fire.

"Because," Malcolm said.

"Not an answer."

Once more something about the other boy startled Malcolm into telling the truth when he knew he really shouldn't.

"Because I didn't want to have to kill them."

7

Frome – the town, *her* town – was convinced Deputy Kelby had been murdered. His car had been found, parked near the diner where Jason worked, but he had, so far, not returned to the home where his elderly mama had spent the last three days crying for him, if maybe not as hard as one might expect. Kelby's logbook was more than two weeks out of date, so that was no help, and he'd told no one where he was going or what he was doing on the night he vanished.

Sheriff Lopez was pulling his hair out. He'd even talked to Jason briefly, as a quick add-on to an interview with Al when Jason was at work the next night (in a clean shirt). Lopez asked Al if he'd seen Kelby park his car, Al had said no, had called to the back, "You see him, Jason?" and Jason had only had to lean out a door and truthfully say, "No, I didn't see him park the car." Lopez had quickly moved on to those citizens of Frome who had way more reason to have a grudge against Kelby than skinny Jason Inagawa.

Town feeling was that Kelby's body was probably buried somewhere deep in the forest that enclosed Frome on every side. Someone had finally had enough of Kelby's hateful nonsense and put him out of his – and no doubt *their* – misery.

Only one person came close to suspecting anything near the truth.

"Tell me again how you fell?" Gareth Dewhurst asked his daughter over dinner.

"Against the counter," she said, wincing at the pain in her jaw. It was bruised and obviously swollen. She hadn't slept after getting home the night it happened (how could she? She might never sleep again) and made sure to rise before her father, listening for him to start downstairs for breakfast. At which point, she dropped herself to the ground as hard as she could, calling out.

He'd come running in, helped her up, taken her to the doctor, who'd confirmed her jaw wasn't broken, though she was likely to lose another one of her back teeth. She'd been off school since. Jason had delivered her homework each day. He told her what the town was thinking, and she told him to try not to panic, that it was an accident, that Kelby was going to kill him, that there was no evidence anyway since Kazimir had...

Well, that was the other thing. She'd been at home three days and the whole time, her father, perhaps suspiciously, perhaps not, had never given her a single chance to be alone with the dragon. The one time she'd tried to sneak out at night, she'd found her father in the kitchen, reading a newspaper by lantern light.

"Can't sleep?" he'd asked.

"No," she said. "Bad dreams."

He hadn't looked up from a newspaper she knew for a fact he'd already read over dinner that evening. "And what might a girl like you be having bad dreams about?"

"Mom," she'd said, which was true, actually. She'd dreamt her mother had been swallowed by a dragon, though a more familiar red than the blue still working their back fields. She wanted her mother so much right now, somehow even more keenly than she had in the two years since her death, if that was even possible.

Her father hadn't said anything to this, just let her go back to bed after a glass of milk, but she hadn't tried to go out again since then.

And now this, the third day in. "Tell me again how you fell?"

"Just clumsy, I guess." She'd made them both baked beans, as it was about the only thing she could comfortably eat.

"Tripped over your own feet?"

"Must have."

"And bashed your face against the counter."

"Yes, sir."

"Nearly breaking your jaw and losing a tooth."

"I must have swallowed it."

"But making no discernible damage to the countertop itself."

"Solid oak."

"Solid oak," he said, quietly. He took a bite of beans, then he stood and walked his plate to the sink.

Where he raised his fist and smashed it into the counter, easily breaking a board out of the top and cracking another.

"Except it's not, is it?" he said, not looking at her. "We're not people who can afford solid oak anything."

She swallowed, forgetting the pain of it until she was halfway through. "Daddy–"

"Do I really want to know why you're lying to me, daughter?"

She was surprised that it was a serious question. She saw him itching his fingers together, for all the world like he wanted to hit something again. Not her, but something specific.

"Did Jason Inagawa lay a hand on you?" he asked.

"No!" she said, startled into making her voice loud. "He would never!"

"Don't think I haven't noticed you two. That you're clearly more than just friends."

"Dad, I swear to you–"

"If he hurt you, I would kill him."

She knew he would. *Knew* it. Not in the way people say they would kill other people all the time. Seeing her father standing there, right this moment, his body tensed and somehow buzzing with an energy only amplified by his stillness, she knew. He really would kill Jason Inagawa. Or anyone else who dared harm his daughter. This knowledge was surprisingly frightening.

"He would never hurt me, Dad, not in a million years."

Another few breaths, then the energy was lessened. Not gone, never gone, but less. "I'm not complaining if you two are more than ... whatever. I'd be the last person telling you that." Then, more quietly, "If not for the pain I know the world will give you for it." He looked up at her again. "But he's not laying hands on you?"

"I swear it. Do you really think I'd ever put up with that?"

He frowned. "No. No, I guess you wouldn't."

"I fell, Dad, that's all."

"You fell."

"Yes."

He walked quietly over to pick up his hat as a prelude to heading out to his farm work. "I wonder where, though," he said, then left before she could answer him.

"Why did he let me lie?" Sarah asked Jason, finally back in school, in the library again. He had no injury, so he'd had to go back the very next day, pretending nothing was wrong.

"We have bigger things to worry about," Jason whispered back.

"Is your dad being weird, too?"

Jason shook his head. "No one saw the shirt but..." He closed his eyes, took a deep, nervous breath. "I'm going *freaky* with this, Sarah."

"It wasn't your fault–"

"Who cares about fault? I shot him. And then your dragon–"

"Lower your voice–"

"*Your dragon,*" in a fiercer whisper, *"ate him."*

"I don't understand it either. I still haven't been able to talk to him."

"What are we supposed to *do*, Sarah? Lopez is going to run out of people who didn't kill Kelby and then where is he going to start looking?"

She glanced around the library. As usual, they were pretty

much the only two students in it, aside from Claudia Caswell, who would pull out her own hair and eat it if she didn't have a book in her sticky fingers. And Miss Archer was ... Miss Archer was there a minute ago.

Sarah turned back to Jason. "We could tell the truth."

Jason rolled his eyes, as he did every time she brought it up. "A dark-skinned girl and a Japanese boy accidentally kill a *policeman* who is then just conveniently eaten by a dragon, who will almost certainly deny everything–"

"We don't know that–"

"We'd be strung up before we ever even got arrested."

"This isn't Mississippi–"

"It's not a bomb," Miss Archer said, slapping a newspaper down between them. Sarah was so startled she cried out, causing Miss Archer's already supercilious eyebrows to rise even further. "You all right, Sarah?"

"Just... You startled me."

"It's not a bomb," Miss Archer said again. "It's worse."

"What's not a bomb?" Sarah said, still shaken.

Miss Archer tapped the newspaper. "The Soviets. It's a satellite."

"A what?"

"A machine that orbits the planet. Sends radio waves." She slowed down for emphasis. "Takes pictures."

At this, Jason finally looked up. "They're going to spy on us."

"What else? They're going to be able to look right down at us. Any time."

Sarah and Jason shared a look.

"Eisenhower won't stand for it," Jason said.

"And they won't stand for Eisenhower not standing for it,"

Miss Archer said, biting her lip with worry. "And that's how war begins." She saw Sarah looking agog and immediately changed the subject. "How's the jaw?"

"Sore. But not broken."

"Count yourself lucky. I had an aunt who broke her jaw and had to have it wired shut. She could only drink soup for three months." Miss Archer got a dreamy look. "Though she did lose thirty pounds."

"Will there really be a war?" Jason asked, still looking at the paper.

"I hope not," Miss Archer said, in a serious voice, which it turned out wasn't the answer Sarah wanted to hear.

"You should ask him about the satellite," Jason said as they walked home. "Dragons aren't going to like being spied on either."

"I told you, I can't get near him."

"I would believe that if you were an idiot, Sarah, but you're not and we both know it."

This backhanded compliment made her blush, which in turn made her angry. "Why would he even know?"

"Because he's Russian."

"With no Russian accent. And he's worked on farms for who knows how long. It's like asking your dad about current affairs in Japan."

"First of all, my dad was born in Tacoma—"

"I *know*, Jason—"

"But he does keep up to date with what goes on over there."

She stopped in the road, noticing with a shudder that it was the same spot where Kelby had accosted them days before, when Kazimir had done the first of what turned out to be a number of unexpected things. "Where would a dragon get that information? Dragon newspapers? Dragon newsreels at dragon picture shows?"

"We don't know how they communicate—"

"And like you said, we have more important things to worry about."

Jason deflated a little. He looked up at the sky at what were so clearly snow clouds they might as well have a label on them. They'd been threatening for a day, having ambled down from Canada, but it finally looked like they were ready to start making serious snow.

"Freaky times, huh?" Jason said, then he dropped his voice to a whisper. "I killed someone."

"*We* did."

"It wasn't your hand on the gun."

"He wouldn't have been there if it wasn't for both of us."

"Yes, he would've."

"And that would have been better? That he get you alone? And beat you to death with no witnesses? He was a bad, stupid man."

"A bad, stupid man who I killed."

He looked so sad there seemed nothing at all to do except kiss him, right there, out in the open, in the middle of the road.

"Ow," she said.

"Jaw?"

"That was nearly broken by a man who would have murdered you."

"Sometimes you just have to feel bad about a thing. Sometimes that's the only thing that makes you human."

This, she understood. Good God, did she. She carried the pain of her mother around her like an undershirt. No one could see it, but it covered her body.

They pulled apart as they heard a car coming up the road.

"You have to be kidding," Jason whispered, as they saw it was the Sheriff's own patrol car.

"Just stay calm," Sarah said, though it was fake bravery. She felt her whole world sliding away as the Sheriff pulled to a stop and rolled down his window, like the ground was crumbling and there was nowhere to run. But it wasn't to Jason he spoke.

"Your daddy hired a dragon, I hear," he said.

Gareth Dewhurst didn't trust the dragon, which was only prudent. He was never going to trust *any* dragon, and when Hisao Inagawa said it was a blue – from where? Who'd ever heard of a blue anywhere in this godforsaken state? – Gareth hadn't even believed him, had thought his abrupt, frequently unlikeable neighbour was teasing him, which, knowing Hisao Inagawa, seemed improbable.

But a blue it was. Story on the blues was that they were mischievous, snide, imps. Everyone knew reds were imperious, would treat you like lowly subjects in a royal court even when you were paying them a single gold coin to dig you a new latrine. But blues were intelligent troublemakers.

"Where the hell did you find a blue?" he'd asked Hisao, way back when it first came up.

"The broker I got that red from a few years back recommended him," Hisao had said. "Said he'd just shown up one night, asking for work."

"Don't you find that odd?"

"Since when have either of us been able to afford to refuse something just because of its oddness, Gareth?"

Which was true. Which was fair. After Gareth had married Darlene, it was something that had become even truer and fairer. Hisao Inagawa – difficult, angry, stern Hisao Inagawa whose life the government had, to put it delicately, screwed over pretty hard – had at some point become Gareth Dewhurst's closest friend, for what it was worth, because Gareth was the only other person in Frome who might understand that.

So Gareth had contacted Hisao's broker and been told, yes, there was a dragon looking for work, and yes, that dragon was a blue, but no, they were actually hard workers, and any reputation they might have had was built on such little actual knowledge as to be close to worthless.

It was only after Gareth had handed over what was damn near his last ten dollars to the broker for his commission that the broker gave him the letter.

"What's this?" Gareth had asked.

The broker shrugged. "Came here, had your name on it. Letter of recommendation, probably. Some of the claws have them sent along."

"That's an ugly word," Gareth said, distracted, opening the envelope.

He read the letter.

And now, right now, on this cold just-February day,

he watched the blue dragon work in the second field, having completed initial clearing on the first far faster than Gareth had expected. He'd assumed the job would take a month, but this dragon would be done in under two weeks. This damnable dragon who had done not a single thing wrong in the time it had been working on the farm. This dragon who, indeed, seemed to have saved his daughter during an encounter on the road with the missing and not much missed Deputy Kelby.

This dragon Gareth had been asked to kill for five thousand dollars.

We know you are a peaceful man, the letter – which he'd now read countless times – began. *We know you want nothing more than to provide for your daughter. We know that this has not been easy for you since the death of your wife.*

We also know, it further said, *of your distinguished War record. You are a man of action, Gareth Dewhurst, especially your noted exploits in France.*

How did they know any of this? And who were "they"? The letter had no name, no postmark, nothing but a simple sheet of paper with clear, printed handwriting.

We do not believe we are asking this of a man who would perform this action cavalierly or with any pleasure. We believe this is why you are the right man to ask. We certainly understand that you will hesitate and that there is a good chance you will refuse us. We would, however, implore you not to.

This imploring had taken the shape of five hundred of the five thousand dollars showing up in his bank account, free and clear, the letter told him, regardless of his final choice. It was an outrageous windfall, and even though the farm was so far in debt it wouldn't even come close to saving it, five *thousand* might. Might even be enough to have a little left over to buy his daughter a damn jacket that would fit her. It filled him with shame to see how badly he was failing to keep her even properly dressed.

The letter said the death of the claw should look like an accident. Dragons were protected by the same treaty that protected humans. If one side could just go around killing the other, then war was inevitable, and mutual annihilation followed.

We will not reveal ourselves to you, Mr Dewhurst, not even after the action is finished. The balance of the money will simply appear in your account. You may explain it to the authorities as you see fit. We will never resurface to contradict you.

Were they Believers? Gareth didn't know much about the religion, but *everyone* knew the death of a dragon was the worst sort of blasphemy to a Believer. They'd sooner kill themselves, and occasionally had. But who else had the kind of money in this post-War decade besides churches and the government?

Know, sir, that this is a bad dragon. We do not say this lightly. Nor do we say it in the way that people often speak negatively of dragons – of their supposed indolence, of their pettiness and greed, of their dangerous superiority. We mean that this specific dragon will act in a way that will bring danger, not just to the world in general, Mr Dewhurst – though it will – but to you and to your daughter, personally.

This sounded like prophecy, which he knew Believers trafficked in, but again, no Believer would ever even conceive of harming a dragon. This had to be some sort of bizarre con, though a very expensive one, even if the five hundred dollars was all that came from it.

You must do this before February's third Sunday. If you do not, so much more will be lost than you ever thought possible, Mr Dewhurst. We suspect you are not a man to be convinced by an anonymous letter and a little bit of money in your bank, so we ask you to watch for the signs. Does the dragon take an interest in your daughter? Does she take an interest in the dragon? Does she begin to keep secrets from you?

It had, she had, and she obviously did, but so what? How was any of that not to be expected between a curious girl and an unexpected beast? For all that humans resented dragons, it was ninety per cent sheer jealousy at their power. No wonder there were religions around them. No wonder Sarah's school friends would sometimes argue about what dragon they'd like to be. Adults did it, too, just more discreetly. All of that was normal. But then came the question that moved this whole thing from baffling speculation into something else altogether.

Does she ever come to mysterious harm?

How could they know? Unless they were the ones who hurt her and had always planned to? Unless they scared her so badly she would refuse to tell him the truth, even when he threatened Jason, who a blind man could see she was fond of?

Either whoever wrote the letter could see the future, which was absurd, no matter what the Believers claimed, or this letter and offer wasn't a bribe.

It was blackmail.

Someone was offering him a huge amount of money to kill a dragon.

Someone was (possibly) threatening his daughter if he did not.

Gareth Dewhurst hadn't felt this much impotent rage since the death of his wife.

Through the window, he watched the dragon breathe fire on the day's toppled lumber. A controlled stream of heat and light and flame, like a welder's arc, too bright to look at directly for long. That was supposedly how they died. A rupturing of that organ. The main reason their skin was so hard to pierce, to protect this part of them that made the impossible, horrible miracle they breathed.

But there were ways. Ways that could be made to look like an accident.

And then what? Gareth Dewhurst wondered.

A question he'd found no answer to in the past weeks and days. A question he still had no answer to when Sheriff Lopez came driving onto his farm, his daughter in the passenger seat.

"I am armed, dragon," Sheriff Lopez said. "I have bullets that will harm you."

Kazimir looked, as always, slightly amused. The Sheriff, Sarah, and her father stood about twenty feet away from where he rested at the edge of the field. Smoke still twined in the air from the burnt lumber.

"Are we declaring weapons?" Kazimir said. "For my list is long."

"It's a courtesy," said the Sheriff. "My state of being armed is implied to all humans, but I declare it to dragons so that there are no surprises."

110

"There are always surprises, Officer," Kazimir said. "That is the nature of the word."

"He always talks like this," Sarah's dad said to the Sheriff, then to Kazimir: "The Sheriff wants to ask you some questions about the disappearance of Deputy Kelby. You remember him, don't you?"

"You met the Deputy on the road out there, I gather," the Sheriff added.

At this, Kazimir looked at Sarah, though she kept having to remind herself she was the only one who knew the dragon's name. "*I* didn't tell them," she found herself saying, then was deeply embarrassed by the sceptical glance the Sheriff gave her.

"Indeed she didn't," he said. "It was the Deputy himself. Said you'd been insubordinate."

"As I am not his subordinate," said the dragon, "how would it be possible to act in any other fashion?"

"Enough of this," Sarah's father grumbled. "Did you kill the Deputy?"

"Mr Dewhurst," the Sheriff warned.

"I did not," Kazimir said, almost casually. "Who is saying that I did?"

"No one, Mr...?" The Sheriff left a blank for Kazimir to provide his name. A cue the dragon either didn't understand or pretended not to.

The Sheriff was not obviously unkind. He'd driven Sarah down to her farm and had been respectful in his questions to her about the dragon: if she had ever known it to leave their farm, if she had in particular known its whereabouts the night Deputy Kelby was thought to have vanished. She'd offered no information that would have incriminated anyone. If the Sheriff had thought she was being evasive, he didn't show it, just mentioned that he'd known her mother slightly. "A smart lady. I was sorry to hear of her passing."

"So was I," was all Sarah was able to say in return.

"We found a dragon footprint," the Sheriff said now. "Well, half a footprint. In the dirt by the alley behind Al's diner, not too far from where Deputy Kelby's patrol car was parked. As there are no other dragons working in this county right now to my knowledge, and as that footprint is too small to be a red—"

"It is interesting, this word 'small'," Kazimir said, opening his wings some. "It is accurate to say that I am smaller than my red brethren." He stepped forward, like he did that night at the gas station, making himself look enormous, terrifying. "It is inaccurate to say that I am small."

Sheriff Lopez held his ground with a smile. "I mean no offence. I merely want to confirm that it's yours and to hear your explanation for making it."

"I cannot confirm, not having seen it, but I have, yes, walked through your town in your sleeping hours. You know little of my kind, but where I come from, we are famous for our curiosity."

"And where *do* you come from?"

"To the point at last," Kazimir said. "You would like me to say that I am Russian, as if the nations of men have any meaning to a dragon. You would like to think that I am a spy, if not a murderer. I am neither, Officer, and do you know why?"

"Tell me."

"Because I will outlive you," Kazimir said, simply. "If I

took a human life, my own would end, but why would I bother when my life is so much longer than yours? I win by simply outlasting you. For the same reason, why would I ever care about the fate of your nations, except when they would limit the freedom of mine? Why would you ever be so significant to me?"

"You work for us," Sarah's father said, and she could hear the anger. "You want our gold."

"You work your hogs," Kazimir said. "Yet you want their meat."

Sarah winced. This did not feel at all like the right thing to say.

"And do you want *our* meat, Mr Dragon?" the Sheriff said.

Kazimir lowered his head on that long neck, careening it down to their level. "It does not suit the stomach," he said. "Too much grit."

"*Did* you kill Deputy Kelby?" the Sheriff asked. "*Are* you a spy?"

"No," Kazimir said.

"No to which?"

Kazimir only smiled.

There had been little more after that. The Sheriff had no real evidence or, it seemed, any real belief of a connection between the dragon and the death of Deputy Kelby.

"But that might not matter to some people," the Sheriff told Kazimir. "I'd be careful, if I were you."

"I am always careful around men," the dragon had answered. "You are dangerous animals."

113

After that, Sarah and her father walked the Sheriff to his car.

"Do you really think it was the claw, Sheriff?" her father asked.

"Not especially. We found a human tooth in the alley and signs of a scuffle. The Deputy no doubt finally said the wrong thing to the wrong person."

He tipped his hat at them and left. They watched him drive away. She and her father were alone. Like they always were. Like they had been since her mother had passed.

"A tooth," her father said. "Isn't that interesting?"

"Dad–"

"Whatever it is you're too afraid to tell me," her father said, still watching the Sheriff's car head off into what was now falling snow. "I'm braver than you think."

He didn't wait for her to answer. He just headed back towards the house, leaving her there. She let that sink in, knowing she deserved it but wondering what to do. She found no answer. She moved to follow her father, but she felt Kazimir's footsteps behind her, terrifyingly quiet for a creature so large.

"Time to open your eyes, Sarah Dewhurst," he said, as if whispering into her ear. "The days grow short."

"What days?" she said, still watching the house her father had vanished into.

"The days until you meet your assassin."

She *did* turn at this, eyes wide.

"He is coming," the dragon said to her. "And he is going to kill you."

8

"But what do they mean?" Nelson said, tracing his finger along the tattoos down Malcolm's chest.

"That feels really nice," Malcolm said, a catch in his voice.

"And why do they stop here?" Nelson's fingers didn't stop at Malcolm's waistline, where the tattoos did. He carried on down through the uninked skin and hair.

"That feels nice, too."

They were at the border, waiting for the night to get late enough so there was no chance of traffic. It had taken most of three days to get there, even in Nelson's truck, not just because of the increasing snowstorm but because Malcolm had agreed to go to a crossing much farther east, all the way over in Montana, that Nelson said wouldn't be manned.

Their first night after the campground, with no tent and a fire a risk too far, they had huddled together in the truck for warmth, turning the engine on every hour or so to bring in a little heat.

"We're going to have to get close," Malcolm said, "or we'll freeze to death in our sleep."

"You sure?" Nelson said, with a little smile that Malcolm hadn't understood. Or *told* himself he didn't understand, when in fact he understood perfectly well and had hoped his voice didn't give it all away when he made the suggestion.

What on earth was he doing? Where had this come from? And why had those questions evaporated so completely when Nelson snuggled in behind him and started talking about his family, breathing a sad story into the back of Malcolm's neck? His parents had found him with someone. They didn't approve of that someone in a very violent way. His father had beat him, his mother had told him to never come back. Nelson had left, taking the truck he'd bought from his grandfather with money from farm work.

"Where are you going to go?" Malcolm had asked, wanting the breath to continue.

"Right now, I'm going to Montana with you."

"And after that?"

Nelson didn't answer, Malcolm turned around to see why, and it happened. Despite the freedom of the Believers, Malcolm had never been kissed, by anyone at all, until Nelson. Shy, questioning, but unambiguous, Nelson tasted warm and slightly sour and of tobacco and warm again. Then Nelson, in the relative warmth of the truck cabin, had started to undress him.

This was not in the preparations Malcolm had been given. He'd been warned of predatory men and women who might seek this in exchange for favours, favours like a ride to the border. He'd been warned about those who might try and take this from him by force. He had nodded and understood and accepted properly the wise words he had been given.

But this didn't feel like that. At all.

He was only ever supposed to accept a ride with someone when he was in deep extremity and only then for the briefest possible time. But he had happily agreed to another day's ride from Nelson. And then another day after that. And here they were again, Malcolm shivering in the cold while Nelson traced the tattoos on his skin.

"They're down your legs, too," Nelson said. "And you've had them a while." Nelson gently ran his fingers across Malcolm's inner thigh. "Your leg hair has had time to grow back."

"They start when we're very young," Malcolm answered. "They're our scripture."

"Like the Bible."

"In a sense. But it's more about your dedication to what you believe. The more you commit yourself, the more scripture is written on your body."

"And you know this when you're a child?"

"Believers don't think age is a barrier. Some of our most important preachers are children."

Like me, he didn't say. He had preached since age seven, been acclaimed for it. It had made him the obvious selection for this mission.

He pushed the thought of the mission firmly out of his mind.

Nelson kept looking – between Malcolm's legs, around his hips – seemingly more out of interest than lust. "It's a little cold to be all the way naked," Malcolm said, gooseflesh appearing everywhere.

"Only for a second. I want to see." Nelson glanced up. "If that's all right?"

Malcolm smiled. Nelson had become almost an entirely different person after the kiss. Softer, younger, like he'd thrown off the burden of having to defend himself against possible attack. Malcolm wondered if he would ever experience that feeling himself. His defences were for something else entirely, not for who he wanted to kiss, wanted to touch like this.

The second day, they had literally spoken to no one else save for a gas station attendant midway. Malcolm used his cash to fill the tank and buy them enough food for the road. Nelson's eyes had widened at the money.

"Is that why those people are after you?" he asked. "Did you rob a bank?"

"No," Malcolm said. "It's all mine, free and clear."

They got back on the road, going as fast as the snowstorm would let them. Malcolm felt some anxiety at their pace and that they were going in the wrong direction, but an unmanned border crossing was clearly high priority after being chased out of the campground. Besides, he was finding it hard to feel anxious about much in the presence of Nelson.

"So why are they after you?" Nelson asked carefully that second day, driving and eating the sandwich Malcolm had bought. "You never said."

Malcolm sighed. "I haven't done anything wrong, if that's what you're asking. People don't really like Believers. Officials especially. We rarely even leave our Cell compounds any more."

"Then why did you say you didn't want to kill them?" He glanced over. "Was that for real?"

"I wish it wasn't," Malcolm said, quietly. "I have to be somewhere. Soon. It's more important than I could even say. They would have stopped me. Tried to."

"You don't mean..." Nelson ate the last bite of his sandwich, trying to look nonchalant. "You don't mean actually *kill* them, though."

Malcolm watched him, watched his handsome profile, watched the way he cleaned his lips with thumb and pinkie. The question of attraction had barely come up in his training. It was a religious mission, not unlike priesthood or a nunnery. Relationships were never meant to enter it. That had been drummed into Malcolm since he was a boy. He had been surrounded by women, too, almost exclusively, his entire life, and though he knew about this feeling, there had almost literally been no opportunity to even entertain it, much less act on it.

He barely knew Nelson. Nelson knew him even less. But the connection had been so instant, so strong, that he already worried about disappointing him.

"Not actually, no," he lied, and his heart leapt at Nelson's disguised relief.

That night, lying together again, Nelson had said, "I never thought this was possible. I never thought this would ever happen."

Malcolm heard him crying, but Nelson wouldn't let him turn around to comfort him. He kept talking, though. "I always thought it would have to be rough. And violent. And full of shame."

Malcolm didn't ask why he thought that, but he could have taken some guesses.

119

"But this," Nelson said. "Like this." He choked up again. "I just don't believe it."

With that, he had finally allowed Malcolm to hold him. Malcolm pushed away all thoughts of the mission, of the very short time he had, of how he would – without fail – have to leave Nelson behind.

But not that night. And not this one either. Not just yet.

"And down over your feet," Nelson said, moving his hand across Malcolm's toes. Malcolm giggled involuntarily.

"Yeah," he said.

"Turn over."

Malcolm did, somewhat clumsily in the limited space, and felt Nelson's fingers moving down his bare back, along his spine, between his buttocks.

Oh, Mitera Thea, he thought, praying before he could even stop himself, but why shouldn't he? If it was all ordained? If it had all been seen and decided long before he was born? *Thank you,* he prayed, *thank you for sending me this.* And why wouldn't she? Was she not benevolent? Was she not the holiest Mitera Thea there had ever been? It was a secret for now, but when the rest of the Cells found out she had not only convinced a dragon to fly him to the start of his journey but actually incinerate two men so the mission wasn't lost, well, no Mitera Thea had achieved anything like as much in two hundred years. She truly, truly had the power of dragon blood in her, enough to change the world. Why wouldn't she be able to do this for him, her humble servant, if she chose? *Thank you, Mitera Thea, thank you.*

"You're *really* committed then, I guess?" Nelson said, still looking, his voice unsure.

"Does it bother you?"

"My experiences with religion aren't good."

"We think sexuality is healthy." He turned his head back around to look at Nelson. "That it's the dragon part of us."

Nelson grinned, shyly. Malcolm found his heart thumping just at the sight of it.

"I like that," Nelson said. "The dragon part of us."

He smiled again, and that was it, Malcolm's heart was lost.

"Goddammit," Agent Dernovich said, not for the first time.

"I would ask you to watch your language," Agent Woolf said, also not for the first time.

"I *am* watching it. I'm watching myself swear because we *had* him. We had the little fucker and now–"

That word, apparently, was too much for Agent Woolf, who got out of the car with her notebook and headed back to her hotel room. The last hotel room they were probably going to get out of this trip. The APB – or whatever equivalent the Canadians used – had found no truck, no boys, no sign of what Agent Dernovich was now completely convinced was their would-be assassin.

"How can they not have found him?" he'd asked, a hundred times in the last seventy-two hours.

"It's a big place," she'd replied. "Lots of roads to cover. And they're not happy we're here."

That was an understatement. The Canadians were fuming. They knew, of course, that Bureau agents were in the country, but had diplomatically looked the other way as long as they kept their heads down and stayed on the sidelines. The APB had violated that, especially when Dernovich connected it directly to the murder of two of his own who had been melted on a road. The Canadians had also been less than happy when Dernovich had used the word "assassin", and even less so when he couldn't say who the assassin was supposed to assassinate. He had stopped short of telling them about the threat of all-out war.

Cutler had been called on the carpet by his bosses, who'd been called on the carpet by the Canadian government. There'd been a lot of carpet-calling, all of which had landed back down on Dernovich. Which would have been fine if days hadn't kept passing with that bastard Believer kid still not being seen.

Dernovich went to his own room. It was late. Woolf was right to be pissed off at him. He was frankly pissed off at *her*, as she'd been spending more and more time in her notebooks, going through those damn runes that had offered nothing but gibberish. On the other hand, maybe that's not what she was doing at all. Maybe she was writing up a report about her no-good partner.

He put a nickel in the TV to watch the news, but had barely heard the first headline when his hotel room phone rang.

"Is that Agent Dernovich?" a Canadian voice said, politely.

Dernovich made a disgusted sound. "You guys ever heard of a tapped phone line?"

"I'm sorry," said the voice, still polite, affecting not to hear Dernovich's sarcasm. "Is that Agent Dernovich?"

"It is."

"Think we found your truck here, Agent."

Dernovich sat up so fast his head spun.

"You still there, Agent?" said the voice.

"Where?" was all Agent Dernovich replied.

Even before properly waking, Malcolm knew the knock on the truck window wasn't friendly. He opened his eyes and looked straight into the beam of a powerful flashlight picking its way over Malcolm's face, his bare shoulders under the blanket, the bare shoulders of the now-waking Nelson behind him.

"Oh, no," he heard Nelson breathe.

"Whatever moves you're about to make," said a voice behind the flashlight, "you're going to make them nice and slowly."

"We're not doing anything wrong," Nelson started.

"Not what it looks like to me," said the voice. "Put your clothes on. No sudden moves."

"Oh, no," Nelson kept whispering, "oh, no, oh, no, oh, no."

"It's okay," Malcolm whispered back, gathering the clothes that lay scrunched around them. He was shivering. It had really been far too cold to stay naked, but how could you not when it felt that nice?

He wondered if he would ever feel that way again.

He sat up, seeing the man holding the flashlight. He was an RCMP and had a pistol in his other hand. Nelson saw it, too, and raised his own hands in response.

"As long as you just get dressed and don't try anything," the Mountie said, "I'm not going to shoot you."

"Then why are you pointing a gun at us?" Nelson asked, pulling on his shirt.

"He's not pointing it at us," Malcolm said, also dressing, but keeping his eye on the Mountie. "He's pointing it at *me*."

"How did they find us?" Nelson asked.

"Maybe this border isn't as unwatched as you thought."

"That's what my grandfather told me–"

"I'm not blaming you," Malcolm said, calmly. "I'm really not." He smiled at Nelson. A true one. *Let there be that, at least,* he thought.

"Hurry up in there," the Mountie said. "It's not getting any warmer."

Malcolm put on his thick sweater, feeling the sleeves as he pushed his arms through.

"We're getting out now," Malcolm said. "Don't shoot us."

"That depends on you," said the Mountie.

Malcolm opened the door. Nelson did the same behind him. Malcolm stepped out into the snow, his hands in the air. Nelson started coming around the front of the truck.

"You stop right there for a minute," the Mountie said to him. Nelson did. The Mountie turned back to Malcolm. "Is your name Malcolm?"

"No," Malcolm said, simply, as this was actually the truth.

The Mountie's face hardened a little. "I'm looking for a teenage male Believer in a rusted brown truck making for the American border." He shone his flashlight in Nelson's face, making him squint. "Possibly in the company of another teenage male." The Mountie brought the flashlight back to Malcolm. "And you're telling me you're not him?"

"No," Malcolm said, "just that my name isn't Malcolm."

"Are you playing smart with me?"

"No."

"No, *sir.*"

"No, sir."

The Mountie glanced again at Nelson. "Your kind disgust me, you know that?" He spat in the snow at Malcolm's feet. "Fruits."

"Watch your mouth," Nelson said.

The flashlight was back on his face in an instant. "What was that?"

Nelson's face was suddenly angry, *very* angry. Malcolm got a terrible feeling in his stomach and silently adjusted his sleeves.

"I took enough of that from my dad," Nelson said. He hooked his index finger in his mouth and showed him an empty tooth socket that Malcolm's tongue had recently visited. "That's what the last person who called me a fruit did. I promised myself no one would ever do it again."

"Well, now, that's a pretty speech," said the Mountie, "but I'm the one with the gun. I can take as many of your teeth as I want to."

Quick as he could – which was *very* quick, as he'd been trained for this, as he'd nearly been trained for *only* this – Malcolm shunted the blades from his sleeves to his hands, and before the Mountie even saw what was happening, Malcolm swung his arm out in a single arc.

Efficient. Exact. His arm was already back down to his side as if nothing had happened.

The Mountie blinked in surprise and put the palm of his flashlight hand up to his neck. The light accidentally illuminated the blood now spurting from the incision Malcolm had made in his jugular. It pulsed with the beat of the Mountie's heart, letting out a little spray every time that muscle contracted.

"You fffff…" the Mountie said, swinging the gun towards Malcolm. But he never made a shot, and they never knew what the "f" was going to stand for – nothing good, probably – because the Mountie slumped to his knees, dropping the gun. The flashlight lit the sprays of bright red being flung onto the snow and onto Malcolm's trouser legs. The Mountie made a terrible swallowing noise and fell, face first, between Malcolm's feet.

Then all there was to hear was the snowfall, which was silent as a breath, and nothing to see but the shadows across Nelson's horrified face.

"Can't they go any faster!" Agent Dernovich shouted at the RCMP Security Service vehicle ahead of them, an unmarked Oldsmobile, just like theirs; did all Secret Service drive Oldsmobiles? Did criminals know to be on constant lookout for them?

The RCMP had granted them use of a helicopter to get out here, but the snow was so bad, the pilot would only land back at base, leaving them an hour's drive to the border.

"They're Canadian," Agent Woolf said, face still in her notebook. "I would trust them to know the fastest safe speed in snowfall."

"I grew up in the Cascades, Agent. I know a thing or two about driving in snow." He only just stopped himself from smacking the horn in anger. "The boy will be long gone by the time we get there."

"The RCMP said he was going to detain them until we arrived."

"And no one's heard from him since."

"It's practically a blizzard, Paul," she nearly snapped, then looked as surprised as he was that she'd used his first name. "Sorry. Agent Dernovich."

"Not a problem." Agent Dernovich scowled. "*Veronica.*"

Her voice was innocent as a lamb. "Is it the Polish spelling? Pol?"

"No. Dernovich is Croatian. I'm named after my father's brother who died in the Great War."

"All wars are great if you're in them."

"Do you have anything helpful to say, Agent Woolf?"

"I mean no disrespect," she said. "My mind is elsewhere."

"No kidding your mind is elsewhere. You've hardly looked up from that page for the last two days. Those runes aren't going to tell you anything different."

"Yes, but..."

"But what? But *what*, Veronica?"

She blew out a thoughtful breath. "The Mitera Thea won't speak to us."

"She won't speak to anyone. We've only gotten written responses out of her, even though we've been clear on the possible ramif–"

"Let me finish."

She said it so calmly, he was surprised into silence.

"What if she sent the assassin herself?" she said.

"That's our whole working theory, Woolf!"

"Not as Mitera Thea, not as a representative of all Believers, but as herself. One person, acting independently."

"What difference could that possibly make?"

"The Believers are riven with sects. Sects that compete for primacy. We've always known that the current Mitera Thea is from a sect that relies heavily on prophecy." She raised a hand to ward off his interruption. "Which is how this investigation first started, yes, you don't need to tell me. Now, prophecy is usually vague nonsense. Worded so broadly it could mean nearly anything. Any time anything does happen, the prophecy can be pretty much made to fit in retrospect."

Dernovich finally butted in. "So how is that helpful in the middle of a Canadian blizzard when we're on our way at a frigging snail's pace to apprehend what might be the assassin we're looking for. Who is maybe a teenage *boy*. God, just saying it out loud makes me hear how crazy you people are."

She pressed on, wincing slightly, as if she was politely ignoring a fart. "If the Mitera Thea wanted to hide something from us, she'd simply call diplomatic immunity and that would be that, but if she wanted to hide it from other Believers, what would she do?"

"Leaving aside the question of *why* she'd want to do that, you tell me."

"She might hide it in plain sight. The Believers are believers in red dragons, always have been, but there are five dragon breeds in the world, each of them with a similar but not quite identical language that each uses the same pictographic, runic alphabet."

"What are you telling me?"

"The languages have a lot of overlap. I've been trying to

translate those runes via the language of reds. They make enough vague sense that way to feel like prophecy, certainly enough for the Believers to build entire Cells around. But what if it's *not* in red? We'd never considered it because that makes absolutely no sense for the Mitera Thea. She'd disregard anything in any other dragon language."

"But if she was doing it on her own–"

"It turns out that the runes also make a vague prophetic sense if you translate via the language of the greens and the whites. They make no sense at all via the desert dragon language." She finally held up her notebook. "They make perfect, almost exact sense if translated via blue."

Agent Dernovich's eyes raced over the page. "Holy shit. Hidden in plain sight."

"No one would ever dream the Mitera Thea would follow a prophecy of the blues. It would fundamentally go against who she is. She would, in fact, not be the Mitera Thea if she did so."

"But she did."

"And if she did that, who knows what other rules she might break?"

"Hire a dragon to kill humans? It would take a lot of gold to break that taboo."

"Believers hand over all their worldly wealth when they join. Paying for it wouldn't be a problem."

Dernovich's heart sank right down to his belt. "My God, if she's gone that far–"

"Then we have to stop her. Fortunately, I think I've figured out her target."

"Who?"

"I'm not exactly sure of the name, but I know where and when."

"What about *why*?"

Agent Woolf looked surprised. "Why ever else, Agent Dernovich? Because that's where the end of the world begins."

9

"What you must remember through all of this," Kazimir said, "is that you are not special."

"Well, that's just terrific," Sarah said, shivering in the gathering snow. Though the moon was well hidden behind what was probably miles of clouds, the whole farm seemed to glow from the white that covered everything. It was the fourth night in a row she'd tried to get answers out of him. The constant lack of sleep and overall tension were wearing on her. She'd even told Jason about the assassin, even though Kazimir had warned her not to. The fact that Jason hadn't even doubted her was yet more proof of how strange life had become. "When are you going to tell me something practical, like exactly when this supposed assassin is coming or–"

"You are merely lucky," Kazimir continued, ignoring her.

"*Lucky?* How has any of this been lucky?"

"You have no special abilities. You have no special bloodline – or what passes for bloodline among your species. You have no history or strength or intelligence that would mark you out in any way."

"Okay," Sarah breathed against the snowfall. "Now, you're just being mean for the sake of it."

"Do not misunderstand me," the dragon said. "You may have those things in abundance in other areas of your life. You certainly have shown a resourcefulness and a capaciousness of character I have found most surprising, but for the purposes of your death, there is no intrinsic reason why you should be the one and others not. It is merely a coincidence of timing."

"So you've said, but I don't know why I need to be insulted–"

He grunted in what finally seemed to be frustration. "Because there is a prophecy about you, Sarah Dewhurst."

She stopped. "Me?"

"Not you in particular." The dragon looked around at the farm, the snow, the forest, the steel antenna and great shadow of Mount Rainier hidden somewhere beyond. "But this time. This place." He looked back down on her, his eye seeming to glow, and not for the first time she was reminded of the old wives' tale of dragons being able to hypnotize you. "This *exact* time. This *exact* place. And a girl."

"What's supposed to happen?"

"A moment in which war itself pivots."

"War?"

He looked frustrated, but not at her. "Presumably. The language of prophecy is never so clear. It is always 'worlds colliding' and 'worlds ending'. Which is why they should usually not be taken seriously."

"I shouldn't take someone coming to murder me seriously?"

"On the whole, one should worry less about prophecies and more about the lunatics who believe them."

"So I have a *lunatic* coming to murder me?"

"That is accurate."

"Because he believes a prophecy that isn't true?"

"That is what is so troubling. This one has proven quite true so far." He frowned. "My breed are scholars, and as such, rather more sceptical than others. We freed ourselves from the Goddess long ago and feel no allegiance to the furious dictums she left behind."

"You have an actual *Goddess*? I thought that was just something the Believers made up–"

"But this particular prophecy, the only one clearly in my own tongue, has been coming true in pieces for decades. We kept it secret, again not for itself but for those lunatics, mostly among your own kind, who might act on it. Yet somehow it was found. As, in fact, it was predicted to be. And so here I sit, watching it unfold further, intervening where I must."

"Why you? Who are you that intervention is your responsibility?"

He didn't answer at first, clearly deciding how much he would. "Dragon magic is wild," he finally said. "It is so untameable and dangerous it only properly exists beyond this world. The dragons you know are, in essence, safe containers of it. If the magic came here unfiltered, it would destroy everything."

"I didn't know that," Sarah said, an understatement.

"Most humans do not. It would make our relations even more difficult if you did, but the truth is, we exist as a sort of safety valve between you and it. It is a balance that must be maintained or all is lost, for dragon and man alike. But much of the knowledge is forgotten. The blues are the guardians of what remains. The prophecy suggests that this place – and a girl within it – is the pivot of a war that could wreck that balance and destroy us all."

"So they sent you–"

"To do what I can, if I can."

"If?"

He ruffled his wings in a way she guessed was a shrug. "Our theology believes that everything that happens has already happened, somewhere, sometime, and will happen again and again, somewhere, sometime. In an infinite number of other worlds. We have felt echoes of this happening before where it went very, very badly. We have a vested interest in trying to prevent that happening again."

Sarah swallowed. "And killing me is part of this particular prophecy?"

"You are the pivot," the dragon said, and for the first time ever, he sounded *kind*. It was almost more upsetting than being told her death was coming. "If your assassin kills you, then there is no hope at all."

Gareth Dewhurst watched his daughter and the dragon through his darkened bedroom window. He couldn't guess what they might be talking about, but he didn't believe it would hurt her. It had helped her with Kelby at least once and – as was seeming more and more likely – in a very final way a second time.

But another letter had arrived.

The time draws close, Mr Dewhurst. By now, it is likely your dragon will have performed the first of his prophesied deeds, that of taking an action to spare your daughter's life. We do not know the exact circumstances of this, but we suspect you know of what we speak.

How did they know? No one could tell the future, and those who believed they could were lunatics.

Do not be deceived. He protects your daughter for his own purposes. He will befriend her, but he will lie to her. He will appear as an ally, a confidant. He will not be.

Gareth Dewhurst was not a stupid man. He knew full well the letter could contain equal lies as the ones it was accusing the dragon of spinning. How could you possibly take an anonymous letter seriously?

There are larger issues at stake than your daughter, but we know that will not be true for you personally. We appeal to you through her then. She is in danger. The dragon will not harm her directly – we cannot lie, though it would be easier to convince you if we could – but he will, by his actions, cause her to be harmed.

And if this wasn't true, if the dragon didn't harm her...

We ask for action from you, Mr Dewhurst. If not, we will be forced to take matters into our own hands, which would – through no fault of your own – cause great difficulties for you and your family.

There was the threat. If he didn't do it, *they* would, and screw you, Gareth Dewhurst.

He was certain they would carry it out, too, for they had sent a delivery to his doorstep this very day.

* * *

"I don't understand any of this," Sarah said.

"There is no need for you to," said Kazimir. "There is only need for you to prepare."

"I kind of feel like *I'm* the one who decides what I need to understand. If I'm the one whose life is at stake."

He cocked his head, watching her anger as if he was deciding something. "So be it. Very soon, Russian humans are sending a machine up into the sky, far higher than any other before. Higher than even your aeroplanes, which have made dragon flying so dangerous."

"You mean the satellite?" Sarah asked. "How do you know about that?"

He didn't answer. "When that happens, men believe dragons will no longer have dominion over their lives. That you will know all our secrets."

Sarah realized how true this probably was. A side effect of humanity's race to destroy itself, but–

"Oh, my God," she said. "Dragons won't put up with that. There will be war–"

"We have suffered the spies of men for centuries," Kazimir said. "I would have hoped we could find ways to protect ourselves. But the prophecy says war, a war that will be the end of men and dragons. What occurs here in this very place, in a very few days' time, will decide whether war happens or not. And because of where you are and *when* you are, you will be in a position to stop it."

"But how could I possibly stop a war–?"

"Others know this about you. It has been foretold. They believe that if they can stop you at the precisely correct moment, then the prophecy will be averted. And war will be upon us, men and dragons finally unleashed. This is why the assassin comes for you."

"He *wants* war?"

"*They* do. He himself may not even know. The prophecy suggests he might believe the opposite, which would give his mission a holy imprimatur of peace. If so, he would be coming as a religious fanatic, the most dangerous lunatic of all."

She crossed her arms against the cold. "So what do I do then?"

He shifted from foot to foot. "You will know."

She glanced back up at him, realizing. "Oh, my God," she said. "You don't know either."

The plough might do it. It was old, but it had been built to last, being mostly iron. Dragonhide was notoriously tough, but the plough could break it, if there was any way to get it moving fast enough. There was an old belief, possibly not more than a folk tale, that if you rammed a dragon in the exact right spot, their fire-generating organ would burst, killing them from the inside. There were absolutely no authenticated dragon deaths by this method, but Gareth had put idle thought into how he might tie the plough to the front of his truck.

This new letter, though, told him differently. Apparently, he would have to poison it. That's what had been delivered today. Three large bags labelled "fertilizer" which weren't fertilizer at all. The letter told him it was a chemical that mixed violently with that same fire-generating organ and, in sufficient amounts, would corrupt its bloodstream, killing the beast. As dragons were sometimes known to die (on the rare occasions that happened at all) of a similar condition on their own – something like a human having a heart attack – there wasn't much chance of a human action behind it being uncovered.

The letter suggested slaughtering a pig and filling its stomach with the "fertilizer", then feeding it to the dragon, hoping it would swallow it down like dragons tended to do with their food. In order to throw off suspicion, the letter suggested, he should slaughter all three of his pigs as if they were the ones who'd been poisoned, leaving the fertilized one as the second.

Such a clear plan. It might even work. Sarah would be devastated at the loss of Bess, Mamie, and Eleanor, but with five thousand dollars in the bank, he could buy as many more as she wanted. And if the letter was right, she'd at least be alive to be devastated.

If the letter was right.

"You don't know what's supposed to happen or what I'm supposed to do."

The dragon looked unhappy. "It is somewhat unclear," he admitted, grudgingly. "The future shifts. It changes. It's why prophecies are so vague, so that they may fit whatever circumstances come and still look true. We blues are right to treat them with suspicion. But this one describes things that went on to happen. More than once. It did not, however, fill in every connection or – as you keep demanding – *why*. Perhaps those events even happened not because they were foretold but because someone read the prophecy and *caused* them to occur. Regardless, the stakes are high enough that it cannot be ignored."

"Who says it's prophecy anyway? Who *made* it?"

"Our Goddess, of course, as I've said."

"There's no 'of course' about it, Kazimir. Everyone knows Believers worship one. No one knows dragons do, too."

"We do not *worship* her." He made a grumble of disgust. "She created us and then tried to destroy all Creation."

"Why?"

"Because she is the untamed magic I spoke of. It exists just out of your sight, but it rages against your world like a tempest. *She* was the one who reached into it and brought all dragons into being in the blink of an eye. We contain only a fragment of that magic; she channels it *all* and cannot exist in this world for long without destroying it. She is fire without boundary and would devour everything. It is the nature of gods to do so. They must either be defeated or trapped in the confines of something like your human minds lest everything they touch turn to ash."

"You defeated your own Goddess?"

"We did what was necessary. Millennia ago. But that does not mean that there are not those who would carry out her mission no matter what the cost."

"But if we know it, know it's coming, couldn't that stop it?"

"Knowing the future is part of that future's past. Perhaps the foreseen happens because we try to change it."

"I don't see *any* future," Sarah said, truly fed up. She found herself thinking of Jason, how much she wanted him to be here now, hearing this. Not that he'd know any better, but he'd be a nice ... touchstone. That's a word her mother used. Touchstone. She used it about her father. A rock you could

139

count on. A rock you could launch from and feel confident you wouldn't fall.

"Nevertheless," the dragon said, "the future is coming. A killer is coming. For you. I will try to stop him."

She looked up at this. "Try? Doesn't the prophecy say if you succeed or not?"

"It says both yes and no."

"That's just great."

"Indeed, it says both yes and no about the ultimate outcome as well. We are in the hands of Goddesses and madmen, Sarah Dewhurst."

"You know," she said, "I'm beginning to wonder why I even got out of bed."

Gareth Dewhurst watched his daughter stomp angrily away from the dragon.

He made his decision.

10

Nelson had said almost nothing for nearly four hours.

They were now in Montana. They had left the body of the Mountie where he died, in the red spray across the snow, then Malcolm had corralled Nelson into the passenger seat and had taken the wheel of the truck himself. They'd crossed the border, empty now that its single guard was gone, and driven into the mountains of the United States of America.

They were on a road that led to a town called Kalispell. Nelson had only pointed when Malcolm asked him directions. Every once in a while, Malcolm would catch Nelson looking at the blood that still stained Malcolm's trouser legs. Nelson would look away again hurriedly and refuse to answer any of Malcolm's entreaties.

Malcolm felt an ache in himself, an ache that missed the closeness of Nelson, even though he was right there; the smell of him, the weight and warmth of his body and his hands. So near still, but across an impossible barrier now. He swallowed away a tightening in his throat as they drove through the increasing snow. If they could get to Kalispell, maybe he would have a chance to explain. Maybe he could share his mission with Nelson. Maybe he could–

"I want you to get out," Nelson said, so quietly Malcolm had to ask him to repeat it. "I want you," he repeated, his voice rising, "to get the hell out of my truck!"

Malcolm didn't stop driving. It would have been difficult anyway, a long, slow process of braking and waiting, so he just kept on, while Nelson began to weep.

"He would have killed us," Malcolm said, quietly.

"You don't know that," Nelson said, his voice thick with tears.

"He would have killed *me*."

"That doesn't make any sense."

Malcolm didn't say that the Mountie would have killed him because he would have fought until the Mountie was forced to. Perhaps this wasn't the same thing.

But if he didn't complete his mission, the Mountie and Nelson and everyone and everything they ever knew was dead anyway. The Mitera Thea couldn't state that enough. The mission was the only way for there to be peace, she said, no matter what anyone else might tell him.

Perhaps that wouldn't make any sense either.

"You heard what he said to us," Malcolm said. "You heard his disgust."

"It was only right," Nelson said, his voice despairing.

Now Malcolm looked at him. "No. No, it wasn't."

"We're fruits. We're disgusting."

"We are *not* disgusting."

"How can you say that?"

142

* * *

"Believers have a much more relaxed view of human sexuality than almost everyone," Agent Woolf said.

"I really don't need to hear any more of that kind of talk–"

"It doesn't matter what you want to hear, Agent Dernovich. If you close your mind to something that may bring this case to a conclusion, then you don't deserve to be on it."

Agent Dernovich gaped at her. Not just at her words – "sexuality" being the least of them – or her tone, which was calm but firm, but at the utter confidence with which she spoke them. She knew she was right, and she was never going to apologize to him for his own wrongness.

He tried to keep his voice under control. "We are standing at a murder scene, Agent Woolf. Of a fellow officer–"

"Yes, and the murderer is driving away, with another boy who could be his lover–"

"Or captive, Agent Woolf. Or accomplice."

"He would never have an accomplice."

"I don't understand what possible point is made by bringing perversion into this–"

"Because if he has feelings for this other boy, it might give us a way to capture him."

He wanted to strangle her. Not literally. Maybe literally. Her damnable calm, for one, in a snowstorm that still hadn't managed to cover all the blood that had flowed out of Royal Canadian Mounted Policeman John C. Callahan, married father of four children. Then there was also her rightness. Again. As without force or aggression, she simply described

143

the obvious next plan of action. He had no idea how she had made the leap to their boy being *that way* but...

If she was right.

They were surrounded by a horde of angry Mounties, understandably furious at the loss of their colleague. They wanted answers, specifically how the hell this had happened to an eighteen-year veteran at the hands of a teenager. So cleanly, so brutally efficient. But most especially, they wanted to know exactly to what degree these two Americans were responsible for it.

The RCMP Superintendent, who hadn't even said hello when they arrived and who was demanding every five minutes to know what the US was doing to find the murderer, approached them again. "We've got an ID on the licence plate Sergeant Callahan radioed in," he said, though he certainly didn't make it sound like a prelude to good news, which it wasn't, given that it was Sergeant Callahan's last ever official act.

"What did you find?" Agent Dernovich asked him.

"And why would I keep you informed about a Canadian police matter when you don't see fit to–?"

"Superintendent–"

"There are enormous issues at stake, Superintendent," Woolf broke in.

"More than the death of my officer?" the Superintendent fumed. "More than some crazy Believer assassin you tell me we've got running around?"

"I'm afraid so," Woolf said, her calm catching the Super-intendent's attention the same way it had so often caught Dernovich's.

"Perhaps you'd care to share those issues with me, Agent,"

the Superintendent said, addressing only her.

"Above my pay grade, but I can tell you we are authorized to stop him with extreme prejudice."

We are? Dernovich only just kept himself from saying out loud. Whether that was true or not – and boy, was he going to find out – it was working on the Superintendent, who finally seemed to think he was getting some proper support.

"Plate came back to a family in Vancouver," he told them.

"Long way from here," Dernovich said, trying to add something to the conversation. The Superintendent ignored him.

"Parents say their son–" and here he read from his notes– "Nelson Arriaga, seventeen, took it when he left home last week."

"Why did he leave home?" Woolf asked.

The Superintendent read again. "Parents say he was, quote, 'an abomination against God'."

Woolf's eyebrows raised. She looked over at Dernovich, who asked, "What do they mean by that?"

"Fruitcake. Found him with another boy. Threw him out." The Superintendent looked at them seriously. "Do you think that might be something we can use?"

The Superintendent clearly thought it was, so Dernovich said, "Yes, yes, we do," before Woolf could beat him to it.

"Believers take a different view of what humans do together than most people," Malcolm said.

"Obviously," Nelson said, the bitterness apparent, even through the tears.

"I don't mean that. We're not killers."

"Could've fooled me."

"I'm ... on a mission."

"One that involves killing policemen?"

Malcolm hesitated, then said, "If need be."

Nelson looked back out his window at the snow and empty road. "Get out of my truck," he said again, but the anger had gone.

"The world... It's on a knife edge, Nelson. Something's coming that will send it one way or another, and if it's not sent the right way... All of this, the snow, this truck, you, me. All of that vanishes. Ends. We all die."

"You're crazy."

"Believe me, I wish it weren't true."

"How are you different from my parents, then? Huh? They said the world was ending, too." His voice dropped. "They said I was part of it."

"How am I different?" Malcolm put his hand gently on Nelson's thigh, not as a prelude to anything physical, just as a comfort. "I would have thought that was clear."

"You killed that man."

"I wish I didn't have to."

"You didn't–"

"Nelson–"

Nelson pushed his hand away. "You ruined it. For a minute there..." He looked miserably out the window again. "You ruined it."

Malcolm didn't reply. It seemed he *had* ruined it. The sob in his throat threatened again, and he swallowed it down, like he had been trained to. He would drive to Kalispell, and then he would leave Nelson to his truck, wishing him the best.

Though it was the truck the police were undoubtedly now

looking for, he thought, and Nelson had no training to avoid being captured. Malcolm looked back over to the boy he'd so recently been close to, whose body he had explored and been explored in return. Now probably doomed, all because he'd helped Malcolm.

He really *had* ruined everything.

"What's the name of the town again?" Dernovich asked as he drove. They'd left almost immediately, Woolf putting off the RCMP with mutterings about "top secret missions", again in language Dernovich would have very much liked to use out loud himself.

"Kalispell," Woolf said. "About sixty miles from here."

"They've got half a day's head start."

"Yes, but in a snowstorm."

"A snowstorm that affects us, too, Agent."

She sighed, clearly impatient. When had the power shifted between them? When had she gone from his subordinate to someone who could sigh so contemptuously without fear of reprisal? Maybe it had always been like that and he was too stupid to have noticed.

"It matters not," she said, actually using those words, like a Henry James novel, not that Agent Dernovich had ever read one. "We know where he's going. The other boy will be useful if we can find him, but the road still ends at the same place."

"Frome, Washington."

"Frome, Washington," she confirmed.

"And you're sure about that?"

"It's not just the prophecy," she said, taking out that

infernal notebook. "I had a hunch and got all the intel Cutler had on this satellite the Russians are launching. They've moved up the date. It could be tomorrow or the day after, at the latest."

"What?" he said, genuinely surprised. "What the hell does that have to do with the price of fish?"

"It's a spy satellite, Agent Dernovich."

"Yes, of course it is, but again I say, so what?"

"In all the tension between the US and Russia, we never considered that the dragons aren't going to like being spied on, either."

"So the dragons get the Believer Pope they've always ignored to suddenly send an assassin from Canada to a nothing town in Washington? Make a connection that works, Woolf, or quit wasting my time."

"It's going to launch from a remote station in Siberia."

"Is there anything in Siberia that couldn't be called remote?"

She ignored that. "Intel has gathered info from its sources in the country and has plotted possible first orbits of the satellite. Guess where almost all of them cross more or less first in the continental US?"

"Frome, Washington?"

She nodded.

"Why? What the hell's there?"

"For the Soviets? Nothing. Just an entry point on its way to DC. For the Believers, though." She ran her finger over the dragon runes in her notebook again, looking somewhat uncertain for the first time. "As best as I can translate..."

"Yes?"

"They say it's the tipping point."

"So I'm lost either way?" Nelson said, looking surprisingly small on the motel room bed.

They'd had no choice. The roads were getting more and more impassable in the snow; they hadn't enough fuel to stay in the truck without freezing to death; and there was no campground left open in the entire state, it seemed. They had taken the cheapest motel room possible and just had to hope the police wouldn't find them in the storm.

"I can protect you," Malcolm said, "if you come with me. But the police will be looking for your truck and for you."

"I didn't do anything."

"I'll tell them that. After my mission." He did not add, *If I survive.*

Nelson put his head in his hands, running two anguished fists through his hair. "This is hell. This is actual hell."

"I'm sorry."

"Well, that makes everything better."

"Does it?"

Nelson looked up at him. "Who even are you?"

"I'm Malcolm."

"Is that your real name?"

"I don't have a real name. Malcolm is as real as it can be."

"That makes no sense. They had to call you something."

"The Mitera Thea never needed to. She always knew who I was."

"Isn't she, like, your Pope or something?"

"Mitera Thea? She is the source of it all."

"All what?"

"Knowledge. Power. The future and the past. Hers were the first words I heard in the morning and the last at night. She'd leave me recordings when she had to travel. I still pray to her. And sometimes she comes to my aid. As, I hope, now."

Nelson looked at him, his eyes red and sad. "You're talking about someone sending a dragon, aren't you?"

"If that's what it needs to be."

"Coming here?"

Malcolm was unsure of this, but he *had* been praying. Mitera Thea worked in mysterious ways. "Maybe," he said.

"You actually expect a dragon to come here and help you?"

"Help *us*."

"Why?"

"Because I asked."

Nelson was incredulous. "And that's enough, is it?"

Malcolm could barely stand the still-stinging sadness in Nelson's eyes. "We believe they're angels. Heaven on earth." But even as he said it, he knew that didn't quite cover it. Anyone could believe that without dedicating their life to the Belief, without living in a Cell, without offering up unquestioning commitment to a mission that would require man's laws to be broken and for Malcolm's own life to almost certainly end.

What *could* explain it? That he'd known nothing else? But that was like saying he'd known nothing else but life on earth. There *was* nothing else. He had been cared for. He had been nurtured and protected. Now, he would do the same in return. It was hardly even a sacrifice.

Believer was an ironic name. Like he'd said to Nelson,

it was an unnecessary word when what you believed in moved among you. It merely distinguished them from all the unbelievers who had to take on a kind of bizarre anti-faith *not* to believe. He pitied the rest of the world.

He also pitied Nelson, but in a different way. There again was the sob threatening to break free. He had not expected this. Had not expected to feel so fast, so deeply.

"Will the dragon burn us?" Nelson asked, slumping down into himself. "Will it burn this all away?"

Nelson sounded like that was exactly what he wanted, and Malcolm's heart broke afresh.

"We can't possibly be this lucky," Agent Dernovich said.

"Why not?" Agent Woolf said, as they idled the Oldsmobile in the motel parking lot.

Where they were blocking in the rusted brown truck they'd been seeking.

"Why not indeed?" Agent Dernovich said, taking out his gun.

"It might burn things," Malcolm said, gently, "but it would spare me. And you."

"I don't want to be spared."

"*I* want you to be spared."

Nelson began to cry again. Malcolm waited a moment, then moved to the bed next to him. This time, Nelson didn't pull away. He allowed Malcolm to put an arm around him, and then another, allowed himself to be brought into an embrace. Once again, Malcolm's nose was filled with the smell of him, and oh, how his heart reached for that smell, *longed* for it, as if it was an answer to a question Malcolm never knew he had been asking. He breathed in Nelson.

Oh, Mitera Thea, he prayed, *save him. If not me, him. I beg you.*

Nelson suddenly looked up. "Do you hear something outside?"

"You don't want to wait for back-up?" Agent Woolf said, as they stood outside the motel room door, directed there by an alarmed manager who Dernovich had sent scampering.

"Back-up from where, exactly?" he said. "The Canadians are an hour away in heavy snow and, need I remind you, we're in Montana now. They have no jurisdiction here."

"We had no jurisdiction in–"

"Back-up from the Billings office is even farther than that. We need to stop this. Right here, right now."

She considered for a moment, then nodded at him and took her place on the other side of the door frame. His blood was jumping, but finally with something other than bafflement and missed opportunities. *This* was the stuff he knew how to do. Apprehension, interrogation, extreme prejudice, if necessary (though it still galled him *she* was the one who got to say it out loud to the Superintendent). Her expertise was what got her put on this job, but he had expertise, too.

As the little murdering shitbag who had made a new widow today was about to find out.

"Ready?" he asked.

* * *

"Go into the bathroom," Malcolm said, urgently, with such solemn command Nelson barely even hesitated, just looked frightened (*I've lost him,* Malcolm thought then, and knew it to be true) and started moving–

It was too late. The door burst open with the boot of a man who was clearly a colleague of the two men who'd tried to kill Malcolm in the woods. A woman was with him. Both had their guns drawn.

"Freeze!" the man yelled. Malcolm heard Nelson cry out, but he didn't look around. He kept his eyes on the man as he stepped a little in front of the woman, who had her own gun on Nelson. "Drop it," the man said, for he had seen the blade Malcolm held in his hand.

Malcolm did not drop it, his heart pumping. *Guide me,* he prayed. *This cannot end here. I know you will not let it.*

"Drop it, or I will kill you," the man said.

"We need him alive," the woman said.

"That's up to him. *Drop it.* I'm not going to count to five. I'm just going to shoot you, all right?"

Malcolm looked at the blade in his hand. It seemed so far away, so oddly quiet amongst all this shouting. Almost like it was a secret, a whisper.

He dropped it.

I am in your keeping, Mitera Thea. I hand myself over to you.

"Cover me, Woolf," the man said. His gun was still out as he approached, but he lowered it slightly to take a pair of manacles out of his coat pocket. "I'm going to put these on you," he said, "and if you try anything, anything at all, she'll shoot you dead." The man addressed the woman without looking at her. "You got him?"

"Affirmative," the woman said, her gun now pointed at Malcolm.

The man lowered his gun.

Malcolm released the second blade he held in his left sleeve. It fell silently into his hand. The man took Malcolm's right, raising the open cuff of steel to slap on him. Malcolm moved his left arm back to start the swing.

"No," Nelson said, seeing, "don't!"

The man's eyes met Malcolm's.

Malcolm swung the blade.

A gunshot filled the room like a wave, unbelievably loud in the small space.

Mitera Thea, he said. *How does the world end?*

It ends in fire, of course, she said. *But we will change its destiny. We will change it entire.*

What is my role?

You are the tipping point. You will nudge history in the right direction, and it will be changed.

And all will be glorious?

All will be glorious.

Mitera Thea?

Yes?

Will I die?

I will guide you and protect you and guard your path. Do you believe me?

Yes, Mitera Thea.

Do you Believe?

And he raised his eyes, and he said, *I do.*

The man lay on the floor of the motel room, astonishment on his face along with the blood bubbling on his lips. He was alive, but Malcolm could see that he would not be for long.

"Woolf?" the man said, looking at the woman.

The woman who had shot him.

"You have to hurry," the woman said to Malcolm. "The time frame has changed. You must leave right this moment." She nodded towards Nelson. "Take the boy. I'll make sure you're not followed for as long as I can. Do you understand me?"

Malcolm didn't answer her, just held his blade and looked at the dying man.

"Do you understand me?" she said again, but gently, no anger or harshness there.

Malcolm turned to her. "Yes, Mitera Thea," he said.

11

"But how?" Sarah said, distraught. Eleanor, Bess, and Mamie lay dead in the snow.

"Rat poison," her father said, pointing to the granules scattered across the sty.

"Someone did this on *purpose*?" She turned to her father. "Why?"

He didn't answer, just looked shamefaced, which, she supposed, was its own answer. Why? Why had the Dewhursts always had a tough time of it? Because her mother and father had been different races. Because they were poor. Because they were forced to hire a dragon to try and save their farm. Did there need to be any other reasons?

"I'll report it," her father said, "but I wouldn't get your hopes up."

Sarah had no illusions about what happened to animals on farms, had regularly been served pork and beef, was responsible for the welfare of the piglets they sold to the butcher every year, for heaven's sake. So why should the loss of these three hurt her so much?

Because they weren't for butchering – or if they were, it was so far into the future as to not be real yet. Because they'd greeted her every morning when she fed them. Because they were as clever as dogs, she knew. They learned and they recognized.

They were hers.

"Someone actually thought this through," she said, her voice hiccuping. "They sat down and figured out how and took the time to see it done."

Her father sighed behind her. "We can get more," he said.

"With what money?" she asked, not really caring.

"I'm sorry, Sarah," he said, "but you might as well feed them to the dragon when his workday's done."

"But they're poisoned."

"Rat poison isn't going to hurt him." He was already walking away. "Trust me."

She knelt down by Eleanor, put a hand on her chilly hide. Pig skin was usually so jumpy, giving a start whenever you touched it, no matter how gently, that this was the thing that really drove home how dead her pigs were. It was stupid, crying over them. She cried over them anyway.

The crying occupied her enough that it took her a few moments to realize that her father had told her to deal directly with the dragon herself.

"Did something happen?" Miss Archer said, the instant she saw Sarah's face.

"Someone poisoned her pigs," Jason said, following Sarah into the library.

"What? Why on earth–?"

"Because human beings are mean and pointless and will destroy anything nice that they see," Sarah said.

She and Jason went to a study table. Miss Archer came and sat down heavily beside them. They were the only three people in the library today. It was a wonder the graduating class knew how to read. "Is it worth going to the police?" Miss Archer asked.

"For pigs?" Sarah said, and was annoyed that she needed to wipe her eyes again.

"I guess not," Miss Archer said. "With Kelby still missing and everything." She paused in a heavy way that made Sarah's stomach start to curl. "People know the Sheriff interviewed the dragon. You don't think–"

"The dragon didn't have anything to do with it," Jason said, fast. Too fast, really.

Miss Archer was surprised. "How are you sure about that?"

"Because ..." Jason scrambled, "no dragon would risk their life on someone as worthless as Deputy Kelby."

"It could be why they poisoned the pigs, though," Sarah said, quietly. "If they think the dragon did it."

"Why would anyone care that much about Kelby?" Jason asked.

"It wouldn't be that. It would be humans versus dragons."

"It's like when you have a terrible relative," Miss Archer said. "You can complain about him all you like but when an outsider does..."

Jason frowned. "Outsiders complain about my family all the time."

"Yes," Miss Archer said, "I guess that was a bad example." She rubbed her chin distractedly. "You hope for good in the world, you know? You always hope. And then someone kills a Deputy and someone else poisons your pigs. Back and forth it goes, on and on, getting worse and worse. It's like the US and the Soviets now, over this satellite business."

"What happened now?" Jason asked, getting out his textbooks. It seemed impossible to Sarah that, with all that was going on in her life, there was still schoolwork to do.

"Did you see today's paper?" Miss Archer said. When they shook their heads, she got up to find it.

"I still don't think anyone would care enough about Kelby to take it out on you," Jason said.

Sarah shook her head. "It's not a reason. It's an excuse. Might have even been Mr Svoboda. He knew we couldn't afford to pay him sire fees this year."

"Maybe it was this assassin who's coming–"

But Miss Archer was on her way back. "Eisenhower's threatening retaliation if they launch without proof they won't be spying on us," she said.

"That's like asking for proof the sky isn't blue," Jason said, picking up the paper.

"Don't you feel helpless sometimes?" Sarah said, not looking up. "Caught in the middle of other people's decisions? All these important things they do, not caring that people they'll never meet get hurt?"

"It's always been that way," Miss Archer said. "Just what humans do."

"Yeah, well," Sarah said, "if the world ends in a couple weeks, at least *that* part will be over."

"Tomorrow," Jason said.

"Tomorrow what?" Sarah asked.

"Not a couple weeks." Jason tapped an article with his forefinger. "The Russians moved the launch up to tomorrow."

"Tomorrow?" Sarah yelled at Kazimir. "Does that mean the assassin or whoever is coming tomorrow, too?"

"These pigs are poisoned," Kazimir said, sniffing the three carcasses – such a harsh word for them, but carcasses they were, if she had to harden herself enough to let the dragon eat them.

"Yes, I know," Sarah said. "That's what I've been saying–"

"Not rat poison. Different."

She looked up at him, confused. "Different how?"

The dragon sniffed again, then put a claw forward, tapping the body of Mamie. "This one."

"What about her? He *can't* come tomorrow. I'm not prepared. You haven't told me how to be prepared–"

"There is nothing you can prepare for. You must simply act as you think best." He pressed his claw into Mamie's side, on the bloat of her stomach. The claw cut the flesh, letting out a terrible hissing sound. Sarah covered her nose at the smell–

Then she stopped. "That doesn't smell like rat poison."

"As I said."

Sarah inhaled a few times, not too much as the stench was quite strong. "That's fertilizer. Ammonia and–"

"A disguised poison for much more than rats," Kazimir finished.

Sarah gasped. "Someone was trying to kill you. They knew we'd feed you the pigs."

"Yes," Kazimir said. "Someone."

She followed his gaze as he turned it back to the house. "No," she said, suddenly. "No, I know what you're thinking–"

Kazimir laughed, deep and low, a vibration she felt in her spine. "Trust me when I say, you do not know what I am thinking."

With a swoop of his wings, he left her there, tumbling back into the air as if she were the least of his concerns.

"Did you poison my pigs?"

Her father looked up from where he was oiling the leather of his boots, boots that should have been replaced at least two winters ago. "Of course I didn't, and I'll thank you not to speak to me in that tone of voice, missy."

There was a pause before he said it, though, a pause when her eyes caught his, where anything could have been going on behind that stone face.

"You're trying to poison the dragon," she said.

"And have seventy tons of dragon meat rotting on my farm? No, thank you."

"Mamie isn't full of rat poison. It's something else."

He affected surprise at that. She knew he was affecting it. She could see the falseness right there. "Well, whoever gave it to them–"

"You."

162

"Not me, and that's the end of it."

"Why are you letting me talk to him now?"

"What?"

"This whole time, it's been, 'Stay away from him, don't even tell him your name' and all of a sudden it's 'Feed him the pigs, Sarah.' You wanted *me* to do it."

"Well," he said, turning back to his boots, "with the way you've been sneaking out and talking to him at night, I figured you'd taken over the job."

He knew. Of course, he knew. It was foolish of her to think otherwise. How often could she sneak out without the one other person on the farm noticing?

"He saved me and Jason from Deputy Kelby that day," she said. "I wanted to thank him."

He looked at her now. "Just that one day?"

She swallowed. "What's that supposed to mean?"

"Kelby is missing. The Sheriff was around here talking to the dragon. And your jaw is still sore from your 'fall'."

"That was against the counter."

"So we're still lying to each other, are we?" He put one boot down and started on the other. "Good. Makes things easier."

"What are you lying about?"

He glanced back up at her. "What are *you*?"

Here was the chance. She *wanted* to tell him. The burden was heavy, the confusion even heavier. And if Kazimir was telling the truth? If someone was coming to kill her? Tomorrow?

"This is crazy," she whispered to herself.

"I can agree to that," her father said. He set down his second boot, looked at the floor for a moment, and sighed in that

163

way of his. "I've been getting letters. Letters telling me exactly what kind of bad news that claw out there is, Sarah."

"From who? Small-minded people, I bet. People who've never liked us, Daddy."

He looked at her again, calmly, almost sadly. "The letters said he would win you over."

"If by winning me over, you mean saving my life, then I'll take that kind of being won over."

"Big words for getting you out of a conversation with a Deputy."

And here it was again. Another chance. She held her breath.

She took the plunge.

"He was going to kill us."

"Who?"

"Kelby. He had his gun out and he was going to shoot Jason."

"This was on the road?"

She shook her head. "Outside Jason's work. At night."

His look darkened. "And how did you find yourself outside Jason's work at night?"

"Is that the thing you really want to know?"

"I will. At some point."

"Kelby caught us."

"Doing what?"

She raised her voice. "Just being together! Standing in the same place! It's bad enough that I'm black, apparently, but if I'm seen with a Japanese boy, well, then."

She could see how much he knew this to be true. He calmly waited for her to continue.

"There was a fight," she said.

"Who started it?"

"Who do you think?"

"I've seen Hisao Inagawa get angry. I wouldn't be surprised if Jason could, too."

"And don't you think they have the right?"

"The law doesn't care much about your rights when you look like Jason Inagawa."

"Or me."

"Or you. Yes. I'm sorry."

She ran her foot along the floor of the kitchen. Dusty. Her fault, though between the two of them, they had to do the work of a farm that required at least five. Maybe they could hire the dragon to mop when he was done with the fields.

She saw her father was flexing one fist. "He hit you, didn't he?" Flex, flex. "Kelby hit you in the jaw."

"Yes. With the butt of his gun."

The fist still flexed. "And the dragon ... took care of him?"

"No."

Her father looked surprised. If this was truth-telling, it might as well all come out, right?

"Jason got into it with him. The gun went off..." She suddenly found it difficult to say any more.

"Jason shot Deputy Kelby?"

"He didn't mean to!" She was upset now, like a dam was bursting. "Kelby was going to beat him. I think kill him, maybe."

"Sarah?" Her father was standing now. He came over to her. "Sarah." He held up her chin so he could look her in the eye. "If Jason stepped between you and Deputy Kelby, I'm never going to regard him as the problem, okay?"

"It was an accident. But the police would never believe that. Not even if it was Kelby."

He let go of her chin, but not before a gentle rub on the still-fading bruise on her jaw. "No," he said, "I don't reckon they would. But Sarah? Sarah, you've got to trust me now and you've got to tell me the truth, okay?"

"Okay."

"What did you do with the body?"

She slowly turned from him, looked out the window and into the snow, out over their farm, where the dragon slept.

"And he says someone's coming for you?"

"Yes. Tomorrow."

"And that he'll protect you? As if I'd let anyone dangerous get within a mile of you."

"That's what he says, but I can't get any more out of him. Only that it's got something to do with the satellite the Russians are launching. Somebody using it as an excuse to start a war between men and dragons. Maybe the spy part of it is going to see something it's not supposed to. I don't know. I don't think he does either."

They were standing on the back porch, both wrapped in blankets against the cold. She had told him everything. He had told her all about the letters he'd received, the money they'd paid, told her what they'd predicted, how it had all come true so far.

"So who do we believe?" she asked him now.

"The letters have been right about everything so far."

"So has the dragon. *And* he saved my life."

"Maybe he was supposed to."

She turned to her father. "Even if the letters are right, he did save me. You can't kill him. That wouldn't be... Honourable."

He stood next to her, and she could almost feel the tension still there. "The people who write these letters, they're not going to be happy about not getting what they want."

She glanced out towards the dragon. "You think he will be?"

"Between a dragon and a dark place," he said.

"What do we do?" she asked again, though knowing neither of them had any answers. "Maybe we should just get out of here and let Kazimir handle things."

"Kazimir?" her father asked. "That's his name?"

She nodded.

"Well, first of all, I'm not being run off my own farm. Second, if they want to find us, they seem to know how. I'd rather be here." He put an arm around her. "And who knows, maybe your dragon will turn out to be the hero after all."

"He isn't my dragon," she said. "I don't think he's anyone's."

He breathed out through his nose in that way of his. "That, my daughter, might be the whole problem."

12

Nelson went silent again as they drove out of Montana in the middle of the night and across the panhandle of Idaho. Malcolm hadn't forced the issue, not even when he stopped for food and gas, not even when Nelson had to help Malcolm push the truck out of a snow bank after they crossed the border into Washington. He wouldn't meet Malcolm's eye. He wouldn't answer Malcolm's questions. He'd just do what Malcolm asked (never commanded, always asked) without hesitation or a word.

It was as if Nelson had died.

"I'm sorry," Malcolm said. Over and over. "I'm so sorry."

And he was. He still believed in his mission, even more so when the Mitera Thea herself had shown up in the motel room, dressed in a way he'd never seen before but it was her, speaking commands, telling him what to do.

Answering his prayers. Again.

He was a Believer. He believed in her.

169

But.

"I'm sorry," he said again, as they approached the southern pass through the Cascade Mountains – a ten-hour drive that had taken over twenty in this weather – which would lead them towards Tacoma and then the little town of Frome where...

Where he would do his work.

The pass turned out to be nearly snowed over. If they'd arrived a day later, they wouldn't have been able to cross it at all. *Another blessing,* he thought. They'd put on the tyre chains Nelson (and every Canadian) kept permanently in their cars, and Malcolm drove the truck up the increasingly steep and snow-covered road.

"I'll make sure you're free after this," Malcolm said, meaning it, but wondering if he could keep the promise. "I'll make sure your name is forgotten. Or that everyone knows none of this was of your doing."

Nelson whispered something.

"What did you say?" Malcolm said, too fast, too eager to hear from him after all the silence.

"I said, it doesn't matter," Nelson whispered, just a little louder. "It's too late. There's no going back."

"Don't say that. Please, don't say that."

Nelson turned to look at him, his face so lost, so hopeless, Malcolm had to stifle the sob again. "You think they're just going to let me go?" Nelson said. "You think your Pope woman is going to protect a Guatemalan queer wanted for the murder of two Federal officers?" He turned back to look out at the endless snow. "You really are a Believer."

Malcolm said nothing until they reached the summit. And then, he could only say "I'm sorry" one more time.

* * *

"You're planning to kill someone else, aren't you?" Nelson asked, some hours later. The sun was rising, somewhere behind miles of clouds, not that it mattered when the landscape glowed white at every corner. They were being held up by an overturned semi-truck coming down the western half of the pass, surrounded on all sides by trees that looked like creatures waiting to pounce.

Surprised as he was by Nelson's question, Malcolm didn't answer, hoping he didn't have to.

"Those knives in your sleeves," Nelson said. "The easy way you cut that Mountie. Who are you going to kill?"

"Blades," Malcolm said quietly. "They're blades, not knives, and I hope I won't have to kill anyone."

"That's a lie."

"It's not. I don't *hope* to kill anyone."

"But you expect to." Nelson's gaze was steady. "You can talk about hope all you want, but you expect to, once we get wherever we're going."

Malcolm looked back out into the snow. There seemed to be some movement much farther down the zigzag road, brake lights coming off, then coming on again a moment later.

"I do expect to," Malcolm said.

"Who?"

Malcolm didn't answer.

"*Who?* You could at least tell me that. At least tell me why my life is over."

"It's meant to save your life. It's meant to save all our lives."

"And you believe that, too."

Malcolm let his foot off the brake. Nelson's truck slowly rolled down the opening left by the car in front. "Something has to happen. Something that can't be interrupted."

"And you're going to make sure it happens."

"I am."

"By killing someone."

"If I must."

"Oh, you *must*, all right. I've seen what you 'believe'. So who is it?"

Again, Malcolm didn't answer. He didn't know the girl's name. The Mitera Thea felt it was easier if he never learned it. It would make the killing somehow less personal, which was an absurd, obscene idea, but one that had stuck.

He didn't feel he could say this to Nelson, though.

"This is madness," Nelson said. "How can any of this make sense to you?"

"It's been foretold."

"By who?"

"Dragons. For thousands of years."

Nelson said nothing at that. The car ahead of them moved again, and Malcolm followed, down the long hill, the mountains around them hidden entirely by the mist and snow.

"You really believe that?" Nelson asked, after a moment.

"I do."

"And you believe that if you don't do this–"

"Everyone will die. Everyone."

"How?"

"What?"

"How will everyone die? Exactly?"

Malcolm turned to him, though taking his eyes off the road even for a moment was hazardous. "In fire."

"I've seen men who were dragons, you know," Nelson said, after another half-hour of silence. "Under their skin."

"That metaphor is a little blasphemous," Malcolm said, uncomfortable.

"I don't care. Everyone's got a little dragon in them, that's what my grandfather says. We all want to be dragons so much that's probably what created them."

"No, there was a Goddess–"

"He also said, some people are more dragon than others. Some people, you just give them a scratch, and underneath, they're pure dragon."

He glared at Malcolm as if he was "some people". Malcolm concentrated on the road. "We can talk about something else–"

"Your beliefs have killed two cops and destroyed my life. I have a right to insult them."

"There's a greater plan."

"You've read it? You've approved every word? Know your entire role in it?"

Malcolm drove on. The roads were ever clearer. The sun itself might even show (the moon definitely would, it was foretold).

"You haven't, have you?" Nelson asked, not even taunting, just asking.

"Faith is belief without proof," Malcolm said. "It's a leap, an act of bravery. If I had proof, I would have no reason to believe. I can't tell you how many times I've reaped the benefit of that faith."

"You really believe this Thea person watches over you?"

"She sent a dragon," he said, remembering the woods on his first day. "No human has been able to do that with a red for fifty years or more." He also remembered the kindness of the lady at the drugstore when he was injured. He remembered finding Nelson (his heart panged) just in time to get away from the agents that hunted him. And of course, the Mitera Thea herself in the motel room at the moment all was lost.

He had been saved. He had – despite his own words – what he considered ample proof.

He had no doubts.

He had few doubts.

"I have no doubts," he said.

Nelson looked back out the window as they picked up speed, heading south-west now, towards the end. "My parents didn't have any doubts either," Nelson said.

As they passed through Tacoma, then through a much smaller town with an unpronounceable name, Malcolm reflected how little walking he'd ended up having to do. His bag – with the item still in it, the item without which all was lost – sat in the space behind the truck seat, almost as if it had been planned this way.

She must have known. He had enough days allotted to walk the whole journey, but he'd found Nelson and the truck and *then* been informed he was running out of time, that the day had been moved forward.

She must have known. Must have seen it all, arranged it all.

She hadn't said what he should do with Nelson or how long to keep him as companion. She had only said to take him, so presumably she must know of a purpose Nelson would serve.

At the end.

I'll protect him, he vowed to himself, though again wondering how much power he would have to keep that promise.

He shook his head. There was the mission to think about. There was the world to save. If he didn't succeed, Nelson wouldn't be saved either.

He must focus. He must *re*focus.

He had a job ahead of him.

They found the town easily, the farm as well. He had been told where to go, told where the blue dragon would be working, where the girl and her father were living.

If the dragon is still there, Mitera Thea had told him, for the hundredth time, over so many years and months and weeks of training, *as it will be, for the father will not be able to send him away like we ask, no matter how much we offer. Then the day will come, the hour, the moment. And you will act.*

"Who are these people?" Nelson asked, after they parked on a side road, watching the farm as the skies cleared and the farm's two inhabitants – three, Malcolm corrected himself – the farm's *three* inhabitants went about their daily business, as if nothing was going to be different than any other snowy day. They had watched for hours, Malcolm prepared to follow the girl to school if need be, but she had made no appearance on the main road. He had fed Nelson on the rations from his bag, and they'd warmed themselves in the extra clothes he had remaining. He didn't want to move unless he had to. He had waited all day. Dusk was coming. The moment was growing so very near.

"They're no one, really," Malcolm answered. "An accident of geography. It might have been anyone. It had to be someone. It was them."

"*What* was? What's going to happen here? Why can't you just tell me?"

Why couldn't he? He had been forbidden discussion of the mission – for so many, many obvious reasons – with anyone outside their Cell, and even within, only Malcolm and the Mitera Thea knew all the ins and outs. Most of the Cell thought he was on an evangelical mission, trying to recruit more Believers to the cause. All young Believers did at some point, so it wasn't beyond possibility.

But if Nelson was a part of it now? The hour was drawing close. What could possibly be the harm? He took a deep breath and began to explain.

"Tonight, the Russians will launch a satellite–"

There was a loud thump on the driver's side window. Both Malcolm and Nelson jumped. Malcolm turned to look. A teen-age boy of Asian descent thumped it again and angrily said, "Who the hell are you?"

Without even thinking about it, Malcolm slid the blade from his sleeve to his hand.

13

"It is today," Kazimir said.

"Yes," Sarah answered. "You've told me. Do you mind? I'm trying to feed the chickens."

Not a single one of the idiotic birds would leave the coop if the dragon was near. Well, maybe it wasn't idiotic, now that she thought about it.

"I do not know exactly when he will come for you."

"Or what he's going to do. Or what *I'm* supposed to do. Or my dad–"

She hesitated there. She hadn't told Kazimir about her father or the letters or even his plans for the day. He'd told Sarah she wouldn't go to school but they should both go about their farm duties like normal, in case the people who wrote the letters were watching. Then he would wait in the house with his shotgun. For what? No one seemed to know exactly, not even the dragon.

"You'd have stopped me, anyway, I'll bet," she said. "If I'd tried to run."

"You would not have run," Kazimir said.

"I might have."

"It was foretold that you would not."

"Because you would have stopped me."

"You begin to understand the madness of prophecy." He suddenly raised his head, looking firmly out towards the road hidden by the barn, his ear cocked. "I think," he said, starting to beat his wings to climb into the air, "it has begun."

"Don't," Nelson said. "Please, don't."

Malcolm looked at him, but kept the blade in his hand and rolled down the driver's side window.

"You were here this morning," the boy said. "I saw you parked. Who are you?"

"We're lost," Malcolm said, brightly. "Could you please direct us to–"

"If you hurt her," the boy said. "If you so much as touch a hair on her head–"

"I don't know what you mean–"

The boy pulled around the bag he carried over one shoulder and took out what Malcolm could not know was the gun of the late, unlamented Deputy Kelby.

Agent Woolf – for she still thought of herself that way, it was snappier than "the Mitera Thea" all the time – nearly broke her steering wheel in frustration. The sky had cleared, the roads had been ploughed, and still some idiot driving a truck full of what seemed to be toilet tissue had overturned, blocking nearly the entire freeway.

The sun was getting close to setting.

It would happen. It would happen soon.

And she was going to miss it.

She honked her horn again, but as everyone who honked a horn knew, it did no good other than as a channel for her anger. Which, she supposed, was some small good after all. Her anger, when properly riled, was quite a thing to behold.

Dernovich was dead. She was sorry for that, genuinely. He acted stupider than he was. She had diverted his attention numerous times – the drugstore for one, the campsite in a manner that allowed the boys to escape – but he had doggedly kept up his pursuit. Which was why she had shadowed him so closely. What better way to keep close enough on Malcolm's trail to see when he needed assistance, while also feeding his strongest pursuers just enough information to stay one step ahead? She had no doubt Dernovich would have eventually found Malcolm on his own, and the information he had unknowingly provided in return had proved most fruitful.

But the mission had to continue. It must.

She honked again and uttered an expletive. Then she took a long, long breath, uttering a low chant as she exhaled, clearing her mind, clearing her thoughts. She'd always felt a duality within her. It gave her strength.

Instead of honking again, she turned the wheel sharply to the right. There wasn't enough room, so she bumped the car in front of her, reversed, bumped it again, and broke free just as the owner of the bumped car was getting out with a shocked look.

She drove down the shoulder of the freeway, skidding

some on the ice, but increasing her speed towards a policeman waving his arms, trying to stop her. There was barely enough room. She thought she might have knocked the policeman down as she roared past.

But she didn't look back.

Sarah ran up the long drive from the farmhouse to the road.

"What's going on?" she heard her father shout from the front steps. "Sarah? You're not to leave!"

But she couldn't stop.

She'd come around and seen the dragon flying towards the parked car.

She'd seen Jason standing beside it.

She'd seen Jason holding the gun.

"I don't want to hurt you," Malcolm said, getting out of the car, slowly. "But I will if I have to."

"He's not kidding!" Nelson shouted. "Get out of here! Call the police!"

"Don't call the police," Malcolm said, still calm, taking a step towards Jason, who took a step back. "The police would only make things worse."

"Stop talking," Jason said. He held the gun, but he looked very nervous. "I've shot people before."

"I don't believe you."

"You should," said a voice from the sky. The dragon landed in the road in front of them. "You are the assassin," he said to Malcolm, simply.

"Yes," Malcolm answered. "And you, oh, Great One—" he moved his arm so that the item he'd hidden in his other sleeve dropped into his free hand— "are exactly what is needed."

Gareth Dewhurst, still holding his shotgun, stopped himself from running after his daughter. The dragon was on the road now. Whatever important thing everyone had been waiting for was now clearly happening. His daughter was running right towards it.

He took off for the barn where he'd parked his truck.

After tying the steel blade of his plough to the front.

"Jason, don't!" Sarah shouted as she neared them: Kazimir, Jason, what looked like a teenage boy getting out of a truck, and was there another in the passenger seat? Surely, these couldn't be assassins?

Kazimir's neck was arched, his wings out, like a cat that had been threatened and was showing how big it could get. For Kazimir, this was very, very big.

"These are the guys, Sarah!" Jason yelled. "Stay back!"

The boy who had got out of the truck turned to face her. He had a look that suggested he'd known her for a long, long time.

Kazimir put out a wing, abruptly stopping her progress. "No closer," he said. "He is more dangerous than you could possibly imagine."

"He's a *boy*."

"He is a boy with power."

Sarah was shaken more than she thought possible by the fear she heard in Kazimir's voice.

"What are you talking about?"

Kazimir swung that great, one-eyed head back towards the boy, who she now saw held a blade in one hand and ... *something* in the other.

"He has the Spur of the Goddess," Kazimir said.

Malcolm felt no fear. True, the other boy had a gun on him. True, the dragon could incinerate him with a single breath, but he held his blade in one hand.

And the Spur of the Goddess in the other.

Sacred nearly beyond speaking, a holy relic to every dragon the world over, regardless of colour or mythology, missing for centuries. A dragon claw, blackened and ancient, believed to have been torn from the Goddess herself, and carried for these many days in Malcolm's travel bag, the item without which all this was lost.

Dragons were not quite of this reality, were they? Even Believers acknowledged that. Breathing fire, living for a possible eternity (Malcolm believed in that eternity, so did the Mitera Thea, so did Kazimir), intelligent, obviously historic but somehow with no past evidence in the geological record. They were, for all that science could confirm, *sui generis*.

They were not of this world. And then they were.

The Spur was the proof of their power. Believers had stumbled upon it in the Wastes, indeed it was the artefact that had founded the whole religion. They had kept it hidden away all these years.

In the right hands, it held power unimaginable.

"I do not wish to harm you, Great One," Malcolm said with reverence that was not manufactured, "but I will if I must."

"And what do you plan on doing if I allow you to continue, boy?" Kazimir asked, trying to keep up his haughtiness, but Sarah could tell there was a strain behind it. That fear again.

"You don't know?" the boy holding the claw asked, surprised.

"I know the result that you believe. War between men and dragons. War unceasing. The death of us all."

Malcolm's eyes widened in astonishment. "No, oh, Great One, that is exactly what I'm here to *stop*. I'm the only chance at peace."

Jason's voice was strained. "Well, both can't be true."

"Oh, they can," Kazimir said, ruefully. "Prophecy is slippery, dangerous, open to fatal misinterpretation."

"I'm not afraid of fatal," Malcolm said. "I only wish to do my duty."

"And there is no doubt in your mind that you will complete it?"

"None," the boy said, firmly. "It's been foreseen."

"Well, then," said Kazimir, "I suppose there is nothing but to let you get on with it."

The boy looked astonished.

"*That* was not foreseen," Kazimir said, the playful tinge Sarah was familiar with back in his voice. He raised his long head, looked directly at Jason, and said, "Shoot him."

Jason Inagawa raised the gun. The boy with the claw turned to him. In fact, *everyone* turned to him.

"Jason!" he heard Sarah shout, but just his name, no call of yes or no. She was clearly as confused as he was.

"Jason is your name," the boy with the claw said. "Mine is Malcolm. I have a great work to accomplish."

"One that involves killing Sarah," Jason said. "I'll shoot you before that happens."

"Shoot me then," the boy with the claw said, opening his arms. "I won't stop otherwise."

"Do it," Kazimir said to Jason.

"You said Sarah was the important one," Jason said.

"She is, and believe me when I say, only one of them will live to the end of this day."

"I don't think either of us will, Great One," Malcolm said, somewhat sorrowfully. "But you will. That's what's important."

"Then why did those who sent you wish for me to die, oh, Believer?"

Malcolm was immediately angry. "We would *never*, Great One, it would be sacrilege–"

"This girl's father tried to poison me, I can only assume through blackmail, as I could practically smell the struggle in him. Your leader wanted me out of your way."

"The Mitera Thea would *never* harm a dragon!"

Kazimir got right up into his face. "Your Belief will let you down."

"It won't." Malcolm flicked the blade with impossible

speed at Kazimir's face. Kazimir could only flinch fast enough
to have it cut just his chin. He roared back, but the blood was
already dripping. Malcolm expertly caught some of it in the
hand holding the claw.

Which started to glow.

"Thank you, Great One," he said.

And Nelson struck Malcolm on the back of the head with
a rock.

Agent Woolf sped along the dirt road where Sarah and her
father had been picked up by the dragon and flown home.
She would have warmed to the synchronicity of this, had she
known.

She rounded a corner and could see the antenna on a far
hill, barely more than steel and wires, the whole arbitrary
reason why all of this was happening here. She had no doubt
Malcolm would use the Spur of the Goddess to complete his
mission. Blue dragon or not, prophesied girl or not, whether he
lived or not. She had trained him herself. She knew the desire
in him, the absolute Belief. She had worried at first at his pairing with the new boy, but on balance, she felt it gave Malcolm
even further incentive to succeed.

He would save the world.

She smiled to herself. It was the least happy smile Agent
Dernovich would have ever seen had he lived. It was grim,
a smile of the gallows.

Because she knew the world Malcolm was saving was not
his own.

She heard police sirens behind her.

* * *

Malcolm dropped the claw. That was the worst part, not the pain or the blood on the back of his head, not his certain knowledge that it was Nelson who had struck him (a beat of sad, inevitable betrayal he felt beyond the pain from the rock), but that the Spur of the Goddess was falling, falling, falling to the frozen ground. Malcolm intoned the words he'd been taught, dragon language itself, hoping it would work even if he wasn't holding the Spur.

It worked.

The tip of the Spur struck the ice, piercing it as if it were aflame. A light opened above it, shimmering, almost as if something was trying to open.

"You fool," the Great One said, still bleeding.

Malcolm heard cars, coming from both directions.

Agent Woolf had her gun on the passenger seat, ready to use it the moment this podunk cow-jockey of a Sheriff tried to make her pull over. She didn't even slow; on the contrary, she pressed the accelerator as far as it would go, nearly reaching the floor.

But whatever the Sheriff's Department was investing in its police cars was clearly a scandal, as it reached her with ease, then raced right by as if she were standing still.

The grim smile was gone. This could not be good news.

"What's happening?" Sarah asked, as the aura around the claw grew, now as big as an orange, now a grapefruit. The sirens were getting nearer, as was what she guessed was her dad's truck, on its way from the farm.

"This fool," Kazimir said, meaning Malcolm, "thinks the Spur is a weapon. One that will stop the satellite and save this world for dragons. But that is not all it is."

"What is it then?" Jason said, nervously, his eyes on the aura, too.

"It is a key," Kazimir said.

The aura rising above the claw was now pig-sized, and Sarah thought she could actually *see* things in it, a change of light, shadowy ground...

"A key to what?" she asked.

"The satellite's moving into place," Malcolm said, his voice distant. "The moment is arriving."

Sirens blared as the Sheriff's car screamed into view, its headlights – when had it grown dark enough for headlights, Sarah found herself wondering – lighting up Jason.

Jason, still holding the pistol.

"Throw the gun down!" the Sheriff himself shouted, getting out of his car, holding up his own gun. "Throw it down, *now!*"

"What are you doing here?" Sarah found herself asking, as if that was the thing to be curious about.

"Your librarian saw a gun in Jason's school bag," said the Sheriff. "One that looked an awful lot like a Deputy's sidearm."

"It's not what you think, Sheriff!" Sarah said, moving forward.

"Do not move!" the Sheriff snapped, and Sarah froze. The Sheriff had seen the aura above the claw, still growing, still shimmering in light. "What the hell is that?"

"Dragon magic," Kazimir said, simply, dread in his voice.

"I suggest you stop it right now," the Sheriff said, in a way that made it clear it wasn't a suggestion at all. "And *you*," he said to Jason, "I said, put the gun down, son, and I meant it."

"You don't understand," Jason said, gun still on the boy Malcolm. "This guy is here to kill Sarah."

"What are you talking about?"

Malcolm had stopped when the Sheriff got out of his car, but Sarah saw him slowly leaning towards the aura again, his hand getting closer and closer to the claw.

"Stop!" Jason shouted at him.

"*Everyone* just stop!" the Sheriff ordered. "Even you with the rock!"

The boy who'd struck Malcolm on the back of the head dropped it. "He murdered a Mountie," the boy mumbled, sadder than anything Sarah had ever heard. "He did it right there on the road."

Sarah saw the Sheriff's eyes going back and forth among them all, trying to figure out this scene. But there could be no figuring. Nothing here made sense. The sun had set, the moon was up – the snow clouds had vanished somehow, going against all the weather she'd ever seen in her state – and nothing, nothing, nothing made sense.

"There it is," Malcolm said, turning his eyes to the sky.

They all looked, almost involuntarily, even the Sheriff. A little light blinked among the stars, faint but there, *blink, blink, blink*.

"The satellite," Sarah whispered.

"The world is watching us now," Malcolm said.

188

* * *

Agent Woolf pulled up to a stop behind the police car. No one seemed to note her arriving. They were all looking up.

Ah, yes. The satellite.

She took her gun and got out of the car. This was what she had worked for. Why she had folded herself into the FBI with her dazzling dragon expertise, disappearing for months at a time to do "research" that only dazzled them more when she returned, the gullible idiots. It had been tricky, to say the least, balancing her role as Mitera Thea and being undercover, but she had needed their best information on the satellite and what they knew about her and her mission. Taking over the search for herself and any potential assassin had seemed only natural. Then after a while, it was simply fun, the best way to keep Malcolm safe while he fulfilled his destiny.

His destiny not as assassin. The *real* destiny he had remained unaware of even up until this moment he was about to fulfil it.

Oh, no, he was definitely not the assassin.

She was.

She was about to murder the entire world of men.

So many things happened at once then, so many terrible, terrible things, that it was only later, after the world had already burned, that Sarah could sort it out completely and even then, she could only see her small part in it.

The satellite was first.

While they were all looking at it, Malcolm had – of course

he had, of *course* – used their distraction to move for the claw, as he frantically muttered in a language she didn't understand.

"No!" she heard Kazimir growl.

And then she heard–

Oh, God–

She heard the dragon start an inhalation of breath.

"Don't touch it!" Jason shouted, *still* pointing the gun at Malcolm.

"You don't even know what you protect," Malcolm said, almost sadly, his hand an inch away.

"I protect *her*," Jason said, seeing Sarah move out of the corner of his vision.

"I will shoot *both* of you if you don't stop right now!" the Sheriff yelled.

Malcolm ignored him and continued talking to Jason. "She'll try to stop me," he said. "If she doesn't, no harm will come to her."

"No harm will come to her anyway," Jason said.

Malcolm lunged for the claw–

Jason cocked his pistol–

The Sheriff fired first.

"Jason! Get out of the way!" Sarah shouted, leaping for him.

She meant the fire she knew Kazimir was about to breathe. There was so much shouting, she didn't even hear the gunshot, only saw the pistol flip out of Jason's hand, saw the blood erupt from his wrist. Then a second eruption from his back as he turned from the force of the first. It was only pure luck that neither bullet struck her as well, another thing she would only realize later.

For now, she was catching him in her arms, noting the look of complete surprise on his face as he slumped. He said her name, "Sarah," but it was more exhalation than word, a *wet* exhalation, small bubbles of blood floating out on his breath.

"The dragon," she said, still not quite understanding what had happened. "He's going to fire."

Malcolm could hear the blue drawing in its breath, knew there was oblivion coming–

But also knew victory was his.

He felt more than saw the blue rise above him, the great chest expand, the head pull itself back in the preamble to incinerating Malcolm and pretty much everything within a circle large enough to include the girl the dragon was supposed to be protecting.

But the prophecy had been wrong. The girl had *not* interrupted. She'd run to the other boy instead, right at the critical moment. And something was happening to the other boy, he was falling, falling–

Malcolm had no time for that, no eyes for anything but the Spur of the Goddess. He grasped it. He spoke the final words, words of pure dragon, thinking of the blinking eye in the sky above them.

His mission was complete.

* * *

There was a pulse. And a light.

Kazimir exhaled, and the flames ceased just past his mouth. The pulse and the light from the Spur of the Goddess stretched the aura to swallow his fire as if it was nothing more than mist.

The pulse and the light rocketed into the air above them all, in a spiral to the antenna on the hill, which lit up like the transmitter it was, shooting an even bigger spiral up to the cold, improbably clear sky, twisting around itself farther and farther, faster and faster. Until a small flash of light, high up in the atmosphere, signalled the end of the satellite the Russians had sent to spy on America...

America, thought Kazimir. *The satellite was destroyed by a weapon fired from American soil.*

Oh, no.

Oh, what have I done? he thought.

He realized his mistake. His unforgivable, irredeemable mistake, the truth that had been sitting right in front of him the whole time.

The prophecy wasn't about a war between men and dragons. It was about a war between men.

The Russians would see the destruction of their satellite as an act of aggression, and if it took them time to understand that that aggression came not from the United States, but from the world of dragons, how could that matter if the bombs were already falling? This world was over. It was only a matter of days now, perhaps hours.

The Believers hated humans. The Believers worshipped dragons, dragons who might not survive a direct hit from a warhead, but who could withstand radiation humans could not. The Believers thought they were giving the world to dragons. A world without humans.

They didn't know what doom they had started.

"You have not saved us," he said to the boy.

He raised his wings to fly, though he had no immediate answer as to where, just somehow to get to the right humans, to tell them where the real fault lay if they would even believe him, to stop the bombs that might even be falling by morning. He made to rise, taking his first muscular swoop to leave the ground. He turned to get away from the ever-growing aura around the Spur.

The truck with the plough attached caught him just offside his chest, mere centimetres away from where a direct blow would have punctured his flame sac, killing him terribly, in agony. Instead the blow was glancing but managed to knock him off to the side.

Into the aura.

Where he disappeared completely.

Agent Woolf saw the blue make to rise–

Then just like that, he was gone.

That would make things *much* easier in the short term. She cocked her own pistol and shot the Sheriff in the back.

"Jason?" Sarah tumbled to the ground with him, unaware that a light was now rising into the sky, unaware that Kazimir had started to breathe fire, unaware even that her father was less than fifty metres away and closing fast. "No, Jason, please."

He couldn't speak. The second bullet had angled down his back and out through his lung. Every breath brought more blood to his lips. He looked up at her, and still his main expression was of surprise.

"I don't understand what's happening," she said to him, crying. "I don't know what I'm supposed to do–"

His eyes widened at something behind her. She turned and saw Kazimir, all seventy tons of him, vanish into the aura as if he'd tripped through a door.

"What on earth?" she said.

When she turned back to Jason, he was dead.

"Sarah?" her father shouted, getting out of the truck. "Sarah!"

Gareth Dewhurst didn't know what the hell had happened to the dragon, didn't know who the hell any of these people were, or what the hell this huge glowing *thing* was in front of him. He only knew that his daughter was in the midst of it, surrounded by danger.

"Sarah!"

He also didn't know he'd been shot until he slumped to one knee.

Malcolm waited to die.

(*You have not saved us.*)

He'd thought it would be in the fire from the blue, but the Spur of the Goddess had stopped that, the aura swallowing it all, and in doing so, turning the aura from him.

Towards where the girl held the boy.

"Malcolm?" he heard Nelson say.

"I'm still alive," he said, astonished. He turned to look into the face that made his heart lurch with what so briefly *might* have been. A future outside the destiny he had been given. A future inconceivable, impossible, yet real for a few shining moments.

(*You have not saved us.*)

"Nelson, I... What did he mean?"

"That woman is here," Nelson said in horror, looking behind Malcolm. "She just shot the policeman and that man from the truck."

"Daddy?" Jason was dead in Sarah's lap, an idea so big she couldn't yet feel it. The aura from the claw was close to her now, and she felt wind buffeting her hair. The edges of the aura were ragged and strange, as if curtains were opening and closing over a road that looked a lot like – but was not *exactly* like – the one where this was all happening.

The dragon had gone. Her father had pushed it ... *somewhere*. Her father, in the truck where the plough had been tied as a weapon. He had gone that far in considering how he might kill the dragon for the invisible people who'd written the letters, she thought.

She watched him jump out of the truck, start running towards her, then he fell to one knee, his hand going to his chest. He looked up at Sarah with the same surprise as Jason, before he fell to the ground and didn't move, his eyes dying just like Deputy Kelby's.

"Daddy!" she screamed and started to rise.

The aura surged around her, the curtains of light flapping in whatever torrent of wind was driving them and wrapping her away.

She was no longer there.

"Damn," Agent Woolf said. "Damn and damn and damn."

She should have shot the girl first, but she had been obscured by the aura from the Spur, an aura that now seemed to have taken the girl completely.

Well, never mind. Malcolm had done his work. It was complete. This world and all of its human inhabitants would be highly inconvenienced, but that mattered little to Agent Woolf.

She moved towards her trained assassin. The boy who had travelled with Malcolm moved away from her, behind the truck. He would need taking care of after Malcolm. She doubted anyone would believe whatever he might say about what he'd seen, but why leave a loose end?

"Malcolm," she said, stepping forward.

"Yes, Mitera Thea," he said, his hand still on the Spur.

She stopped herself, curious. "Why did you stay with the name Malcolm above all the others?"

"I grew accustomed to it," he said, still not looking back at her.

"It's dangerous to grow accustomed to things," she said. "You find them harder and harder to discard with each passing day."

"But there will be no more passing days for me," he said, finally turning, "will there?"

The boy was clever. Which, of course, was why he had been chosen so young, selected out of all the orphaned children at the Cell, the ones even now innocently knocking on doors, collecting money and second-hand clothes for a cause they would never know the full purpose of.

"And why do you say that?" she said, to his question.

"You have not saved us," he said, and she didn't know what he meant. "I accept my ending," he said, turning back to the Spur. "I have killed, Mitera Thea."

"It was needed. It was what you were trained for."

He didn't answer that right away and finally just repeated himself. "I have killed."

"It's a burden," she said, softening her voice, not out of sympathy but because she knew softness would aid her approach, help her in dispatching what was, after all, an exceptionally trained assassin. "One that I've had to share."

Malcolm looked around. At the bodies of the Sheriff, the young man, still visible under the swirling aura that had taken the girl, and then her father, face down on a road, no longer moving as the blood pooled around him. "Why?" Malcolm asked.

"You ask your Mitera Thea why?" she said, affronted.

Without turning around again, he said, "I do."

She would have to be careful now. Very careful indeed. There was doubt there. It was probably only knowledge of the end; no matter how much he may say he had accepted it, it was only human to struggle. He probably couldn't help himself. She wondered if she could outfight him. She had trained him after all.

"They cannot see into the hearts of dragons," she said

now, taking another slow step behind him, her hand returning to her gun. "They wish to. They've tried for centuries. And even when some of them knew better, even when some of us *worshipped* dragons, worked to protect them, they still wanted to know, to look into their hearts."

"The satellite," Malcolm said.

"It is only the beginning." She took another step. "They will not stop."

There was a dangerous pause. "But you have stopped them."

"I have. *You* have." With every sentence she took a step. "You will go to glory, Malcolm. It awaits you."

"No, it doesn't. You told me this mission would bring peace. That it would stop war between men and dragons."

Again, troubling. "And so it shall. Forever. A lasting peace for the dragons without any humans to bother them again. It was the only way. Listen to your Mitera Thea. She knows."

"I have killed, Mitera Thea."

"In a just cause—"

"And I have harmed one who might have loved me, given time."

Ah, there it was. The other boy. One who had clearly turned Malcolm's head away from his purpose. "You wouldn't have arrived here had you not met him," she said, "even with my help."

"He's more than a circumstance, Mitera Thea. He's whole and complete on his own."

"I'm sorry your heart's been bruised. Your capacity for caring only shows how right we were to choose you."

"And how were *you* chosen, I wonder," he said.

Now, Agent Woolf felt real danger. This wasn't just insubordination, this was heresy, as impossible for Malcolm to do as breathing fire. It was time to end this.

"I won't harm you," he said, still not turning back, his hand still on the Spur. "You may shoot me as I know you intend to. Though I don't know why."

"Because humans are weak, no matter how much they profess their love for dragons. You would eventually talk, which might stop the world ending in fire."

"And you? You won't talk?"

"I will not be here."

He turned at that. A full understanding was dawning, of how thoroughly he had been betrayed. She saw it, tumbling across his features like an explosion underwater. She had the gun pointed directly at him, no more than three feet away. She would have shot him already, but his hand was *still* on the Spur. "Did you try to have the blue killed?" Malcolm asked her. "You said you would just drive him away."

"Sometimes one must commit even the vilest blasphemy for the greater good, my child."

"How can a Believer say that? How can a Believer believe that and still call themselves a Believer?"

"You must let go of the Spur of the Goddess, Malcolm," she said. "You must do it now."

"Who *are* you?" he said, fear in his voice.

She lowered her head, looked at the ground, letting out a sigh. The gun lowered, slightly, too. She felt him relax a little, she felt hope reach from him.

As she had intended.

"Time's up," she said, raised the gun and fired.

* * *

But Malcolm knew a defensive deception when he saw one. By the time her gun was level with his head, he already had a blade out of his sleeve, slashing at her hand.

The gun went off as he cut her, sending the shot astray, his blade going so deep he severed her forefinger altogether. She cried out and dropped the gun, right next to her lost finger.

The fight was on.

He leapt at her, was surprised that – despite her obvious injury – she was already leaping back at him. The fist at the end of her uncut arm struck him hard on the temple. He absorbed it, stayed standing, and slashed at her again. She jumped to avoid it, and he took his advantage, slashing more and more.

She got back out of his reach, then looked up at him with a smile. "You let go of the Spur."

She tumbled to the road, nearly somersaulting to avoid another swing, but getting past him and almost reaching the Spur. He made to jump on her back, trying to break her spine with both his feet, a bit of brutality she had taught him herself–

Which made her know just when to roll to avoid it. He swung his hand down in another slash, but with surprising strength, she caught his wrist, holding it there, sweat now covering both their faces.

"You made me kill," he hissed at her.

"The cause was just," she hissed back.

"What was the cause?"

She kicked at his knee, giving it a painful crack that made him stumble. She scrambled up towards the claw, but he threw himself at her, shifting his weight until she fell. He knelt on her arms, her face below him. "What did I kill for?" he demanded.

"You killed," she panted, "to save the dragons forever."

With a powerful kick of her legs, she bucked him off, catching him a blow across the face as he fell. Now she stood over *him*, the claw directly behind him, the aura still growing, pulsating, reaching out across the road.

He rose and she struck him again. He felt a tooth knocked from its root and spat it out onto the road. She grabbed him, the bloodied four-finger fist around his throat, the other holding her gun, which she had picked up with terrifying speed.

"Who are you?" he gasped again.

"I've told you," she said, putting the barrel of the gun against his forehead. "I am your Mitera Thea."

"What happened to my real mother?"

She paused, clearly not expecting this. "You were an orphan. Like all the others."

"A lot of orphans in the Believers," he said. "If you think about it."

"Now? You ask this now?"

"It's because I can see Nelson sneaking up behind you with a rock."

She spun. She knew she shouldn't spin, but she did. She had him in her grip, she had the gun against his forehead, she could pull the trigger at any second, but turning away from him, even for an instant, was a risk. And he was probably lying–

Nelson struck her in the face with a stone.

She felt her nose break, along possibly with her cheekbone, but the worse outcome was that it knocked her off balance, the gun sliding up–

She could feel Malcolm on her even before she reached the ground, felt him break the forearm that held the gun, felt him wrench it from her grip and fling it away. She shunted aside the pain as best she could, but only looked up in time to see him over her, the blades in both his hands, ready to strike.

"I believed in you," he said, and she could see tears in his eyes. He drew back his hands.

"No," the other boy, Nelson, said. "Don't do it."

To her surprise, Malcolm immediately stopped.

"She'll kill you," Malcolm said to the boy. "She killed the two men here today. She killed the man in our motel room–"

"Isn't that enough?" Nelson said. "Haven't enough people died? The boy over there, too. And what happened to the girl and the dragon? They're just ... *gone*, Malcolm. Somebody has to say stop."

She saw Malcolm swallow. She wondered if she could back away from him while he was distracted–

He put a foot on her hip to keep her from moving.

"And you're saying it?" Malcolm said.

"Whatever that claw thing is doing," Nelson said, looking beyond them, "it's getting bigger."

Malcolm turned to look, too, and Agent Woolf found herself unable not to look as well, though forever keeping her mind on any chance to escape.

The aura was increasing. Malcolm had clearly got a large quantity of blood from that blue. She'd have to stop it soon; the other boy was right to be afraid of it. She would find an opening to make it so. She would or there would have been no point to any of this.

"It will swallow this world," she said, "and everything in it, including this boy here–"

Malcolm didn't even look at her, just pressed with his foot to cause her enough pain to stop talking.

"You saved me," Malcolm said to Nelson, marvelling at the fact. "She was going to shoot me."

"I told you. I want it all to stop."

Malcolm looked back down at the Mitera Thea. She was in a bad way. Blood across her face, blood flowing from one arm, the other newly broken. But she was looking back up at him with eyes that signalled no defeat. He knew how dangerous she was.

He thought he knew what to do next, though. He knew *she* probably knew, too, and that she would do her very best to prevent it.

But it would stop all this. For however long, it would stop this.

Which is what Nelson wanted.

"Then I'll stop it," Malcolm said, and stepped to the Spur of the Goddess, taking it in his hand.

He disappeared along with it.

* * *

"No!" Agent Woolf screamed. She scrambled to her feet, cursing at the pain in her arm, but again trying to shunt it away.

"Malcolm?" Nelson asked, but there was no sign of him at all.

The aura itself was rapidly shrinking, too, like a tornado disappearing down a drain. There was no time to waste. No choice. She'd have to go through and take what consequences would come.

"Where did he go?" the boy demanded of her.

She took a step back to gain momentum, then ran at the ever-shrinking aura.

"What are you doing?" Nelson yelled.

She leapt.

She was gone.

There was a sudden quiet, one that for a moment made Nelson think he had gone deaf, so complete and sudden was it. The aura had vanished, but the spiral in the air was still dissipating. Nelson could see the fading splash of the explosion that had happened way up there, miles above the earth.

It was only the sound of sirens in the distance that stirred him. Surely the spiral in the air had been seen, surely *someone* had heard all the gunfire.

Police were on their way. Lots of them.

And Nelson was standing alone in a road, surrounded by dead bodies.

Part 2

14

Sarah's world had disappeared, but somehow also not. There was a moment of shimmer, as if she were underwater, and the world above stretched and ebbed until she broke the surface. But broke the surface where? For all she could tell, she was on a road that for most of its length looked just like the road to her farm. The turn, the small hillock beside it, the gravel, all the same.

But it was daylight, and the hillock was in slightly the wrong place.

There was the usual uniform grey cloud of the Pacific Northwest winter obscuring all horizons, where it had been completely clear just a split second ago. If there was a Russian satellite flying overhead, no one here would ever see it. She looked back down the road.

"Daddy?" she said.

He was gone, too. She'd seen him put a hand to his chest, stumble to the ground. She'd seen his eyes go out.

Then he was gone.

So was Jason, no longer in her lap. The cars were gone as well. Her father's truck, the Sheriff's car, the truck that had belonged to the boy with the claw. Who was also gone.

From the utter madness of what was happening, from a crowd of friends and strangers *at night*, from a bloodbath and a dragon and some sort of world-warping magic thing, she was – in an instant – alone on her road.

But also not her road.

She got to her feet. She could see the roof of her barn from here, a sight so familiar and comfortable it was all but invisible to her on her thousands of walks home to it. It was now taller than it should be, with a second-floor hayloft door looking out at the road. She also shouldn't have been able to see her house from where she stood, but the rise that crops of onions had curved over for her entire life was now a dip of land instead, still filled with onions, but now leaving a clear view to the farmhouse.

Which was painted white, not the natural wood it had always been. The fields beyond, too, had none of the clearing that Kazimir had done. They were still thick forest, as were the fields next to them, which had been waiting for sugar beets to be planted until a moment ago. The clouds were so low, she couldn't see Mount Rainier and had a panicked moment wondering if it was there behind the clouds at all.

"What is this?" she said, to herself, to no one, turning in a full circle. Was she just waking up? Had she sleepwalked out here and dreamed a different landscape that had felt so real the one she was seeing now was causing doubts?

But no. Jason had died in her arms. His blood was still all

over the front of her work dungarees. Oh, no. Oh, nonono, Jason, her *father*–

"It is not as I expected," she heard a voice say, the voice of a young man but oddly deep. She saw him walking side-on to her out of a ditch that also hadn't been there a few moments before. He was looking around, seeming as befuddled as she was. "I thought it would be..." He turned to face her. "Smaller."

He was about eighteen years old, with wavy blond hair and one impossibly blue eye, the other seemingly sewn shut, plus a cut on his chin that bled dark black blood.

He was also completely naked.

"Try not to scream, Sarah Dewhurst," he said. "I am Kazimir."

"You're young," was the first thing she said, after her legs had given out from under her. She hadn't fainted, she didn't think, but it felt like all the air had left her body, making it a weight she could no longer support.

It wasn't what he'd said. It wasn't the eye-stitching or the blood or that he knew her name. It was that *she had believed him*. She felt the truth of it hit her like a stone. Of course, he was Kazimir. That he looked human, spoke like one, had the shockingly exposed anatomy of one, didn't seem to matter at all; she immediately knew it was true. It was *this* that had caused her to tumble. If Kazimir was different but still himself, then she really was elsewhere.

"I am the age I ever was." He stooped beside her, somewhat bemusedly checking to see if she was all right, but checking nonetheless.

"You were a teenage dragon?" She moved to get up, but had to stay down.

"I *remain* a dragon," he said, more seriously. "It would be wise not to forget that, no matter how I am shaped." He put a hand on her arm, helping her up with what seemed like effortless strength. "As for my age, we are different than you." He said it as if that sentence would explain everything.

She was on her feet, a bit wobbly still, but at least standing. She glanced at his body, then glanced away very quickly. "How are you ... like this?"

"Unclothed? Dragons do not wear–"

"*Human*, I mean."

He frowned, slightly. "Yes. I am somewhat surprised as well."

"What happened?" She looked around again. "This looks a *lot* like home–"

"But it is not."

"Where's my dad?" she demanded, as that came back to her again in another wave. "That woman shot him–"

"He is not here," Kazimir said, and it *was* Kazimir, that certainty resounded a second time. But how? "Or rather," the boy who was also the dragon Kazimir continued, "he is probably here in one way, but not the way that you imagine."

He still had his hand on her arm. She shook it off, violently. "Quit touching me. Where is he then?"

Kazimir stepped away from her, his eye glinting a blue in the way that human eyes never did. He took in a long breath through his nose, smelling the air. "It smells different." He breathed again. "It smells greener."

"Than what?"

"Than the last world."

"Than the what now?"

"Something that has been theorized." He grinned, and if she hadn't believed he was a dragon before, that grin would have eliminated all doubt. It was transfixing; it hinted at secret knowledge that would turn your stomach to jelly. "But not witnessed first-hand in living memory. The prophecy–"

She pulled herself up to her full height, anger blitzing away all the dizziness. "If you don't give me a straight answer, I swear, I will beat you. I'm a farm girl. I'm stronger than you think."

He looked back towards the centre of the road, where so much violence and screaming had recently been, where there was scorching from the flames he had sent through the aura. "Very well. I do not know it all, but I know some. The Spur of the Goddess is deep, deep magic, a channel for the untamed power I told you about. Separated from the Goddess herself in hopes that keeping her incomplete would limit her power. It disappeared, was almost forgotten by humans and dragons. Until today. But it is many things. One of those things is a key."

"A key to what?"

"Other worlds."

"This is another world?" Though again, it was easier to believe than she would have thought. The truth of it felt real. "But it looks so much like..."

"There are an infinite number of universes," Kazimir said. "They exist side by side, made by every choice taken within each, branching off into different possibilities. Four years ago, a mathematician named Erwin Schrödinger suggested the theory to a conference in Ireland." He got a firm set to his lips. "But dragons have known about it for much longer."

"If we're in a different universe," Sarah said, "how do we get back? My dad was *shot*–"

"But not your dad *here*."

"I don't know what point you're–"

"Look how close this universe is to the last one. Do you not think the humans in it will be similar as well?"

Sarah blinked. "You mean... There's another *me* here?"

"Yes." Kazimir frowned. "But not another me."

"I'm not understanding this, and I don't care. How do I get back?"

"The Spur of the Goddess brought us here." He looked again to the centre of the road. "It can take us back. But – and you really must hear me, Sarah Dewhurst – we *cannot* go back."

"What? Why?"

"Because the destruction of that satellite was the first step."

"First step to what?"

"War, of course." He said it in the same patronizing way he'd been speaking from the start, but she could also hear his own solidity in it. He believed this to be true, but he also regretted it. "If not the one I had long thought."

"What do you mean?" she asked, though even as she did, she knew what he said was obviously true. The Russians would think the Americans destroyed the satellite, that they had secret weapons which *could*. Things would escalate. It wouldn't even involve dragons. Humans would destroy one another.

"Oh, my God," she said, realizing. "That was your plan all along."

"*My* plan? Absolutely not, Sarah Dewhurst. I merely saw the wrong thing coming and failed to stop it." He looked angrily at the world again, at the snowflakes starting to fall. "And I have no clear idea how to rectify that failure."

There was a gasp of air, almost like a wind through a particularly leafy tree. The boy with the claw, the boy who had destroyed the satellite, who had come to this little corner of nowhere to assassinate her, was now sitting in the middle of the road.

"It was a lie," he said, looking up at them. "It was all a lie."

"So it seems," Kazimir said, only the slightest surprise arching his eyebrows.

The boy – Malcolm, Sarah remembered now – held the claw in his hand, but there was no aura around it. It just looked like a claw. Nothing more.

"Everything she said," Malcolm continued. "Everything I was taught."

"Not everything," Kazimir said, approaching him. "There would have been some truth or it would not have been believable."

He held out his hand. Malcolm lifted the claw, questioningly, not to give it to Kazimir, but almost as if wondering what it was. "I felt its power before," he said. "Even when it was buried deep in my bag, I could feel it." He looked at Kazimir. "I don't feel it now."

Kazimir reached for it. Malcolm pulled it back, but it was half-hearted. After the smallest of hesitations, he handed it over, a question on his face. Kazimir took the claw and – there was no other word for it – *growled*. He spun it in his hand, feeling with it, stabbing at the air. He then touched it to the drying blood on his chin. There was a brief shimmer of the aura around the claw, but it was gone in an instant. "It is the same..."

"But it's also not the same," Malcolm said. "You feel it, too. Or is that because you're human now, Great One?"

"And how do you know so surely who I am?" Kazimir growled again. "Don't let this shape fool you. I am still dragon."

"Can you breathe fire?" Sarah asked. "Can you fly?"

Kazimir just spun the claw again.

"Take us back," Sarah said, feeling the panic all over, the image of her dad falling, the craziness of the world-that-just-was. "You've got the claw thing, take us back."

"Again, Sarah Dewhurst, that is not a world to be going back to."

"And again, I don't care what you think. Take me back. Now."

Kazimir flipped the claw in his hand one more time. "I cannot." He tossed the claw casually back to Malcolm. "It seems here, for me and for all of us, it is now just a dragon claw."

"What are you saying?" Sarah asked.

"I am saying," Kazimir said, frowning finally, "that it has always worked because of the magic of dragons. Our blood. Blood stronger than what flows through me in my current shape."

"Well, we'll just find a *real* dragon then," Sarah snapped.

There was a tearing sound in front of them, horrible to hear. None of them were sure what they were seeing at first. The woman – who Sarah knew as the one who'd shot her father, who Malcolm knew as Mitera Thea – was somehow running straight at them as the aura opened again. Her arm seemed broken, her other hand bleeding terribly, but she was running, swallowing her pain, and now jumping–

And while a woman jumped *into* the aura–

A red dragon the size of a battleship flew out.

They threw themselves to the ground, the great belly of the dragon passing over them by mere inches, and not even that in the case of Kazimir, who was knocked back into the ditch where Sarah had first seen him.

She watched the dragon pass with awe and horror. She had seen red farm dragons, bigger than Kazimir, certainly, but *nothing* as big as this. This was an eagle to Kazimir's hummingbird. A creature large enough to destroy whole towns, whole *cities*, should it choose. It was favouring its foreleg – where the woman had shown a broken arm – and its flight was uneven, but it was still powerful enough for the downdraught to press Sarah into the ground. The dragon rose, heading east, towards the forest and clouds and the mountain range that Sarah assumed still existed beyond.

"She didn't kill us," Malcolm said, getting up.

"Yes," Kazimir called back, dragging himself out of the ditch. "Why not?"

"She was injured," Malcolm said. "Maybe–"

"What on *earth* was that?"

A voice, behind them. They whirled around. The aura where the dragon had flown was gone. It was now just a road

215

again. A woman with a bicycle she had clearly just been riding was staring at them, mouth open.

"And who are you?" the woman demanded, her frightened eyes alighting first on Malcolm, then on the approaching and still naked Kazimir, before settling on Sarah.

If the sight of a plane-sized dragon wasn't enough to make her drop her bicycle, the sight of Sarah was. The woman put a hand over her mouth, her eyes widening. Then a second hand, as if to stop what she was seeing. "This is a trick," the woman said, her voice taut behind her hands. "This is all some sort of filthy, dirty *trick*."

Sarah felt the world swooning around her again, like it had when she recognized Kazimir, but this time she actually fainted, in the way that people so rarely do.

Because the woman looking back at her as she fell to the ground was her mother.

15

"I don't know who you people are," a distant voice said, "or what trick you're trying to play, but that is not my daughter."

"In an important way," said another voice, one she thought she recognized, "you are correct."

"What's *that* supposed to mean? And why aren't you wearing any clothes?"

"Does anyone have something I can cushion her head with?" said another voice.

The voice of the boy who'd come to kill her.

"Mom?" Sarah said, sitting up too fast. Her vision swam, and she had to close her eyes to avoid fainting again. When she opened them, she was sitting on the road – a road no car had passed in the entire time they'd been waiting – and Malcolm was sitting over her, helping her up. She flinched away from him, scooting back.

"Mom?" she said again, looking around for the woman, finding her, finding that face. The one she hadn't seen since–

"You're alive," Sarah said.

"What do you mean, I'm alive?" the woman said. "Of course, I'm alive, and don't you dare call me Mom."

Sarah could barely breathe. Of all the impossible things that had happened today, this was the most. "You died," she found herself saying.

"How do you think you can talk this way?" The woman backed away, furious and frightened. "How can you say these things to a woman alone in the world?"

"We are not from around here," Kazimir said.

"*You* died." The woman pointed at Sarah. "*You* did."

"What?" Sarah said.

"And I don't know what, what *cruelty* this is..." She stepped back even farther. "And what was that thing? That thing that flew through the air just now?"

"A dragon," Sarah said, as if she couldn't understand the woman's confusion. Which she couldn't.

Kazimir lowered his voice, speaking directly to Sarah. "They do not have dragons here."

"What? You can't just not have dragons. It'd be like not having *pigs*."

"Oh, I can smell pigs," Kazimir said. "But the only dragon I have scented since our arrival is the one that flew past us. Before she arrived, nothing. Not a whiff or a trace in the air."

"That's just around here, though," Sarah said. "The world is huge."

"Not huge enough that dragon scent wouldn't be forever in the air."

"This is crazy," the woman said, picking up her bicycle again. "I want nothing to do with this."

218

"Mom, wait, please–" Sarah started.

"I am *not* your mother."

Sarah was crying now. First, her father. Well, not *first* her father, first was Jason, but who knew how far back the *first*s began. The dragon telling her an assassin was coming? Her mother and the cancer that ate her alive? A town full of people whose skin didn't match her own? Where did it all begin? Where on earth could it all end?

"My daughter is the one who died." The woman was clearly growing angrier now. "How dare you do this? How dare you corrupt her memory? Shame on you. Shame on whoever put you up to this." She turned to Kazimir. "And put some clothes on!"

"Why?" Kazimir asked. "I carry my own heat source."

The woman got on her bicycle. "No, please, wait!" Sarah called after her. The woman didn't stop. Sarah started running. The woman just pedalled faster, but for a moment, Sarah caught up. The woman looked at her once more, her eyes widening, but then she rode firmly ahead.

Sarah only slowed her step because she'd seen that the woman was crying, too.

"We will have to stop her, you know," Kazimir said.

Sarah spun around. "You leave her alone. You leave her *completely* alone."

"I do not mean her."

"He means the Mitera Thea," Malcolm said.

"The dragon?" Sarah said. "That huge dragon that could burn us to dust in a second?"

"And stomp you to bloody gore," Kazimir said. "And tear you to small, shredded pieces. Really, so very many ways you little humans can be killed by dragons and yet for so very, very long have not been."

"This isn't exactly refuting my point."

"She'll try and wreck this world, too," Malcolm said, again quietly, nothing at all like the confident, certain boy who had waltzed onto her farm, intending to kill her and destroying a satellite.

"She will not try," Kazimir said. "She will succeed."

"She's one dragon," Sarah said. "A big one, sure, but other dragons will–"

"There are no other dragons in this world!" Kazimir yelled, the first time she'd ever heard him raise his voice. She realized, beneath all the bravado, all the condescension, he was afraid, like he had been when he was facing Malcolm and that claw. "I could smell another dragon if it was hiding in a cave on the other side of the planet. I am telling you, there are no dragons here."

"That wasn't in the prophecy," Malcolm said, looking lost.

"There is *much* that was not in the prophecy," said Kazimir.

"How can there be no dragons?" Sarah asked, at a loss herself. "That makes no sense."

"The people here would say the same of a world with dragons in it," Kazimir said. He looked around again, not seeming to notice the snow falling on his bare skin. "This world has no dragon magic in it at all except for what's in me and in her." He frowned. "It is like a world without music."

"That's why you turned human?" Sarah asked. "Because it didn't understand your shape?"

"Yes."

"But that can't be true, because a giant flaming dragon just flew over our heads!"

"She was human in the other world," Malcolm said, "but *we* didn't change into dragons."

Kazimir looked even more unhappy. "I do not have an explanation," he said, but in a way that sounded like he didn't have an explanation he was willing to share just yet. "Regardless, she will know all that we know before long. That she is the only flying dragon in this world. That we still have the Spur. If she thinks we can still use it, she will come for us. If she discovers what is far more likely to be the truth–"

"That here," Malcolm said, "her blood is the only thing that can power it?"

"Then we are in even more danger." Kazimir held the palms of his hands together, not quite in prayer but in some sort of consideration. "The prophecy–"

"Ugh!" Sarah shouted. "I don't want to hear one more word of your prophecy."

"The prophecy is that you would stop her from destroying the world."

"Well, that didn't work, did it?"

"The prophecy did not say *which* world."

Sarah put her hands to her forehead. "This is too much. I want you to stop this. I want you to make this all go away."

For the first time since she knew him, as either dragon or the young man standing in front of her, Kazimir looked almost

221

compassionate. "The only thing that may take us back is the Spur, which we have but we cannot operate."

"So we make your dragon use it. Or get her blood or something."

"Indeed. We will also stop her from likely destroying this planet."

"Well, if we're saving planets," Sarah said, sarcastically, "why not ours, too? We force her to take us back and make her confess what she's done."

"She won't," Malcolm said. "She'd kill you before you could finish your breath trying."

"Don't you want to help the boy who was with you?" Sarah said, rounding on him. "He's still there, isn't he?"

Malcolm looked at her, guilt on his face. "I do. Very much. I believe I loved him."

Sarah was confused. "Like ... a brother?"

"No," Kazimir said, "not like a brother."

"He's there alone," Malcolm said. "I did that to him."

"It is of no use to stand here and nurse our wounds," Kazimir said. "You have both lost people. That is regrettable, but there is not one thing we can do to change that, except find that dragon."

"She flew to the top of Mount Rainier for all we know," Sarah said. "Are we going there?"

"If we must," Kazimir said. "But I think she will find us."

"And kill us," Malcolm said.

"I am a dragon, too," Kazimir said. "I know our ways. I may know how to fight her."

"Fighting her is one thing," Malcolm said. "Winning is another."

"And have *you* any plans, assassin?" Kazimir nearly shouted at him. "You knew her as your devoted Mitera Thea!"

Malcolm shook his head, sadly. "She was always just human to me."

"Your species always tell stories of men who you describe as dragons underneath their own skin." Kazimir gestured to his own body as evidence.

"Maybe she wanted it so much," Malcolm started. "Maybe she believed so strongly that–"

"It doesn't matter," Sarah said, bitterly. "She's a dragon now. And I'm not fighting a dragon."

"You are," Kazimir said. "It was foretold."

"Was it foretold that I would go talk to my mother first?" And she left.

Kazimir watched her go, his arms crossed, wondering at all that had yet to happen. The assassin came up to his shoulder, also watching her leave.

"You're considering something," Malcolm said. "A possibility you don't like and didn't want to share with us."

"It is preposterous," Kazimir returned. "It simply cannot be."

Malcolm held out the claw for Kazimir to see. "Torn from the Goddess herself," Malcolm said. "Supposedly."

"Not supposedly," Kazimir said, then asked, "When the red dragon came through, when she was still a woman, I saw her bloodied hand?"

"Yes," Malcolm said. "In the fight, the last one before we all came over here..." He hesitated.

"Yes?" Kazimir said.

"I'm sorry," Malcolm said. "Your nakedness is distracting."

Kazimir rolled his eye. "Humans are ridiculous—"

"In the fight we just had," Malcolm tried again, louder this time. "I used my blades on her. I cut off her forefinger."

Kazimir led Malcolm's eyes to the claw again.

The claw from the forefinger of the Goddess herself.

"Oh," Malcolm said. "Shit."

16

She ached. The snow in the crater of the mountain was soothing, but it didn't stop the pain in her forearm, the one Malcolm had broken, or where he had sliced off her finger, or all the other places that hurt from the fight and from...

The change.

It was an understatement to say she had not expected that.

The pain had been extraordinary, like she was being skinned alive, which perhaps she had been. She felt as if she had exploded from the inside, stretched beyond what was possible for her meagre human body.

That was what had made it so confusing. Even in the intensity of the pain – which had lasted what felt like a lifetime even though it had clearly passed in an instant – she had also felt ... liberation.

All her life she had been driven by a devotion matched only by its accompanying rage. She wanted to destroy men for dragons, knowing all the while it meant her own destruction.

A self-hate so grand it was almost theology on its own. Even so, she'd hoped for her survival somehow. She knew what the Spur was capable of – there was no greater scholar of it in the world than she – she knew it offered an escape, but to another world entirely. Which was a difficult pill to swallow. She would save one world for her beloveds and be exiled to another without them, no credit for her heroism, only the fact of it, which no one would ever know. Unless she could convince the dragons in this new world, make herself indispensable to them, show them what one committed Believer could accomplish. They would know the truth of it, she felt. They would have to.

There *had* been another option, an unlikely one, which embarrassed her to think of now...

But then something wonderful had happened.

She was now dragon. She was now an enormous, red, fire-breathing dragon. She inhaled to try it and made herself cough and cough, the aches ringing out like bells through her enormous body.

She inhaled again, more slowly this time, feeling the fire organ in her chest engage – she knew how to do this, as instinctively as she had known how to fly – and breathed out a blast so strong and hot, it not only melted the top of the glacier but the rocks below, the orange glow of molten lava reflecting back up to her in a brief shine, before the perilously low temperatures froze even the steam, causing a flurry of snow around her.

See her strength. See her incredible dragon strength.

She was not cold. Dragons carried their own heating system, did they not? She could wait up here until the break

226

healed, which she also seemed to know instinctively would not take long. A dragon with a broken foreleg was not a dragon. Their evolution would have made the healing of bones top priority.

So she would wait. And then she would conquer.

She did not know how yet – and that the only other dragon she smelled was that puny little blue who had interfered (and how her nose was like a second brain all of a sudden! How marvellous! How impossibly blind she had always been!) was a matter of some small concern. She would have to seek them out, wherever they might be hiding. She would have to…

She sniffed again. And again.

Well, now. That was unexpected.

There were no other dragons to lead to war over the humans here.

But then again, now that she thought of it, that meant there were no other dragons to share power with after the war was finished.

Fate took away, but fate also gave.

She inhaled another deep breath, not for fire, but to gather herself and her wobbly wings. She flew straight up from the mountaintop, into the clouds, pushing through into open air.

The sun was setting, nearly gone in the far western horizon. To her east lay the night, stars already a-twinkle. Far to the south-west, she saw – and distantly heard – an aeroplane. It seemed commercial rather than military. Any passenger looking in this direction might spot her dark redness against the white of the clouds and wonder what they were hallucinating.

She laughed to herself, then scanned the sky above.

It was empty. Nothing blinked. No satellite flew overhead.

That might not mean anything, of course. It might be in its orbit on the other side of the planet, it might have failed at launch, or that launch might be tomorrow or next month or next year. The point was, she had no satellite yet with which to start a war.

So war would have to come from somewhere else.

She smiled to herself, turning back to the mountain to rest some more and consider what had happened to her.

She had, against all odds and after many years, accomplished the impossible: nuclear blasts would kill a dragon, but only if hit directly. They were immune to the radiation that fell out afterwards. So let men bomb one another into oblivion in a war she had worked so hard to start. With the planet rid of humans, dragons could fly free again, fly free as they obviously should, the top of all Creation.

In all these accomplishments, though, there had been the embarrassing other option. Oh, how she had dreamed, deep in her heart of hearts, never spoken aloud to another soul, how she might be the sole survivor. She would go to the bosom of dragons as the bombs were falling and she would tell them what she had done. They would listen to her this time, these beasts she worshipped but who ignored her devotion. They would protect her, shield her, because they would finally see her for what she always knew she was. She was more than just a Believer (and hadn't she been right? Just look at her now. *Look* at her) and they would know it, too, the human who had given them this unparalleled gift.

Who had given them not just her faith, not just her life, but the whole world.

They would smile on her. They would grant her her dearest

wish. They could do it. There were stories of it happening. Stories over the millennia (but none very recent) of humans who had done great service to dragons and dragons who had done the greatest of dragon magic in return.

They would change her.

"When it turned out," she said now, aloud, revelling in the depth of her voice, its timbre, its *power*. "When it turned out," she said again, even louder, "all I needed to do was cross to a world that would recognize me for what I was all along."

She laughed. And laughed again. And melted more rocks. Then the laughing faltered.

The prophecy had told of a girl who would save the world, *that* girl, the one she'd sent Malcolm after.

Well, that was clearly wrong, yes? It sure seemed so, now that the other world would almost certainly be at war before the week was out. Perhaps the prophecy meant that the girl would go *back* and save it. Yes, that must be it. Who even cared if she did? This world had turned Agent Woolf into a dragon.

But then...

What if the prophecy hadn't meant her old world at all?

What if the prophecy had meant this world? The girl would save this one.

Save it from *her*.

But how? She was a puny girl, and this dragon, this one right here, on this mountaintop, she was the mightiest of the mighty. The mightiest thing – if her nose was right – on this whole planet.

What an unexpected bonus indeed. And what a nasty surprise for nasty little girls.

She had seen Malcolm as she flew past, and he would be

in for a surprise, as well. He would accept her as his proper Mother Goddess now, or he could easily be disposed of. There had been a third with them, too. A boy who...

She sniffed. She sniffed again, deeper. She went right to the rim of the crater and sniffed again.

No.

No, it couldn't be.

The passage through had turned her from human to dragon...

And him from dragon to human.

Oh, how delicious. How perfectly, ridiculously delicious. What a wonderful place this world must be, to recognize your true nature so easily, so beautifully.

Well, wait until her foreleg healed. Wait until she was full strength.

Then they would see. They would *all* see.

They might ask, what could one dragon do to a world?

But that was the great secret, one revealed to her now, this instant, as sure as she'd known how to breathe fire.

She wouldn't *be* one dragon for long.

She rubbed her stomach. In her new dragon state, she could feel them in there. A litter. A proper dragon litter.

Which was impossible. And highly alarming. Agent Woolf had been very much a virgin. She hated humans far too much to touch any one of them in that way.

So, how then?

Destiny, was all she could think. This world had given her every tool to dominate it with this shape, so why not also the means to proliferate? How they must beg for something to worship here.

Very well, then, she would just have to start the new age for them, wouldn't she?

The thumping of her dragon heart told her, made her *know*, that she could.

The dragon that had been Agent Woolf settled in to make her plans.

17

Sarah couldn't settle on whether to run or walk, so she ended up doing both. She would hurry along the road to the farm, desperate to see her mother, then it would all become too much, and she would slow down. Then she'd think again how her mother – her *mother* – was actually within reach and off she'd go.

She was having a difficult day, it had to be said.

She came around the last bend of the drive and looked at the white-painted house and the too-tall barn. Only the bicycle, dropped hastily on the front lawn, its wheel still spinning, showed any clue that someone lived here. She couldn't see her father's truck. Then she remembered what her mother had said about being "a woman alone". Was he dead here, too? Was that the exchange she was going to have to make?

She heard oinking. She looked around the side of the house to the sty, the same place as in her own world. There they were, her three perfect sows. They recognized her, too, as she approached, all three standing their forelegs on the low fence. She put her hands out and they fought to nuzzle them.

Her pigs. Her three not little but quite large pigs.

"Hello, ladies," she said, with a gasping sob. There had been so much going on, she hadn't known how much the loss of them hurt until suddenly here they were, grunting and nuzzling and acting like it was *she* who had risen from the dead and not them.

When it seemed she had. In this world, where her mother hadn't fallen to cancer, something else had come along, some reckoning that clearly stretched across universes to make sure the Dewhurst family was brought low, and had taken this world's Sarah and seemingly her father with it.

"How did I die here?" she whispered to the pigs. Bess, the greediest, was already over to the trough, nudging it the way she did when Sarah was late with their feed. The pigs didn't care. She was here, they were happy to see her, and looking to get a free meal out of it.

"You're not her," she heard. She turned.

"I don't think I am," Sarah said to her mother. Mamie and Eleanor still reached for her with their snouts. She couldn't help but scratch them. "Or if I am, I'm not all the way."

Her mother looked suspicious, a look Sarah didn't like seeing. Darlene Dewhurst had been slighted *plenty* by the town, by the people in it, both overtly and covertly, things Sarah knew all too well herself. Darlene's face had shown anger, and hurt, and fortitude, and humour, and acceptance, and fear, and strength.

But it had never been suspicious. Suspicion corroded, she'd always said. It would grow and take the things you loved with

234

it. What had happened in this universe to make her suspicious?

The death of a daughter and husband might do it.

"The pigs sure like you," her mother said. "You holding food?"

"No, ma'am. I think they just recognize me."

Her mother shook her head, angrily. "I will not put up with cruelty–"

Sarah raised her hands in a kind of surrender. "I don't mean to be. This is hard for me, too, seeing you here." She began to cry again. "It's been two years in my world."

"Your world?"

Sarah shrugged. "That's what they said. A world right next to this one. Almost the same, but not quite. And somehow... We jumped over."

"We? The other two who were with you?"

"Yes, ma'am."

Her mother looked around. "Where are they now?"

Where *were* they now? Sarah had gone off with such purpose, she hadn't looked to see whether either of them was following her. Distantly, she knew that if she was ever going to get back, she'd probably need them, but putting space between her and them right now also didn't feel like the worst idea. How else could a girl gather her thoughts?

"Oh," her mother said, "there they are."

Sarah saw them both hesitating at the end of the drive. Malcolm looking sheepish and sad, Kazimir still naked as the day he was born, staring intently at Sarah, but neither of them coming closer.

"Stay there!" Sarah said, then she turned to her mother. "Can I talk to you?"

"I said, no–"

"My pigs were poisoned." Sarah put her hands back to the still-waiting snouts. "Back in the other world. Whatever and wherever it was. Mamie, Bess, and Eleanor." She glanced back at her mother. "Dad poisoned them. Because... Well it's a long story but I think he knew it was wrong."

"Your father knew a lot of things were wrong." Her mother immediately corrected herself. "*Not* your father."

"I suppose there's no such things as dragons either?"

"Don't be ridiculous. They're only from white people stories. Black folk have more important things to do than worry about dragons."

"Dragons like the giant red one you saw flying less than ten minutes ago?"

Her mother bit her lower lip. "I don't know what I saw."

"You saw a dragon."

"I said I don't know what it was." Then she frowned more. "But I did see something."

"It's dangerous."

"Well, that may be the first thing you've said I believe, missy."

Sarah's heart jumped a bit. She hadn't heard her mother call her "missy" in too long. It didn't matter that she only said it when she thought Sarah was getting sassy; it was like being hit right in the chest. She felt her eyes well up again.

Her mother sighed at the sight of the tears. "You do look so much like her."

"I'm not her," Sarah said, "but I'm almost her." She was really crying now. "I've missed you."

Darlene Dewhurst still looked stern, but she used a thumb

to wipe excess tears from her own eyes. "This isn't right. Whatever this is, it isn't right." She cocked her head. "Is that blood on your front?"

"It's... How do I even explain? There was a boy. And there were guns. And then I saw Daddy..." She couldn't quite say it, but forced it out. "A woman shot him. Right on that road out there. And then I was *here*. And so were you. And I don't know how to get back, if I even can."

Her mother sighed again. "Okay, listen, girl, whoever you may be–"

She stopped at the sound of a truck. It was rounding the corner of the drive, and as Malcolm and Kazimir – who had, somewhat surprisingly, waited where Sarah had told them to – stood to one side, she recognized it. Hisao Inagawa was behind the wheel, looking shocked at Malcolm and Kazimir as he passed, then his eyes widening so big at Sarah she could see them through the windshield. He stared at her as he got out, before looking over to Sarah's mother. "You all right, Darlene?"

"I'm debating that right now, Hisao," her mother said, "but I don't feel under threat if that's what you mean."

"Sarah?" Sarah heard.

She had been staring so hard at Mr Inagawa that she didn't even realize Jason was getting out of the truck next to him. An unbloody Jason, an unshot one. One that wasn't lying (dead, she knew it, she couldn't think the word, but she knew it, dead) in her lap.

"Oh, thank God," she whispered, her heart leaping. She ran to him, wrapped her arms around him, holding him close and hard. It felt like nothing but him, down to the boniness of his skinny shoulders.

237

"It's not Sarah," Darlene said. "It looks like her. It's not."

"Oh, Jason, thank God," Sarah said.

"She knows my name!" Jason kept his arms at his sides but was letting himself be hugged, possibly out of sheer surprise.

"She knows a lot of things," Darlene said.

Sarah pulled away from him. She saw how she'd got blood, his *own* blood, all over the front of his shirt. "I mean," she said, wiping her eyes again, "I know it's not you but... It's just so good to see you."

Jason looked over at Darlene in bewilderment.

"It's not her," Darlene said, again firmly, but not, Sarah thought, angrily. There might be some middle ground here.

"Who are those two?" Hisao said, nodding at Malcolm and Kazimir. "And why is he in the altogether?"

"That I couldn't rightly tell you," Darlene said.

"Did you see it?" Hisao asked.

"See what?" Darlene asked, as if daring him to say the word.

"We saw *something*," Hisao said, frowning. "Looked like it came from your place so we jumped in the truck to make sure you were all right."

"That also has yet to be seen," Darlene said.

"God," Jason said, staring at Sarah now, "she looks *exactly* like her."

"It's not..." Darlene made an irritated huffing sound. "Oh, for Pete's sake, we can't all just be standing here out in the cold. Whyn't you all come inside and we can ... see what's what?"

Sarah looked surprised, as did Malcolm and Kazimir.

"Not him," Sarah said, pointing at Malcolm. "Not him at all."

"You don't get to choose who I invite into my farmhouse, girl," Darlene said, "but, Hisao?"

"Yes?"

"You bring your shotgun?"

Hisao looked serious as a blizzard when he said, "Yes, ma'am, I did."

Hisao sat in a kitchen chair – ones Sarah didn't recognize – with the shotgun across his lap. He stared heavily at Kazimir, now dressed in some of her father's old clothes, removed from a dusty trunk. He had tied a bandanna dashingly around his lost eye. Likewise, Sarah had been given what could only have been her own clothes from before she died. It wasn't even the fourth weirdest thing to happen today.

Darlene, having refused all offers of help, was making hot chocolate, a drink Sarah remembered from childhood. "Let's start from first principles," Darlene said, taking down six mugs. "Like the good reverend always says. This girl–"

"You can call me Sarah, if you want," Sarah said.

Darlene let out a rueful laugh. "Oh, no. No, I don't think so."

"But it is her, isn't it?" Jason spoke up, still staring at Sarah. "How could it be anyone else?"

"Because Sarah died ten months ago, Jason Inagawa," Darlene said, raising her voice into an almost-snap.

"You keep quiet in all this, Jason," Hisao said, in a voice Sarah also recognized. Jason's father never brooked much nonsense.

239

"May I ask what the date is, please?" Kazimir suddenly said.

Darlene looked surprised. "February the eighth."

He nodded. "The same day. Just a few hours different, given that it was light when we arrived."

"What does that have to do with anything?" Sarah asked.

He shrugged. "We might have been off by years. Centuries. Consider it good fortune."

"First principles," Darlene said again, louder this time. She set down a mug of chocolate for Hisao, leaving the others to get their own, which they duly did. Kazimir sniffed his so loudly everyone stopped to look.

"Fascinating," was all he said, and took a drink.

"We all saw something," Darlene said. "That's our first principle. So what was it?"

"A dragon," Kazimir said. "A Canadian red, the largest of all dragons, but large even for that race."

There was a silence, but he just carried on with his chocolate, as if he'd never had anything so peculiar in his life. Which maybe he hadn't.

"Who are you again?" Darlene asked.

"I am Kazimir," he said, as if that explained everything.

"That a Russian name?" Hisao said.

"Yes," Kazimir said, "my name is Russian."

"Are *you*?"

Kazimir took a breath. "Not exactly."

"What was it that we saw?" Darlene said, more loudly, and stopped Kazimir before he could speak. "And don't say dragon."

"Yeah, because *I've* got a first principle," said Hisao. "There's no such things as dragons."

240

"There are plenty in Japanese culture," Jason said.

"You're talking about myths, and you know it."

"That is obviously erroneous, based on recent evidence," Kazimir said.

"It sure *looked* like a dragon," Jason muttered.

"I said, hush, boy," Hisao said.

"And this girl looks like Sarah, but she clearly isn't her," Darlene said.

"It was the Mitera Thea," Malcolm whispered, barely looking up.

"What was that?" Darlene demanded, and Malcolm watched all eyes turn to him.

"The Mitera Thea?" he said again, surprised. Kazimir shot him a look. "Though if you don't have dragons, I guess you wouldn't have her either."

"We don't understand that, son," the woman who was clearly the girl's mother said. They looked so much alike, only a fool wouldn't see it. In all his thoughts bent on assassinating her, in all that time he would have cut her down without a moment's hesitation, Malcolm had never once considered that the girl, of course, would have a mother.

He felt all bound up in words. Kazimir had told him to keep quiet about Kazimir being a dragon and about his suspicions of the Mitera Thea, but maybe he shouldn't even say her title. Maybe he shouldn't say anything at all. Malcolm felt as if all his purpose was gone, all of it. Because it was, wasn't it? If it had all been a lie, and it seemed it *had*, then the Mountie he had killed had been for nothing. And the agent

241

Mother had shot in the motel room. And a whole war started because of ... what?

Nelson had been right to be horrified–

"Nelson," he said out loud, remembering again what the girl had said. Nelson, in the other world, standing alone in the road, surrounded by bodies. "My God, I've killed him, too."

The grown man gripped his shotgun. "You killed someone?"

Malcolm looked at the girl. "It was going to be her. It was going to be you."

"I know," she said, crisply. "And Jason got shot–"

"What?" Jason said.

"And my father. For what? What were you hoping to accomplish?"

"I *did* accomplish it," Malcolm said, feeling a grief so deep it made him dizzy.

"You started a war. If bombs aren't falling already, they will be soon."

"She'll do the same here," Malcolm said. "She'll do it all again."

"By herself?" the girl asked.

"You really have no idea how much damage a single dragon can do," Kazimir said.

"Is this some kind of code you're all using?" Hisao said. "What did we really see?"

"Something code-named dragon and Michael Thayer," Jason said.

"Not code names," Kazimir said. "Well, Mitera Thea might be somewhat of one, but it is more a title, like guru or saint."

"What are you talking about?" the man said. "I'm beginning to lose my patience–"

"It's my house, Hisao," the woman said. "I'll be the one who gets to lose her patience."

"Okay, so you obviously have Russia here, right?" the girl said.

"Of course we do," said the man.

"Well, in our world, they launched a satellite."

There was another silence at this, but not, Malcolm thought, about the satellite.

"Your world?" said the man.

"Another universe," the girl said, clearly not expecting to be believed. "I wouldn't have believed it either before this morning, yet here I sit, in the kitchen of my mother who died two years ago when she insists that *I'm* the one who's dead." The girl glanced at the woman. "Though she never said how."

"Cancer," the boy who'd driven up in the truck said. "In your stomach."

The girl looked stunned. *Sarah,* Malcolm corrected himself. He knew her name now. He should use it.

"You're trying to say you're from another *world*?" the man said.

"You saw a huge red dragon fly across this farm," Sarah snapped. "Surely another world isn't that hard to add on."

"I don't know what I saw," the man said.

"It was a dragon," said his son.

"It was *not* a dragon," the man insisted.

"Yes, it was, Hisao," the woman said, sounding exhausted. "And I think you know it, too."

The man did not relent, but nor did he contradict her. He merely frowned and kept his own counsel.

"So what I'm hearing," the woman said, now looking at Malcolm, "is that *you* brought it here."

"Not exactly," Kazimir started.

"Yes," Malcolm said. "That's true. And I have to stop her." He looked back at the girl. At Sarah. "I'm sorry," he said.

"You're *sorry*?" she said, not sounding pleased.

"I'm sorry for coming to kill you."

"Oh, well, that makes it all right then."

"I ... was misled, but that's an explanation, not an excuse. I'm sorry. To you. And everyone."

"I don't accept," she said. "Your apology is wasted breath. People died. More are going to." Her voice was breaking again now. "What does 'I'm sorry' mean?"

"It means nothing," Malcolm said, "until I can make it right."

"And how are you going to do that?"

"I'll stop her. Then I'll find a way to help Nelson."

"Who in Sam Hill is Nelson?" Darlene said.

"Who is Sam Hill?" Kazimir asked.

"And then," Malcolm continued, directly to Sarah, "if you wish it, you can come back with me. That's how I'll make it right."

"You don't know if you can do any of that."

"I was taught," Malcolm said, calmly, evenly, "that I can do anything I set my will towards. Unfortunately, it's proven quite true."

He wanted her to see the sincerity of his promise. Believers could deceive in the carrying out of sacred duties – he had done so many times, riding the Believer reputation for honesty – but they believed in the fundamental truth of promises. Dragons held them sacred and scorned men who didn't. He would keep his promise. He didn't know how just yet, but that didn't bother him. He would find a way. At the same time, he silently reaffirmed his earlier promise to Nelson.

He made one further promise, probably the hardest to accomplish, but he would. He would.

The man stood, still holding the gun. "Well, I didn't see any dragon," he said, "and I won't sit here listening to any more of this nonsense. Darlene, if you feel safe enough to stay with these people, I'll take my leave, but I strongly suggest you let me escort them from your home."

Whatever the woman was going to say was interrupted by a knock on the door so hard and loud every single one of them jumped. An impatient second knock came as the woman went to the door.

A man in a police uniform stood there when she opened it. Malcolm wasn't sure who he was but hated him in an instant.

"Sheriff Kelby," the woman said, sounding both angry and frightened.

Sarah looked properly horrified. "*Sheriff* Kelby?"

"Well, now," the man in the uniform said, too loud, too false-friendly. "This is a regular camp meeting, isn't it?" He looked around, taking in the room, pausing on Malcolm and Kazimir, and then his eyes widening at Sarah, who had gone quite ashen. His face turned sour. Or rather, more sour.

"Want to tell me what's going on here, Darlene?" he demanded.

Sarah made to answer, but the woman spoke over her. "My niece. I don't have to explain what happens in the privacy of my own home, Sheriff."

"Wouldn't be too sure about that, Darlene," the man sneered. "Not when I see ol' Hisao there with a shotgun ready to go." The man pronounced the name differently than anyone else had, making it ugly.

"What do you want, Sheriff?" the woman said, clearly nervous but also clearly resentful of this man's presence.

The Sheriff didn't like this at all. "What I *want*, Darlene, is for someone to explain to me why the hell I keep getting reports of some sort of *animal* flying outta your farm and up into the mountains."

"We don't know what it is either, Kelby," the man said, still holding his shotgun. "That's what we're here discussing."

"I'd also like to know right now, Darlene," the Sheriff said, purposely ignoring the man with the shotgun, "who these strangers are." He started to remove an ugly-looking billy club from his belt. "And I will get answers," he said, "believe you me."

18

She was hungry, though the word barely seemed adequate. In addition to the literal heat blazing away in her belly and a number of eggs that were rapidly – alarmingly rapidly – nearing maturity, she also had a very empty stomach.

She knew what dragons ate: almost anything. For creatures of such incredible majesty, they weren't too fussy about what they took down their gullets. Up in the Canadian Wastes, she'd seen them eat live moose, trees, even once a standing stone. She considered that such petty concerns must be below such exalted beings, but now she was wondering if they were just so hungry all the time that they stopped caring. The Canadian Wastes hadn't always been wastes, after all.

She had eaten enough snow to no longer be thirsty – dragons needed excessive water for obvious reasons – but her unfamiliar mouth was salivating at the thought of, well, almost anything. She sniffed. There were deer out there, and elk. Nothing especially close by, but she *was* on the top of a mountain. Closer were the muskier scents of mountain goats, not exactly appealing, but she found herself not minding the choice as much as she might have thought.

She took off again, still feeling the thrill of being able to leave the ground, even at this unlikely size and weight. She flew above the clouds once more, twisting and turning, testing out her wings, neither of which ached any longer. The broken foreleg was still sore, but she was mending at a mind-boggling rate, which might explain the hunger.

She headed back down through the clouds, her nose guiding her to the cliffs and caves the mountain goats used. Her eyes were sharper, too, she realized. From three thousand feet away – over half a mile – she could see a mountain goat on a rock, blinking against the wind, its white fur bluffing and huffing. Did they have predators? There were bears here, she thought, and mountain lions, if western Washington was anything like western Canada.

But a mountain goat would never be on the lookout for an eagle.

It was a big male, its horns a pretty prize if a hunter found them, and it didn't look up until the very last second. One frightened bleat and it was in her jaws, her teeth cutting all the way through its body, her mouth filling with its blood as she swooped back into the air, swallowing it whole.

Well, now. That was interesting.

It was more than the taste, for it had only been on her tongue briefly, though the blood still lingered, and it had been still alive, just, when she swallowed, but it hit her stomach like a rush, obliterated in the furnace that was her body.

Oh, yes. More.

She could smell other mountain goats, but wherever they had been, they had fled from this new peril in the skies. No matter. There was a whole forest below.

She went hunting.

The deer were easy. Like the mountain goats, they had no reason to expect a threat from the air, and she picked up a doe in her mouth with laughable ease as it scavenged grass at the edge of the forest. The rest of the herd immediately bolted for the trees, but she merely flew above them, scouted where an opening might be, and dashed down to snatch up a young buck and another doe as they ran this way and that.

My goodness, she felt fine.

She rested in a field, though rested wasn't the right word. There was so much energy coursing through her that she found it impossible to stay still. She veritably *romped* through the snow, digging deep divots with her three legs, still holding her left foreleg up.

But then, why? She stretched it out in front of her. It felt good. It felt more than good. The energy that buzzed through her buzzed down it as well. She placed it on the ground, slowly settling her weight onto it.

It held. Without pain. It was already healed. In only a few hours, it was already healed.

Dragons were even more magnificent than she had ever suspected. She dug through the frozen ground with it, gripping a clump of sod in her claw and throwing it to the side. It flew a hundred feet easily.

She raised her long neck, blew out a stream of fire just for the hell of it and roared so loud it echoed down the canyons of the mountain. She lifted her body up into the sky again against the flow of snowflakes. The winds were tougher here, whipping down the glacier, but she navigated them easily, making the elements accommodate *her* rather than the other way around.

She found the lodge unexpectedly. She had smelled humans in the area, isolated, distant, and there was a small town a few miles farther down the mountainside where a couple hundred humans made the most unexpected stench in her nostrils. But the lodge was just suddenly *there*, in a steep field amongst some trees.

She landed in front of it.

She smelled the man inside.

The wind had been blowing away from it, was the only explanation she could find, because his smell was there now, filling her nose like a living perfume. Then it changed, became charged with a tang, a metallic base note. Fear. That's what it was, she realized. He had seen her, peeking out one of the rudimentary windows on either side of the front door.

The man must have just arrived; he didn't even have a fire going. Yes, there they were, his footprints through the snow, fresh. He had come to hunt the deer she had done exceptionally well in eating or chasing away.

Poor man. She almost felt sorry for him. He would find only surprising quarry here.

She moved closer to the front door, unsure of her motives, but then she reached out the four-fingered claw and, amusing herself deeply, she simply knocked.

The man burst out the door shouting, holding a rifle,

screaming at her as he aimed it. She ate him in one gulp, the rifle going off in her throat, though it felt like little more than the scratch of an under-chewed potato chip.

She flapped her great wings, filled her great lungs, and blew fire hotter than lava onto the lodge. It didn't so much burn as disintegrate, blasting in blazing pieces into the forest behind it, catching a few trees but mostly doused by the snow.

I have just eaten a man, she thought to herself, finding no way of putting it that didn't sound filthy. She laughed again, almost light-headed. Still the energy coursed in her. This learning of herself, this leaping of taboos – sure, she had killed before, but she had never *consumed* – was dizzying.

Why didn't dragons rule the earth she had come from? Why had they put up with their exile to the Wastes for generation upon generation? How could they live day by day with this, this *power*, and not use it?

Because men and dragons had made an accommodation. A wicked one, that made her angry even now.

She turned in the field and looked in the direction where she had smelled the distant town.

A child saw her coming. A child who should have been asleep, but who had grown bored of the long, cold nights that were only just starting to shorten. A child with a father who was pretty strict about bedtimes for eight-year-olds, but who wasn't so strict if she wanted to sneak a book under the covers by the old army flashlight he'd given her from his days back in the War.

She was reading *Little House in the Big Woods.* "You

should feel right at home with it," her father had said, ruffling her hair as she opened it at Christmas. It was the first in a boxed set of books, and by now – early February – she'd already read the whole thing through, including the ones at the end that got stranger and angrier and less good. Her favourite was called *The Long Winter*, which made the winters here in this mountain town seem even more disappointing because no one ever got trapped inside anywhere. There was always Mr Bagshot with his plough to get you out before snow even reached your windows.

But for now, she was back to the beginning, having finished *These Happy Golden Years* just last weekend. Her father had turned out her light promptly at 8:30 (which was late, she knew from her friends in the third grade, so she tried very hard not to moan about it), and she had promptly turned on his flashlight at 8:31. She opened the cover, found her name written there in her father's hand – her father had told her her mother was on a long trip visiting family in Florida; she'd heard the real story from Mr Bagshot's daughter Janet, who no one really liked – and turned to the first chapter.

She hadn't even read the first sentence when a movement at the window, up the white of the mountain – it was never truly dark with this much snow around – caught her eye. The clouds were low. She shouldn't have seen a bird flying, not this late, not in winter, and if it was a plane, it must be in trouble–

It wasn't a plane. Some kind of bat? She got out of bed, still holding her book, and went over to the window. They lived outside the centre of Pinedale; her father having built this little house himself as a gift to her mother for having a job that took him away so often. It didn't work. Now it was just her and her father, who didn't go away all that often any more.

She could see whatever it was skimming over treetops that bent in the rush of wind as it passed. It was big, and it just kept coming, fast and huge. She probably should have called for her dad, but a cold ball of fear held her in place. She hadn't felt like this since her mom had driven off with the electrician, waving out the back window as they disappeared into the forest. They had yet to return.

It *had* to be a bat. The wings were the wrong shape for a bird. Or there was an Air Force base on the other side of the mountains; she knew that, her dad went there sometimes. Maybe it was–

A geyser of flame shot from the thing less than a mile from her house, lighting up the huge ranger tower that stood there, at first as a silhouette in the night but only for a moment before it exploded.

"Daddy?" she said, quietly.

The thing was still coming, so much faster now it seemed. Would it explode their house, too?

"Daddy?" she said again, a little more loudly. He was doing work in the living room, she knew, but it was just that little bit too far away to hear her.

It got closer, closer, then *whoosh* it was over the house and gone. She ran out of her bedroom, down the hall and burst into the living room. Her father looked up from his papers, eyebrows raised.

"Grace?"

She ran right for the front door, flinging it open and

barrelling out onto the porch, which overlooked the town. She barely realized she was still carrying her book.

"Grace, what are you doing?" her father said, stepping out behind her. "It's bedtime."

"There's a monster," she said.

Her father looked out to where she was facing. "My God," he whispered. He put a protective hand on her chest, as if to guide her behind him, but his eyes stayed on the town.

Whatever it was, the giant bird or aeroplane or *whatever*, it was lighting up the night like fireworks, moving from house to house over the few rows of streets where people lived in Pinedale. One by one they all exploded. People were running outside now and, even at this distance, Grace could hear them screaming.

The thing went after them, sometimes blasting them into nothing with the fire from its mouth, sometimes picking them up with that same mouth and swallowing them whole. It chased the people into the centre of town and breathed its fire on the general store and Mary's Diner, destroying both, barely leaving enough behind to burn.

"Go to the bunker," her father said.

"But Daddy–"

"There's blankets in there. You'll be warm."

"What about you?"

He turned to her at that. "I'll be there in a minute, but it's not safe out here for you."

"What *is* that?"

Her father looked back out into the town. The huge thing was flying high up in the air now, then coming back down with a fast plummet to knock the steeple off the little Presbyterian church that served pretty much all the faiths of Pinedale.

"Go to the bunker," he said, not yelling, but firmly enough to make her feet move.

She ran out the back, her bare feet gasping against the cold. He'd shown her plenty of times how to work the bunker door, and she was inside in a moment, though not quick enough to stop her teeth from chattering.

Her father had built it when the Russians first started testing what her ears heard as "the bom". She didn't know exactly what one was, but it was enough for her father to dig out a hollow under their house, line it with concrete, and stock it with food and blankets. Blankets she was grateful for as she buried herself under them, only just now noticing that *Little House in the Big Woods* was still in her hand.

How they ran. How they screamed. It was almost medieval, like in "The Wife of Bath's Tale", where Chaucer described a dragon attack as the travellers reached an inn. That dragon had been talked out of the air, though, and into providing food for the group.

She would not.

The houses smouldered and popped. The shops at the centre of town, too. Even the church had fallen before her. All that was left was a gas station, which she was saving until last. She flew above it, inhaled to blast fire onto two large underground tanks of gasoline that would blow the surrounding area into the sky–

She smelled something...

Something terribly, terribly familiar.

She took another circle of the town. There were outlying

survivors and a few outbuildings that weren't worth her bother. What was the point of an attack like this if there weren't at least a few survivors to report what happened? The war on this world had to begin sometime, and it might as well be tonight.

But that smell. That something on the air. She breathed in deep–

And it was gone. Strong and present, then vanished.

She racked her dragon mind for what it might be, something so familiar yet elusive. She came up with no explanation, and honestly, felt as if one wasn't needed. So what if something smelled like her old world? She wasn't *in* her old world. She was someone new in a new place altogether. She laughed to herself and circled back to town.

The gas station went up like an atom bomb.

"Grace?" her father said, shutting the airtight door to the shelter. She had felt distant booms rumbling through the ground as the monster continued its wave of destruction.

"I'm here, Daddy," she said.

He climbed down the short steps and hugged her to himself. "Is it the bom?" she asked.

"I don't think so, sweetie," he said, keeping his voice light for her, "but whatever it is, we're safe here."

"Are you sure?"

He knelt down in front of her and smiled. "I wouldn't have built it for you if I wasn't sure." He rubbed her hair. "Lie down, baby, try to get some sleep. Daddy has to make a phone call."

She crawled onto one of the two cots her father had put

256

in the shelter, pulling the blanket around her. There was another rumble, a huge one that shook a few cans of food off the shelves. Her father calmly picked them up and she heard him say to himself, "Gas station."

He put the cans back, then picked up the government-issue phone he'd had installed in there. It wouldn't work long in a nuclear war, just long enough for him to make the important calls he needed "if we're the first strike," he'd said. He tapped the button a few times, waited to be connected. She heard him curse under his breath, then he sat up straight as someone finally came on.

"Get me General Kraft," he said. "This is Agent Paul Dernovich. Tell him I'm reporting Scenario 8."

19

Sheriff Kelby didn't wait. He went straight in with the baton, hitting Darlene Dewhurst on the back of her knees, knocking her to the floor. The room stood as one in uproar. Hisao even pointed his shotgun at the Sheriff.

Who just sneered. "And what do you plan on doing with that, *Hisao*?"

Hisao didn't lower the gun even an inch. "My name is Mr Inagawa."

"It's a crime to point a gun at a law enforcement official," the Sheriff said. "I'll be hauling you in for that, but not before I get some answers. Who is this girl really?" He looked at Malcolm and Kazimir. "And what seems to be a vagabond and a fruit?"

"I don't like that word," Malcolm said, calmly, meeting the Sheriff's eye. "Fruit."

"I wasn't talking about you," the Sheriff said, seemingly delighted, "but golly, if the shoe fits."

The Sheriff kept coming, sneering at the upraised shotgun. He stopped, then his hand shot out like lightning and the baton struck the barrel of the gun, knocking it to one side. Mr Inagawa didn't drop it, but the lurch was enough for the Sheriff to deliver another blow of the baton to Hisao's face. His nose broke with a crunch, and this time he did drop the gun.

"Dad!" Jason said, leaping to his father. Sheriff Kelby caught him on the elbow with the baton. The blow was so clearly painful that Jason fell all the way to the wooden floor, not too far from where Darlene still half sat, half lay.

"That's everyone I know," the Sheriff said, looking at the three who remained. "So how 'bout one of you starts talking."

"She told you," Sarah said. "I'm her niece. These are friends of mine."

"Visiting the same night I and every other peaceful citizen of Frome, Washington, see a giant something or other flying straight from your farm?"

"You think I built a flying machine, Sheriff?" Darlene said.

He whipped around to face her. "You laughing at me, Darlene? Because that is something I would not recommend." He spun the baton lightly in the air, then he turned back to Sarah with the ugliest smile in the world. He moved on her, baton rising.

"No," Malcolm said, calmly.

In two steps, he caught the Sheriff, taking hold of his back and the wrist that held the baton. He made the simplest shift in his body weight, and the Sheriff fell, the baton tumbling from his hand, his arm bending back painfully. Malcolm kept the Sheriff's wrist in place until the Sheriff's own momentum caused it to break with an even louder snap than the bleeding man's nose.

The Sheriff hit the floor in clear astonishment. "You broke my wrist," he said.

That's all Malcolm gave him time to say. He kicked the Sheriff in the throat, hard enough to silence him, and in two more steps had one knee on the Sheriff's unbroken arm and the other on his chest. Malcolm moved his arms to release the blades, and in a silky motion, had both tips pressed against either side of the Sheriff's neck.

"Don't!" Sarah yelled.

"I wasn't going to," Malcolm said, and only realized it was true as he said it. "I want no more death on my hands."

"*I'll* do it!" Jason Inagawa grunted, still gripping his elbow.

"No, you won't," the girl said, fiercely. "Not again."

"Again?" the boy said.

"Again?" said the Sheriff.

"I wouldn't speak if I were you," Malcolm said, pressing both blades slightly, drawing two parallel drops of blood on the Sheriff's neck.

"If this is another universe–" the girl started.

"It is," Kazimir said, watching Malcolm with an impressed look.

"If it *is*," said Sarah, "then we don't have to do the same things we did back there. They don't have to have the same outcomes. We could be different." She looked at her mother. "We could be better."

"You have no need to be better, Sarah," Kazimir said, still staring at Malcolm. "You were perfectly fine."

261

"That's a real vote of confidence," Sarah said, flatly, "thank you."

"I told you," Malcolm said again, still calm. "I was never going to kill him." He looked down into the Sheriff's eyes, staring hard.

"What are you doing?" Sheriff Kelby asked.

"I told you not to speak," Malcolm said.

"What *are* you doing, young man?" Mr Inagawa said, holding a napkin Darlene had handed him to his nose.

"Some men are dragon underneath," Malcolm said. "If you just scratch the surface."

Deep, deep, deep in the eyes of the Sheriff, Malcolm saw cowardice, and he saw greed. He saw a fire that burned but stung, a fire like a rash on this man's soul. This man *was* a dragon, in all his fiery yearning, but he would never know. Because he would never know, and because his heart was so clearly a twisted knot of hate and injustice, he would never have a satisfied moment for as long as he lived.

"You're corrupted," Malcolm said to the Sheriff. "Right at your heart."

The Sheriff's eyes narrowed. "You know what, boy?" he said, growling a little at what must have been tremendous pain in his wrist. Malcolm could at least admire the strength, even if it was directed in such warped ways. "You'd better kill me." The Sheriff licked sweat off his lip. "Because if you don't, I *will* be after you. I know how to do a lot of things to wreck every last breath you will take on this earth."

"See?" Jason said. "We *have* to kill him."

"You hush that talk right now," Darlene said, as Jason's father said very much the same thing.

"You think he's just going to let us go?" Jason asked.

Malcolm saw the looks pass around the room, saw real fear there. Kazimir was still looking wonderingly at Malcolm, but it was Sarah who was firm and clear. "Absolutely not," she said. "I've been here before, and I will not do it again."

"Nor I," Malcolm said, "as I've said a number of times."

"Then you're screwed," Sheriff Kelby said, smirking again. "You are well and truly fucked, boy."

"My name isn't boy," Malcolm said. "My name ..." he found himself unable to suppress a smile "... is Agent Woolf."

Sheriff Kelby gave him a surprised look.

"Do you honestly think an actual teenage boy could have disarmed you so easily? That these blades at your throat are standard issue in your public schools?"

Malcolm glanced up. Darlene, Hisao, and Jason were staring at him again. So were Sarah and Kazimir, but in a different way. The lie was so brazen he was amazed it wasn't written all over his face, but when he looked back down to the Sheriff, he saw eyes starting to believe.

"I and my associates–" he nodded at Sarah and Kazimir– "are here under deep cover in relation to what you think you saw flying from this farm."

"I don't believe you–"

In a swift, practised motion, Malcolm repositioned his knees so that one now rested just below the broken wrist. The Sheriff cried out. "I can increase the pain," Malcolm said, doing so with a press from his knee, "or I can decrease it." He did this as well. "Does this, to you, seem like the abilities of a boy, Sheriff?"

The Sheriff turned his face to the rest of the room, as if

263

making an appeal, but even he had to know how little purchase he would find there. He turned back to Malcolm. "No," he said, grudgingly.

"Your deeply misguided actions here, Sheriff," Malcolm continued, "have imperilled our mission. We normally like to work with local law enforcement..." He stumbled a bit as his mind filled with the image of the Mountie falling, bloody, to the frozen ground. "But we can just as easily make your lives very, very difficult. Is that what you want?"

Sheriff Kelby didn't reply. Malcolm applied more pressure to his wrist. Sheriff Kelby screamed and said, "No! No."

"And you won't tell anyone what you saw here?"

"I won't. I promise."

"How do I know you'll keep your word, Sheriff?" Malcolm pressed the wrist again.

"You can put us under surveillance!" Kelby cried out.

"You already are," Malcolm lied.

Kelby looked horrified at that. For the first time, Malcolm realized, he also looked properly afraid. He wondered if it would drive the man to murder. Or if it already had.

"If you breathe one word of this," Malcolm continued, "just one, I'll see you locked up." He pressed on the wrist again. "Or perhaps worse, if you catch me on a bad day."

Sheriff Kelby bit back his cry of pain. "Why didn't you say all that when I walked in?" he grunted out.

"Because I could tell a man like you only responds to force."

Kelby seemed to accept that. After a moment, Malcolm resheathed the blades and slowly took his weight off. Kelby held his wrist close to his chest and scooted back towards the door. He glanced at Darlene. "You're telling me these people are in on it, too?" he asked Malcolm.

"You said yourself it started from her farm."

Kelby reached the door and used it to pull himself up, never turning his back on the group. He looked like he wanted to say many, many things, but ultimately decided to leave without saying any. He slammed the door behind him. Hisao got up from the floor and started heading that way.

"Where are you going?" Jason asked.

Still holding the napkin to his nose, Hisao sighed. "He won't be able to start his car with a broken wrist. I'll at least help him get out of here." He left, too.

"That's a kind man," Darlene said, also rising.

"Yeah," Jason scoffed, "helping the Sheriff who just broke his nose."

"You think Kelby's going to keep quiet?" Darlene asked him. "Even if every word this person with the knives said is true–" she glared at Malcolm– "we still have to live on these farms. Kelby will still be Sheriff. You think he isn't going to make us pay for all this?"

"I'm sorry," Malcolm said. "It was either that or kill him."

"No, no," Darlene said, sounding annoyed at herself. "You did the right thing. So did Hisao. But sometimes doing the right thing comes with a price tag." She sat back down at the table. "What a day." She glanced at Malcolm again. "*Was* any of that true? Are you all spies? Because that makes as much sense as anything."

"It is completely true," Kazimir said.

"It's not true at all," Sarah said, and she and Kazimir glared at each other.

"I *was* trained," Malcolm said.

"Obviously," Darlene said.

"By a religious cult that worships dragons."

She just blinked at him. "I preferred spies. Let's go back to that."

The assassin approached Sarah sheepishly a few moments later, as Mr Inagawa came back in the door. Her mother handed him his shotgun.

"You were right," the boy said to Sarah.

"About what?"

"About not killing the Sheriff. About making amends in this world." He reached into his coat and took out the Spur of the Goddess, which still looked like an ordinary dragon claw. He handed it to Kazimir, who took it with surprise. "I'll come back for this," Malcolm said.

"You know I cannot work it," Kazimir said. "You also know that *she* is the only one who can."

"That's probably true."

Kazimir sounded agitated. "After what I have seen this evening, you seem like you would be a very skilled ally in what we face."

"That may be true, too," Malcolm said, buttoning up his coat. "But it may also be true that it takes a dragon to fight a dragon."

Kazimir said nothing to that.

"I'll be back as soon as I can," Malcolm said.

"You're leaving?" Sarah said.

"I have people to..." She saw him search for the word. "*Save*, if I can."

"Save from what?" Darlene asked as he walked towards the door.

"Save from me."

They all watched him go, Hisao stepping aside to let him pass. Kazimir looked at the claw, considering it, as the door shut again.

"I wonder," Kazimir said to Sarah's mother, "if you might have any paper."

Darlene looked confused, but finally just shrugged her shoulders and went to find some.

It was Jason who finally broke the ensuing silence.

"Isn't anyone going to explain the dragon?"

"I guess I'm staying here tonight," Sarah said to Jason outside later. Darlene was finishing bandaging Hisao's nose, and Kazimir had taken the paper Darlene found for who knew what reason?

"Okay," Jason said. "Sounds good." He kept staring at her. "You really do look just like her."

"I am her. In a way."

"Uh-huh."

Sarah didn't know what to do, exactly. She yearned to hug him again, to be in close and smell that Jason smell, to have him wrap his arms around her like he'd done just a few nights ago, to have it be her and him in a secret moment that the world knew nothing about.

But he was a little awkward here, stand-offish, like he wasn't sure what she wanted. She took a step towards him. He took an uncomfortable step back.

"Jason, I–"

"I don't really know you," he said, looking worried. "This is weirder than anything that could ever really happen, and this is the second time you've acted like you know me super well but..."

"But what?"

He shrugged, still looking worried. "We weren't that good friends, really, me and Sarah. I mean, we weren't enemies, but it's not like we hung around down at the soda shop or anything." He looked away. "You always kind of avoided me at school."

"I did?" she said.

"Yeah, there are hardly any kids there who aren't white, and I always got the impression you thought things were easier for you if we kept separate. Even though we lived down the same road."

"Oh, my," she said, feeling stupid for the grandmotherly phrase. "That's not at *all* how it was for us in my world. It was the opposite. We stuck together. We were friends. We were..." She blushed a little in the dark.

"We were more?" Jason said, and there was so much surprise in his voice that she laughed out loud.

"No one really knew," she told him. "That would have got us in trouble in this town. And *did*. But, yes." She looked into the shadow where his eyes were.

"Huh," he said, his face nearly frozen. She saw him swallow. "I mean, I guess something might have developed–"

"I'm not saying–"

"I did think about it."

"You did?"

268

"Of course. Why wouldn't I? Pretty girl and so forth. But..." He looked away again, then shook his head. "I'm sorry, this is too weird. Just..." He started backing away towards Hisao's truck. "I'm sure I wish you well and all but... Too weird."

He got inside the truck and stared straight ahead, not looking at her. She hugged her arms around herself, until Hisao and Darlene came out, too. Hisao – his eyes already on the way to blackening – nodded at her unhappily as he got in beside Jason. They drove off without Jason ever looking at her.

Except at the very last moment, the very last second.

He looked back.

And they drove away.

20

The dragon that had once been Veronica Woolf slept. Her dreams were dragon dreams.

"Try not to look, baby," Grace's father said. She sat in the passenger seat of their car, seat belt around her, *Little House in the Big Woods* in her hand. It was difficult to disobey her father's instructions – she was so small in a seat meant for adults she could barely see over the window ledge – but she still took quick peeks when he was looking the other way.

Pinedale was gone. There was no other word for it. Fires burned here and there, but they weren't like the time the barn behind the elementary school caught. There was still a recognizable building shape behind the flames, no matter how long it burned, and when it was out, a burnt building still sort of stood there.

The Pinedale houses hadn't burned so much as blown up.

Whatever had attacked them had hit with a heat so hot everything just evaporated, a word Grace had overheard her father use when he was on the phone talking to the General and she absolutely was not supposed to be listening at all.

She saw Mrs Bailey as they passed the wreck of her home, her arm at a horrible angle that made Grace look away. Everywhere out there had awful things to see, no matter where she turned. Maybe her father was right. She sat back in her seat, holding her book to her chest.

"What was it?" she asked him now.

"I'm not sure, pumpkin," he said, but she kept looking at him because she'd heard the phone call, heard how certain he'd sounded. She saw him realizing this, too. "It was ... something that shouldn't be here."

"Scenario 8," she said.

He raised his eyebrows in a bemused way.

"How many scenarios are there?" she asked.

"Ninety-four," he said. "And that's where this conversation has to end, sweetheart."

She was her father's daughter. Even before her mother had left, Grace knew what "top secret" meant and that, though he obviously kept nearly everything from her, she was not to tell any of her schoolmates that her father even *had* secrets.

He respected her enough to trust her. She respected him enough to keep his trust. It made her feel mature, older than her eight years. Older than the very young eight years she felt sitting in the passenger seat in the middle of a town that was no longer there. In his gentle way now – Agent Dernovich was a lovely man, all his colleagues agreed, and a terrific parent in difficult circumstances – her father refused to tell her any more, so she went over what she'd heard him say in the bunker, broken fragments that maybe told a story.

"That's what I said, General...

"Visual confirmation, at least a hundred feet...

"It means we were right, and if we're right about *one* Scenario...

"I agree. Unfortunately, both bases are on the other side of the mountains it seemed to be using as a roost...

"You heard what?"

He had sat up at that sentence and listened for a long time, then he'd glanced at Grace. "I can be there by morning. Grace's grandma is on that side of the mountains anyway."

That was how they came to be in the car so soon after the monster had flown back into the clouds.

"I hate leaving," her father said now. "So many people need help."

"Then why are we?"

He looked at her, touched her cheek tenderly. "Fire engines and ambulances will be here very soon. As will the men your daddy works with. They can handle it."

"And there's something on the other side of the mountains you need to see first."

He looked surprised at her memory, then smiled. "You know, they let women in the Bureau. You'd be amazing, when you're old enough."

She smiled back, warmth flushing her face. A platoon of fire trucks with sirens blazing sped past them in the opposite direction, though there wasn't much good they could do for the corpse of Pinedale.

"Where on earth did you pick up a phrase like that?" her

father said, and Grace realized she'd spoken aloud.

She held out *Little House*. "I've been reading books a little older than this one." Then quickly added, "Not that I don't love it! But the school doesn't have a very big library and I've read all my age year and Miss Archer lets me take out books sometimes meant for older kids."

"I may have to have a talk with Miss Archer," her father said, looking into the night.

"No, Daddy, please!" Grace was suddenly passionate. "I love her so much! She's only doing it to make me smarter!"

"You're already pretty smart, pumpkin." But he was smiling again. "Some eight-year-olds might read a phrase like 'corpse of Pinedale'. You're the only one I know who'd actually say it out loud."

She flushed again, and it was in this rush of good feeling that she asked the question that had tripped in her mind since the shape had flown over her house the first time.

"Was it a dragon, Daddy?"

He didn't answer at first, which was almost answer enough. "It sure looked like one, didn't it?" he finally said.

"Where did it come from?" she asked. "Out of the mountain?"

It wasn't a foolish question. She knew about volcanoes. She knew Mount Rainier would blow up one day, maybe soon, maybe in ten thousand years, maybe after one of the other volcanoes in the Cascades – Adams, perhaps, or St Helens – did the same. Volcanoes were explosions of fire and lava. So was the thing that had killed the town.

"No, honey," her father said. "We don't think it did."

"We?"

They passed an Oldsmobile heading their way, one that looked an awful lot like the one her father was driving. Her father looked in its windows to see if he knew the person behind the wheel.

"We think maybe there are other worlds," her father said. "We don't know for sure. It's only a theory." He saw her not get this word. "A story, kind of. A way of describing something you don't have proof for yet."

"There are worlds full of dragons?"

"Maybe."

"You said Scenario 8."

"That's a phrase I never want to hear you say out loud again," he said, strongly but not angrily. "That's a phrase even a girl as clever as you should not have heard or remembered, and it could be dangerous for you to say anywhere at any time. Do you understand me?"

"Yes, Daddy."

"Good girl."

"But it means you must have thought of dragons."

He laughed to himself, she hoped at her persistence. "There have been ... hints. Things we found that weren't quite evidence. Sounds on unusual frequencies. It was a theory. One of ninety-four."

"What were the other ninety-three?"

"I've already said far too much and you know it. Get some sleep. We'll be at Grandma's tomorrow. You'll like that."

Her clear-eyed father who heard sounds on unusual frequencies had one terrible blind spot: how much Grace liked his own mother. Grace liked her the exact extent that her grandma liked Grace, the living reminder of "that woman" who had hurt her son so. It was a home of doilies and heavy perfumes and the air was filled with unsaid things.

Grace looked out the window. The forest was white in the snowfall, but still seemed to hold more secrets than she had ever thought possible.

That was when she started to shake.

"Don't worry, honey," Agent Dernovich said, gripping all of his daughter's little body in his arms, on his lap. "This is called shock. It's perfectly normal."

He had pulled over to the side of the road the instant she had said, "Daddy?" with alarm. He had kept the motor running, kept the heater on, and taken her into his arms, holding her as she trembled.

"What's shock?" she said, through chattering teeth.

"Something humans do when they see something too big to really understand."

"There was a dragon, Daddy."

"I know."

"It tried to *kill* us."

"I know."

"It killed people in town."

"I know that, too."

He held her while she cried. She never saw how angry his face was. Not at holding her, of course, she was his moon and stars. No, his anger was for the thing that did not belong here. The thing that had killed probably two hundred people in a little under ten minutes. The thing that had made his perfect, beautiful, strange, brainy daughter shake in his arms.

He had met Grace's mother when she was a secretary and he a junior agent. He'd been ordered to Havana – in fact, with a female agent he had long admired for her savvy and resourcefulness – but when he went to the Washington DC office for his final briefing, well, that had turned out to be the day the Canadian spy scandal erupted. The Soviets had an entire network infiltrated into the Canadian Service. This was not a good thing. His Havana trip was cancelled, and he had been stuck for the next three days mopping up the mess, aided by a brand-new secretary who had started that morning.

If the scandal hadn't broken that day, he'd never have known her other than the few seconds he saw her in passing as he went out of his Havana briefing. Were all relationships like this? So predicated on absolute chance? He had moved Linda from the east coast where she'd grown up all the way over to the "other" Washington. Not even a city like Seattle, a tiny field office in his home town in the east where remote stations had been established in the search for a theorized Soviet satellite that could launch any time in the ensuing decade.

She had been unhappy. She had met the electrician. She had left with him, and this had given Agent Dernovich mixed feelings. He hated her for breaking Grace's heart, but he could never, ever regret being left with this girl who made his heart pop every time she asked one of her million questions. That he might never have had her but for the weirdest, slightest vagaries of fate, that she might never have existed at all, made her all the more precious.

So there were indeed huge security risks on the table, and that Scenario 8 had come true – his own scenario, postulated after his team had discovered a potential multiverse

– was very bad and needed immediate addressing (though he knew there were other Scenarios that were much, much worse) and he needed to get to the other side of the mountains.

Despite that, he held his daughter in the car until she cried herself to sleep.

Then he drove through the night, over the Chinook Pass, to Fort Lewis Army Base, which abutted McChord Air Force Base, and into the furious, questioning eyes of a General who wanted to know, please, just what the hell they were going to do.

Grace awoke on a chair wrapped in what she recognized immediately as an army blanket. It was green and scratchy, just like the ones her father had stashed in the bunker. She sat up a little. Her book sat on a side table near her, along with something that smelled like–

"Hot cocoa," a woman's voice said.

The woman sat behind a desk, watching over Grace as she typed, a sound that hadn't woken her, but the smell of hot cocoa had.

"Where am I?" Grace asked.

"Fort Lewis," the woman said. She was a friendly-seeming older lady, her hair pulled back tight in a bun, plus glasses that made Grace like her. "The cocoa's for you. I thought you might want some when you woke up."

"Where's my father?" she asked. The secretary didn't answer until Grace picked up the hot cocoa and took a sip. It wasn't as sweet as Grace normally chose, but it was warm and good in a shivery room.

"Army's finest," the secretary said, with a wry smile that Grace liked even more than the glasses. "Your father's in with General Kraft. He asked if I would keep an eye on you. He said your name was Grace. Mine's Mrs Kelly, so together we make up the movie star."

Grace took another sip of the cocoa. "I was named after my..." She stopped. She'd been named after her grandmother, the one she was supposed to be staying with right now. "Why did he bring me here?" she said, quietly, to herself.

"Well, he couldn't very well leave you in the car," Mrs Kelly said. "If he had, I wouldn't have been able to get you cocoa or take you down to the canteen for waffles, which is what I'm going to do right now."

Mrs Kelly rose from her typewriter just as a door opened behind her. Her father was coming out, another man – Grace guessed it must be General Kraft, a name that was suspiciously close to a really boring hour at school every Tuesday – with him.

"If there's *one* of those things, Dernovich," the General said, frowning.

"There could be more, General, I know," her father replied. "I'll get to the town that reported the first sightings."

The General nodded. "Update me every hour."

He went back into his office, and Grace's father caught her eye. "You're awake."

"I was just going to take her down to the canteen for breakfast, Mr Dernovich," said Mrs Kelly.

"Well, I think that's swell," her father said, looking at Grace. "We can all go."

"Why aren't I at Grandma's?" Grace said, standing up now, yawning.

"I decided I wanted you with me," he said, taking her hand. Then he lowered his voice so Mrs Kelly couldn't hear. "Plus, I know how boring it is at Grandma's."

He winked. She was scandalized, but her father was already leading her and Mrs Kelly towards morning waffles.

The sun broke over the crater of Mount Rainier, finding a sleeping dragon. With a roar in her throat, the dragon woke.

She had never felt more alive. Ever. Not once.

She grinned to herself in the way only dragons can. Today would be a day where this world would learn it had to reckon with a new force. Today was the beginning of a new era here. One with her at the top.

But the second she took flight, the pain began.

21

"I have pencils, you know," Darlene said.

"I find if you want to write dragon runes," Kazimir replied, dipping the tip of the Spur of the Goddess into a small saucer of ink he'd found somewhere, "it's best to use the tools of dragons themselves."

"Dragon runes?" she asked. "You speak dragon?"

Kazimir looked at Sarah's mother with a comically blank face. "I do," he finally said.

"What an interesting world you all live in." Darlene was at the stove making Kazimir and Sarah breakfast. She hadn't allowed Sarah to help with that, but she'd let Sarah feed the hogs this morning.

Little steps, Sarah thought. She leaned over at the kitchen table now and whispered to Kazimir. "What *are* you doing? And where'd you get that ink?"

He looked to make sure Darlene's back was turned, then showed Sarah a fresh wound on his palm. The black scab there matched the one that was already nearly healed on Kazimir's chin. Everyone knew dragon wounds closed quickly, but it was amazing to see it in human form.

"It's your blood?" she said.

He shushed her, still watching for Darlene. "I told her I made it from beets in her larder. Runes have to be written in dragon blood or they do not work."

"Work for what?"

"Never you mind. There are bigger things to be thinking about. I need to write what I need to write before the dragon comes back for the Spur."

"She won't know we'll still have it. She might think Malcolm is carrying it, wherever he's gone."

"No, she will be able to smell it," Kazimir said.

"My oatmeal?" Darlene said, bringing over two bowls.

"No, I meant–"

"I know what you meant." She set down the bowls and returned to the stove. "I'm capable of a joke."

The scent coming from the bowl of oatmeal – cinnamon, a little bit of honey – was enough to get the tears going again for Sarah. Nearly everything this woman did made that happen.

Her *mother*. But also not.

"So she'll smell it," Sarah said, wiping her eyes and looking at the claw he'd set down so he could eat (which he did making all sorts of fascinated faces as he swallowed his first ever oatmeal). "And she'll come for it."

"It ... poses a danger to her." He picked it up, added a bit to a rune he'd made on the paper. When he connected the last corner, Sarah was astonished to see it light up and disappear. "My blood still has a little magic in it," he said, quietly.

Sarah shook her head in wonder. "There's so much we still don't know about dragons."

"With good reason, Sarah Dewhurst," he said, in a normal voice.

There was a clang at the counter. Darlene had dropped the oatmeal pot. "That name," she said, looking into the sink.

"My name?" Sarah asked.

Darlene said, "I can't, I just can't..."

Sarah stood. "This was a mistake. I'm so sorry. We'll leave you in peace–"

She was interrupted by Darlene taking a swift step over to her and wrapping her in her arms. "How can it be you?" Darlene spoke into her neck. "My God, it even *smells* like you. How?"

"I don't really know either," Sarah said, but boy, was her mother right about the smell. Every scent from her mother's body was a lightning flash of memory: of being carried as a little girl, of being sung to sleep in bed, of being shown how to wean the pigs with her mother by her side.

It felt as if she was falling, into a past she'd held at arm's length during the two desperate years when she and her father had been too busy trying to save the farm to ever properly grieve. But now, but this...

Keeping her in the hug, Darlene stepped over to a low bench built into the kitchen wall. She sat them both down, keeping Sarah close to her. "You were gone, my girl," she whispered to Sarah. "Just gone."

"So were you. I missed you so much sometimes I couldn't breathe."

And this was true. Sarah would often be caught unawares by something as small as, say, the smell of cinnamon this morning, or a random brush of her hair before bed, or when she found herself humming a song her mother liked, something from the forties, after the War, after her father had come home safe and sound. Then, for a moment, the world would tumble down, and there would be nothing between Sarah and her loss, just a naked, unfillable expanse that could never be crossed. Until now, until this...

"Do you remember...?" Darlene started. "But I don't know how you could."

"What?"

Darlene smiled. "My Sarah was afraid of geese, which makes sense really, they're terrible creatures, but she, you, *she* once ran all the way home from town after one chased her in the grocer."

"And you were on your bike behind me the whole time?" Sarah said. "And I wouldn't even stop to let you pick me up?"

Darlene's eyes were wide now. "It happened to you, too?"

Sarah nodded. "Except it was geese who were loose out in front of the school where you dropped me off for the first day of kindergarten."

Darlene leaned back and shook her head. "I don't understand this, but..." She didn't finish.

"Yeah," Sarah said. "It's a big but, isn't it?"

They smiled at the feeble joke. Sarah took that moment to ask the question that had been burning in her since she arrived.

"How did Dad die?"

* * *

Starting out the night before had been a foolish decision, Malcolm had come to realize shortly after leaving the farm. There had been no cars at all for the first hour, and by then, it was so cold, he'd had to stop in the trees and make a fire just to stay alive. He considered going back, but he thought Kazimir would apply pressure to make him stay this time. He'd be right, too, and Malcolm would probably do it. He knew the most about the Mitera Thea after all, and he wanted so desperately to get back to Nelson it felt as if someone had sewn a large stone in his chest.

These were good reasons.

But he had something to do here, even if it was a fool's errand – as he had so little information to go on – and he would never get another chance. So he rose at dawn, and found a ride in the first ten minutes with, of all people, Hisao and Jason Inagawa. Jason grumped at having to make room in the truck's front seat, but Malcolm gratefully climbed in.

"You didn't get far," Jason said.

"I will today," Malcolm said, with a confidence he hoped was true.

"Where are you off to?" Hisao asked, his eyes fully black just above a swollen nose.

"Bellingham," Malcolm said.

"Bellingham?" said Jason. "That's a three-hour drive."

"We're just going into town," Hisao told him.

"That's perfectly good, thank you," Malcolm said. He was feeling the loss of his bag now that he was in a truck again. It had been a constant companion on this trip, and without it, he felt a bit naked. He didn't panic, though; he was trained to be resourceful, and he'd kept some cash with him, though it had triggered a worry: he reached into a pocket and pulled out some dollars. "Does this look like your money?"

Hisao and Jason both looked, then looked again. "Almost," Jason said, then pointed at the portrait, "but who's that?"

"Aaron Burr," Malcolm said. "He was President."

"Not here, he wasn't," Hisao said.

"The rest of it's okay," Jason said. "It'll probably work for most places if they don't look too close."

They drove down a long road towards a small group of buildings that made the town of Frome. Malcolm recognized some of it from when he and Nelson drove through it. A church, a small grocery, a small post office, a school. This world's, though, had a large feed store on the main corner, where the last one had a diner. Hisao pulled into it.

"This is where we stop," Hisao said.

"Thank you," Malcolm said, getting out. "I'll find my way from here."

"Are you really an assassin?" Jason asked.

Malcolm stepped away, letting them both out of the truck. They watched him, Hisao seeming as interested as Jason.

"I'll be back," Malcolm said. "I promise."

"Back for what?" Hisao said.

"Watch out for her," Malcolm continued. "The prophecy may come right in the end after all."

With that, he zipped up his coat and headed out onto the main road to look for another ride. Hisao and Jason watched him go.

"Any of that make sense to you?" Jason asked.

"Nope," said his father.

* * *

Sheriff Emmett Kelby was a bad man. His curse was that he was unable to revel in it. His badness came from a fury he could never quite explain, not from any joy at seeing others fear him. He felt no joy at all, not even in triumph. All he felt was the fury.

Which was something to behold. This town knew it. Especially those with darker skin. That Deputy Lopez, for example. A new hire after Kelby had been nearly blackmailed by the County Commissioner, but he was doing his level best to make sure Deputy Lopez was already exploring happier policing options in other counties. It'd be a cold day in hell before *Kelby's* force got muddied up.

It was also true that he had never stopped at just Negroes and Mexicans (or wherever the hell Lopez was from) or the Japanese (and boy was that Hisao Inagawa going to regret offering to help start his squad car). The poor, the rich, the middle class, he'd found his fury boiling over at all of them. They hated him.

They were too afraid not to vote for him, however. Sheriff Kelby knew things that others might not want others to know. Even with that, it had been close. He'd only beaten that weakling Jack Stanton by a couple hundred votes. Victory was victory, though, and four years of Sheriff Kelby it was.

That ragtag group of fruits and vegetables out at the Dewhurst farm were going to find the prospect of Sheriff Kelby's official power very uncomfortable indeed.

"Sheriff!" Deputy Curtis said in deep surprise as Kelby pushed his way through the front door of Frome's Sheriff's office. Curtis leapt to his feet. "We didn't think you were coming in today with the broken arm and all–"

"It ain't bad," Kelby said, barely referencing the cast he'd had put on his wrist last night at Good Samaritan over in Puyallup, where there was less of a chance of being recognized.

"Your ma told us you fell?" Curtis had doubt on his face.

Kelby winced internally. It was the stupidest lie, but it was all he could think of through the pain last night.

"I was breaking up a fight," he said.

"A fight?" Curtis still looked surprised, but then Curtis always looked surprised. "Should I send some men out?"

"It was a private matter, Deputy, and I'll thank you to shut the hell up about it."

"Yes, sir. Any word on the animal sighting, sir?"

"Do I look like I have any word on it, Curtis? Now, are you working or are you just planning on yanking my chain all morning in hopes of coming up a winner? Get me Fort Lewis on the phone. General Kraft's office."

"He the one who fought with your daddy?"

"You're yanking chains, Curtis."

"Sorry, sir. What reason should I give?"

Kelby ran a tongue over his top teeth. "Tell him, I know it sounds far-fetched, but I do believe we might have some treason going on right here in little old Frome."

"He's not dead," Darlene said, surprised. "He left."

"Dad left?"

"Well..." Darlene let her go, looking down at the dish

towel in her hands. "I kind of drove him to it, too. Neither of us is faultless."

"So he's not dead?"

"No, child, what on earth makes you say..." She stopped, then said, "Oh. Because he is ... in that other place."

Sarah nodded, the tears coming again. "It all happened so fast. He was shot and he..."

Darlene hugged her again, had barely stopped, really. "Girl, I may not know exactly who you are or how you're here, but it's obvious you've been through *something*."

"Something that will keep happening," Kazimir said, writing again with the Spur. "Whether we like it or not."

"The dragon will come back," Darlene said, not a question, but as if she was trying it out to see if she could accept it.

"If she is not already on her way," Kazimir said.

"Then we can't be here," Sarah said, wiping her cheeks. "We can't put my mom in any kind of danger."

"She is not technically your mother–" Kazimir stopped at the look Sarah shot him. "But you are incorrect. We *must* be here."

"And what exactly do you propose to do in the face of something that huge?" Darlene said, frowning now. "How do you two tiny people think you stand a chance in the face of a *dragon*?"

"I have some surprises up my sleeves," Kazimir said, "as I believe the expression is."

"You do?" Darlene said.

"You *do*?" Sarah echoed.

He lifted the Spur. "There are two things in this world that are pure dragon. Her. And this. Their connection is inevitable.

I am looking for a way to use that against her."

"How are you all so sure it's a her?" Darlene asked. "Are there ... *anatomical* differences you can see?"

"She was a woman in the other world," Sarah said.

"I beg your pardon?"

"She was a human woman. When she crossed the boundary, that's how she came out the other side. A great big dragon."

Darlene just sat there with her mouth open for a moment. "I'm sorry, *what*?"

"Imagine being so essentially dragon," Kazimir said, frowning, "you override reality itself."

"Sounds like something only God could do," Sarah said.

"Don't blaspheme," Darlene said, as if by reflex.

"Or a Goddess," Kazimir said, almost under his breath.

"You neither," said Darlene.

"Oh, trust me when I say I wish I did not believe it," Kazimir said.

"Believe what?" Sarah asked.

Kazimir took a long breath, and Sarah could just *feel* the bad news coming. "You asked before about our Goddess," he said.

"You said you destroyed her."

"I did not. I said we took care of her before she destroyed *us*."

"Took care of her how?"

Kazimir looked hesitant, like he knew she wasn't going to like his answer. "Using all the dragon magic at hand, we trapped her in the body of a human, doomed to age and die." He took a deep breath. "And be reborn as a woman each generation."

The import of it hit Sarah like a falling brick. "Oh," she said. "Hell."

"Language, missy!" Darlene snapped, much angrier than at the blasphemy.

Kazimir looked at the claw again. "She will come for what is hers. I think we may have made a large mistake letting that assassin go."

A sudden knocking at the door made them all jump again. Darlene went towards it, fear in her eyes. "If it's the Sheriff..."

But it was Hisao and Jason, who Sarah felt another sudden ache for on seeing him again. There was no time for that, though. They'd stopped in the feed store after dropping off Malcolm, and had immediately been asked their opinions on that morning's paper. It was too soon to have photographs, but the headline and story were clear. An entire town just on the other side of the mountains had burnt to the ground.

"Police are saying it was volcanic," Hisao said. "A vent that opened up. But..."

"It was her," Kazimir said, deeply unhappy. "She was taking her first taste."

22

The pain increased as she flew, for she didn't stop, feeling somehow that she might outfly it, an ache in her head like something crawling out from the inside. She managed for a little while, but eventually she had to stop on another mountain peak to rest. The pain was intense enough to make her throw up a bile so acidic the rocks sizzled.

Surely dragons didn't get morning sickness?

Instinct told her (how? She wasn't quite sure; she just knew as certainly as she might know she was hungry) that her time was very near. There would be pain and then a clutch of eggs and then...

Well, she smiled to herself, then this world would be on its way to a proper hierarchy–

She vomited again. And again. Once more, and the pain ceased altogether. Her dragon eye caught the tiniest of sparkles in the mess. The morning sun was brilliant on the mountaintop, and something very small reflected back at her. She hooked the very tip of one claw to lift it.

It was a gold filling.

Just one? She'd eaten many people yesterday—

Then she realized. It was her own. From back when she was Veronica Woolf. The only foreign body left in or on her when she ... *became* who she was always meant to be. Her clothes had torn off immediately, she'd no longer needed her glasses, and the small studs she wore as earrings had long since vanished to who knew where.

This was the very last part of her that had been human, and her dragon body, her *proper* body, was finally rejecting it.

She dug a hole and buried the filling. The start of a hoard. She was a dragon, after all.

Grace did not like Sheriff Kelby. She knew she should have felt sorry for him because of the cast on his arm, and her father would probably say you had to give people lots of room to be who they are if that's what you expect in return.

But she did not like him. Not one little bit.

"Describe for me again what you saw, please," her father said, smiling patiently.

The Sheriff made a weird gurgle of anger. "I told you. A great big *thing* flew over the Dewhurst farm then disappeared up the mountains. But that's not why I called the General—"

"I know why you called the General—"

"There were three people, three *strangers* at Darlene's farm. Two I didn't recognize and one who was the spitting image of her daughter."

Her father glanced up from his notes. "Why do you say 'spitting image'?"

"Well, her daughter died two years ago, didn't she?"

"And you're sure about that?"

Sheriff Kelby's face went hard. It was probably never really soft, Grace thought. She hoped this man didn't have children.

"I know when people in my town die, Agent," he said, with an anger that hadn't let up since they arrived.

General Kraft had caught her father before he'd left the building. They really *were* going to go to her grandmother's this time, as the rest of this mission was no place for a little girl, her father had told her, if in kinder words. But the Sheriff of the town he was going to anyway had just called about some unusual strangers. Her father was to drive there immediately, and he was a man who followed orders. He'd looked at Grace, given her a taut-lipped smile, and back into the Oldsmobile they went. She'd at least had time to eat her waffles.

"How many times do you want me to tell you the same thing, Agent?" the Sheriff asked.

"I'm sure you have the same procedure, Sheriff," her father answered, calmly. "You have someone repeat their story often enough, you get new details."

"Or they make a mistake. Which is what we do with *suspects*. What am I suspected of?"

"You have to admit, these are pretty wild things you're suggesting."

Grace didn't blink at that. She knew sometimes her dad had to tell little lies to get bigger truths out of other people, even if just to catch them off guard or make them really *sure* they were telling the truth. They had seen pretty wild things themselves. Her father just wanted to make sure the Sheriff really had, too.

"The General didn't seem to think so," Sheriff Kelby said sourly.

"Did he not?"

"No." The Sheriff had a crafty look now. "I tell him things that would make my own grandmother think I was soused, and he just says, 'Go on.' Like that. 'Go on.' As if some flying monster and a teenage assassin were normal parts of his morning."

"Teenage assassin?" her father said, and she saw Sheriff Kelby realize he'd let something slip. Having him repeat his story over and over again had worked.

Sheriff Kelby gave him a look. "Which I'm sure your General told you."

Her father smiled. "He did not."

The Sheriff shifted uncomfortably. "Well, that was the one thing he was sceptical about. Not the flying monster, mind you, but the teenage assassin."

"That's an interesting phrase."

"He's a teenager, and he's an assassin. What else do you want me to call him? He's one of yours." Her father didn't answer, just kept the small smile in place. Kelby's own face fell. "He's not one of yours."

"We don't train teenagers to kill, Sheriff," her father answered. "Whatever other horrors you may hear about us."

"Who was he, then?"

"One would have thought you'd be the person to find that out, Sheriff. They're in your town, after all."

"Well, I would have, but..."

"You had your fall."

Grace knew the look on her daddy's face. It was the one

when he caught her in a mistruth and was waiting for her to fess up to it. He never got really angry if you fessed up immediately. She found herself wanting to tell the Sheriff that.

The Sheriff rolled his eyes. "Fine. He did this to me. I got a few good licks in, but he had no trouble at all taking down a full-grown Sheriff. He broke my arm and was threatening to kill me with these blades he kept hidden in his sleeves."

"Blades?"

The Sheriff lifted his chin and showed two bandages on his neck. "They said they were some of your people and that I should leave well enough alone."

"But you didn't."

"Would you?"

Her father looked unsurprised. "No, I don't suppose I would."

"Was he a liar, Daddy?" Grace asked when they were back in the car.

"That's too strong a word, Gracie. You shouldn't call people liars. Say 'economical with the truth' or 'teller of tales'."

"Was he a teller of tales?"

Her father thought for a moment as he pulled from the main paved road onto a gravel one that seemed to head into woods. "I suspect he might be most of the time, but *this* time..."

"We saw a dragon, too."

"Yes, we did."

"We didn't see the sassinam, though."

"Assassin. No, we didn't."

"What's an assassin?"

"Someone not very nice at all, sweetheart."

She could see how serious he was when he said it, so she stayed quiet and let him think. She didn't ask if they were going to her grandmother's, thinking that if she didn't bring it up, he might just keep bringing her along. There was a dragon somewhere, after all. Wouldn't he want her by his side where she would be safest?

He'd said he needed to talk to the strangers out at the farm the Sheriff had mentioned, so she assumed that was where they were going. The roads were empty, though. Forested, like Pinedale was, with farms in clearings. There was still snow everywhere, so she was surprised to see a young man walking by the side of the road going the other way, holding out his thumb.

"Daddy, that boy needs a ride," she said, as they passed him.

"We're not going in the right direction, Grace," her father said, barely listening.

"He looked..." She glanced back at the boy now rapidly disappearing up the road. His clothes were a little odd, like from a slightly different period in history. And the way he walked had a ... she brought up the word "thoughtfulness" and was proud of it, not just for its length but for its accuracy. "He looked different, Daddy."

"Different how?" Her father's attention suddenly snapped to the rear-view mirror.

"He walked with thoughtfulness."

He stopped the car so suddenly, she felt a little afraid. "What do you mean by that?"

She felt even more afraid of his urgency. "He walked like he was older than he was."

Her father looked in the rear-view mirror again, then swung the car around in a U-turn, but when they got back to where the boy had been waiting, he was nowhere to be seen. "Your eyes, sweetie," her dad said. "I should have them insured, they see so much."

Malcolm didn't believe what he'd seen, mainly because he had been watching the little girl who'd kept her eyes on him much longer than seemed normal for a casual glance. She'd watched him as the car approached, watched him as they passed by, watched him as his stomach turned flips when he saw who was driving.

As soon as the car was out of sight, he made for the woods. He hid behind a tree, just like he'd done on the very first day of this journey, what seemed like lifetimes ago, on the day the dragon the Mitera Thea had somehow convinced to help had dropped him, literally, from the sky to start this journey and returned to kill the two men who were threatening him. Two men who maybe had families, maybe little girls. The journey had started in death, and it had just kept going.

Those two men hadn't deserved it. Neither did the Mountie. Or Sarah's father or the Sheriff who'd arrived or the Jason in the other world.

Neither did the man Malcolm had seen behind the wheel of the car he now heard rocketing back up the road behind him, no doubt to look for him. He had watched that man die. Had watched as the woman that man thought was his partner shot him down.

"I'm lost," he whispered out loud. "I'm lost and I don't know where to go."

It was a prayer, but he had no one to pray it to. He prayed to no one that the man and the little girl wouldn't meet the fate of the first two men. He prayed he would find who he was looking for so he could return, and he prayed that on his return, he would find a way to defeat the Mitera Thea herself. So that there would be no more killing.

He would never wash the stain of it from him, and he didn't want to. There was no atonement left for him.

But there might be for others.

He waited until the man gave up and drove away again. Then he hurried on his journey.

Her stomach rumbled, though she didn't feel hungry, despite the vomiting. In the crater of this other mountain – one she could smell was more turbulent than the first, this one would blow in the years to come – she groaned, and the rumbling moved deeper down.

The clutch of eggs was ready.

How? She knew she was close, but she had only become pregnant the day before. Still, they were ready, *she* was ready, they only needed a place for laying.

Well, what better place than a turbulent volcano?

She dug, even as the contractions hit her. She dug under the snow and ice, into the rock, making a cave-like hollow. They couldn't be exposed. The weather wouldn't harm them – there was very little in existence hardier than a dragon's egg – but humans might. Even here, this high, she wouldn't risk it.

The contractions grew painful, then overwhelming. She felt as if she left her body for a time, and when she returned, a dozen steaming eggs, each taller than a man, lay in the cave she'd made.

She collapsed into the snow, spent. She laughed ruefully to herself: the world below was safe for a while because the destroyer that had arrived to claim it needed a little rest.

It was as she was drifting off to sleep that she finally put it all together. The super-accelerated healing, the pregnancy and super-accelerated *birth*, the refusal of her monumental body to countenance one little sliver of her remaining humanity. Even her missing finger, now a missing claw. She'd always suspected it, all those years as a human, those fiery images in her head, her ability to lead others in the Believer cause, to restore them to the days when they stole prophecies and sacred artefacts, though they seemed to have no idea what to do with those things until she showed them. All part of her abilities which finally led even *dragons* to do her bidding.

She'd accepted it as only natural that she'd arrived in a world that couldn't contain her in human form. Though that didn't explain why the blue dragon was down there walking on two legs.

No. This was the realization, and when she thought it, she felt the truth of it ring through her, surge like the earlier energy had.

She was more than dragon. She was the *first* dragon. She was the Creator of them all.

She was their Goddess. And they had contained her in human shape to control her power.

"Not any more," she said, an anger bubbling deep within her. "Not any more."

Tomorrow would be an eventful day for this world, when the Goddess awoke.

23

"It is odd she has not come," Kazimir said, as night fell on the Dewhurst farm.

"Hard to see that as a bad thing," Sarah said. They were out in the cold, looking over the snowy fields. "We have no plan and she destroys entire towns."

"We will stop her," Kazimir said.

"I don't know why you think that."

His eye still scanned the fading landscape, no snow falling, just an increasingly bitter cold. Sarah wondered if this winter would ever actually end. "You were prophesied to do so," he finally said. "She believed it so much, she sent an assassin after you."

"I'm just a girl."

"It is tragic how well you have been taught to say that with sadness rather than triumph."

"I would have thought all bets were off when we came to a whole other world. Things are different here."

"Not so very different," Kazimir said.

"You're a human, my mom is alive, I'm *not*, and Jason barely knows me."

"Yes. Fair points all, but *we* are still the same, Sarah Dewhurst. In our inmost selves, we are still the same, and we will still accomplish this."

She had no response to that, so instead, she asked, "What are these runes you've been writing? Where do they disappear to?"

He pursed his lips, thoughtfully. "May I confess something to you?"

"Oh, no," she said. "Please don't let it be terrible."

"It may be. But it may not. It may just be what always was and all that ever shall be."

"Because that doesn't sound terrible at all." She didn't continue with the sarcasm, though, as she saw the worried look on his face.

"You want to know what I was writing and where the runes go. The first answer is simple. I was recording the story of what has happened, how we got where we are, and so forth. We are scholars, blues. We always have been."

He took a thoughtful breath. "As to where they go, that is harder. I do not like what I think is the answer. I assumed I was writing about the fulfilment of a prophecy, but as I wrote with the ancient claw of a Goddess who had only seemed to lose her finger just before coming to this world, I began to dread that it wasn't fulfilment I was documenting." He looked in her eyes now. "I fear I may have been writing the prophecy itself."

"What?"

"The one that talked about a girl in the other world. The one that led to all that war and loss." Sarah was so astonished to see tears in his eye that she couldn't respond. "I fear I may have caused this. Will cause it. Have *always* caused it."

"How is that even possible?" she found herself whispering.

"All the different worlds," he said. "All the different possibilities. I told you we believe everything happens again and again. It's called recurrence. Dragons know that what affects one world can seep into the next. We know that *very* well, Sarah Dewhurst. And so I ask myself, did a Kazimir in another world write a prophecy for ours? Did I write one for another? For *this* one, perhaps? Have I always done this, in every world?"

"But the time frame is so different—"

"The runes go into the accumulated knowledge of all blues. Does that reflect across worlds? Across times? Did what I write, *will* what I've written, be interpreted and reinterpreted over the millennia until it becomes as vague and dangerous as any prophecy, bringing me to a place where I will write it again after it has happened? Or is there now a clearer version in another world where this story has yet to unfold, waiting to do so because I have 'foreseen' it?"

"Kazimir—"

"Dragon magic is about the realization of unrealizable possibility. That's why it's *magic*. It subsumes reality, subsumes what is real, while all the time worlds spring up again and again, playing out infinite choices in infinite varieties. Am I the thread in that variety that has caused this to happen?"

His tears had never fallen, perhaps that they'd even reached his eye counted among dragons as weeping. He held up a hand, cutting the planned comfort he saw on her face.

"The truth is," he said, "I do not know for sure and almost certainly never will."

"Then all you can do is your best. Always. That's it."

He still faced away from her, but then he cocked his head. "Someone is coming."

"I don't hear anything." Then she did. His ears were unnervingly sharp. A car – not the Sheriff, not the Inagawas – was coming up the road. An Oldsmobile. They watched it pull around a bend and slow as it saw them. A man in a fedora was behind the wheel, a solemn little girl in the passenger seat.

"Hello," the man said, rolling down his window. "Can you direct me to the Dewhurst farm?"

He seemed so friendly, so confident, that Sarah found herself on the verge of answering, before Kazimir interrupted. "Who might be asking?"

The man still smiled, his little girl watching seriously. She had a book with her. *Little House in the Big Woods*. "I read that," Sarah said. "*The Long Winter* was my favourite, though."

"Mine, too," the little girl said, quietly.

"Well, now, see?" said the man. "We're already friends."

"People who say that out loud tend to be no man's friends," Kazimir said.

The man stuck the tip of his tongue on his top lip, as if thinking, then Sarah saw him turn to his daughter and raise his eyebrows. The little girl shrugged, and her father – if that's who he was – turned back to her and Kazimir.

"I'm wondering," the man said, still friendly, "if you two in particular might be people who could tell me a little something about dragons."

306

Kazimir and Sarah exchanged a look, then he surprised her by saying, "That depends upon how committed you are to stopping one."

It had only taken Malcolm four different cars to get all the way to Bellingham. All four drivers had been single men. One of them tried to convert him to Christianity, and two of the others had asked for sex, one obliquely, circling into it through jokes and small attempts at dirty talk, but the other had unzipped his fly and taken himself out before they were five minutes down the road. "You want a ride, you gotta pay," he'd said and tried to force Malcolm's face down. A blade held at the man's jugular was good for silence for another twenty miles, but the whole thing left Malcolm feeling so dirty – for the man's actions, for his own, however "justified" they might be – that he made the man drop him off long before the promised destination.

What was wrong with this world? There were no dragons. Did men think they needed to take their place?

Fortunately, the fourth man just seemed decent. "I used to travel by thumb," he said. "I remember it being less fun than I thought it would be."

"You're not wrong there, sir," Malcolm had replied.

After a pleasant final leg of more than two hours, the man had dropped Malcolm off at a phone booth in Bellingham. The man leaned out of the car as Malcolm left it and said, simply, "I hope you find what you're looking for, son."

"Me too," Malcolm said.

He waited until the man drove off, then went into the

phone booth and took out the phone book. He was playing a very long shot, but if there was even a chance, even the remotest chance, he had to try. This town, near the border with Canada, had slipped from the mouth of the Mitera Thea more than once over the years, in enough subtle ways that Malcolm came to understand that it was from here he probably came, where his parents were lost, where a Believer – the Mitera Thea always said it was herself – had found him and adopted him into the life of the church.

He was also working on a hunch from a single name mentioned a single time over his seventeen years of life, when the Mitera Thea had a rare cross moment with him, saying he was lucky she didn't send him back to the "vicious distant relations of poor dead Mr and Mrs Ottaviano–" She had caught herself and stopped, refusing any further entreaties from him and never making the slip again.

But he had never forgotten.

Ottaviano wasn't a common name.

There was one, just one, in the Bellingham phone book.

He walked to the address given, sure it would be a mistake, sure that the phone book would be out of date or that, even if not, this would clearly be a "vicious distant relation", but he went anyway, to a tidy little house in a nice neighbourhood, watching it from across the street.

He hadn't been waiting more than half an hour, when the front door opened, and Malcolm watched himself walk out.

"Here's another stranger in my house," Darlene said, handing a coffee to the man who'd identified himself as Agent

Dernovich, "Federal Bureau of Investigation, ma'am." She handed a hot chocolate to the little girl he had with him, so obviously his daughter she might as well have been wearing a name tag.

"I'm sorry to put you to trouble, Mrs Dewhurst," he said, "but I'm guessing my appearance at your farm might not be all that much of a surprise?"

"A day after a dragon flew across my property?" Darlene said, sounding almost amused to the ears of Sarah. "A day after my dead daughter walked right up to my door?"

"Yes, ma'am, that sort of day." He took out a little notebook. "I'd like to ask you all a few questions, if I may."

"We agreed to an exchange of information," Kazimir said. "That does not mean we just answer your questions."

"I didn't agree to anything that I recall," Darlene said.

"He knows things," Sarah told her. "He might be able to help us."

The man had been surprisingly forthcoming about the threat of a dragon and his endeavour to stop it. He was looking for anything, any answer, any help, that would prevent the disaster of the mountain town from happening again. Kazimir had unilaterally decided the need was "too great to equivocate" and asked the man inside.

"Help you what, exactly?" Darlene asked.

"Stop a clear and present danger to our lives, ma'am. And I do not say that lightly in front of my daughter."

"That's okay, Daddy," the little girl said, glancing up from her book. "I saw what it did to Pinedale."

"That town in the paper?" Darlene asked. "You were there?"

"It's our home," the man said.

"Was," said the little girl, firmly looking at the pages of her book. Her father placed a gentle hand on the back of her head and stroked it once.

"So you saw her first-hand," Kazimir said.

The agent perked up. "Her?"

Kazimir smiled. "As I thought. You know less than you promised."

The agent smiled back. "I see. Clever." He cleared his throat. "Well, perhaps we should start with what I *do* know, and then you good folks could fill in any gaps." He took a deep breath, then jumped in the deep end. "What if I told you this wasn't the only universe?"

The shock was visceral. Malcolm moved behind a rhododendron so he would not be seen. He thought he might actually faint, so at least he could do it in the privacy of a bush.

The Other Malcolm locked the front door, and came down the walk, spinning the key ring around his finger. He was beefier than Malcolm, almost strapping, clearly having been better fed recently. His hair was a touch longer, too, enough to have a style to it, with a combed-back front.

His aspect, however, was the most different. There was no furtiveness. No subtle but constant checking of his environment. No tension in his body in case he needed to spring suddenly towards or away from a threat. This Malcolm carried himself with a distracted lightness, a phrase no one would have ever used to describe the Malcolm who'd been trained his entire life to kill.

And what even of the name? This Other Malcolm would have a proper name. A name given from birth. Malcolm suddenly ached with all his heart to know it.

"Excuse me?" he said, before he even knew he was going to.

The Other Malcolm started at a voice emerging from a bush. "Who's there?"

Malcolm cursed himself. This was the worst possible choice for an approach, but he had no time and there had never been any question about his bravery.

He stepped around the bush, faced himself, and said, "Do you know me?"

"We've known of the other universes for about a decade," Agent Dernovich said. "Since we started investigating satellite technology."

"Those machines that are supposed to fly around the world one day and spy on us?" Darlene asked.

Agent Dernovich grinned. "Yes, ma'am, among many other things. Communication, television signals, eventually we'll even put men up there. Then onto the moon."

Darlene snorted. "And pigs will fly."

"Dragons *did* fly," Sarah said. Darlene gave a little scowl but didn't offer a rebuttal.

"Well," Agent Dernovich sighed, "we started sending out test signals. Not just through the radio towers that carry everything now, but out there." He gestured up towards the ceiling. "This was a one-way test, mind you, bouncing signals off the moon, seeing what trajectories we needed, et cetera. We weren't supposed to hear anything back."

"But you did," Kazimir said.

Agent Dernovich nodded. "First we thought it was just echoes because they were so similar to what we were sending out. But on closer look, they weren't exact matches. Which was impossible." He lowered his voice, as if remembering the awe of it. "On certain frequencies, we were hearing *ourselves*, our own voices, but saying and sending different things."

He paused, clearly for the effect. "On one of those frequencies, men and women talked about dragons as if they were the most normal thing in the world."

The Other Malcolm backed away, one hand still gripping his key ring, perhaps in case it needed to be used as a weapon.

"I won't hurt you," Malcolm said.

"Damn right, you won't."

"I'm too far away for you to lunge effectively," Malcolm said. "I could tip you off balance and overpower you with punches to the head."

"So you *do* want to hurt me?"

Malcolm held up his hands. "The exact opposite."

"How do you have my face?" the Other Malcolm asked. "Is this some kind of stupid joke? Did Terry Haskell put you up to this? Because I told that bully–"

"I don't know who that is. My name is Malcolm."

"I don't know any Malcolms."

Malcolm sighed. This really couldn't be going any worse. "I am you," he said, simply, deciding to go for bare honesty. "If your circumstances had been very different."

The Other Malcolm still looked angry. "I don't have time for this. Lunch is almost over, I have to get back to school."

"You're in danger," Malcolm said. "We all are."

"From who?"

"Did you read today's newspaper? The little town that burned to the ground?"

"So? So what? Sometimes volcanoes erupt. Why do you have my face?"

Malcolm closed his eyes. If he'd had proper time to plan, how would he have gotten through to this person? This version of himself one hair's breadth and a universe away? How would he make him believe? And most importantly, what was the very fastest way to do this?

"When I dream, I dream of men," he said, quietly, eyes still shut. "When I love, my love is for men." He opened his eyes. "Does this seem like the truth of you, too?"

The Other Malcolm looked horrified, and now here was Malcolm's own familiar furtiveness, one that made Malcolm curse himself for coming to find this boy who had maybe even been happy just moments ago.

"You need to get out of here," the Other Malcolm said. "If you come near me again, I *will* hurt you. I'm a hell of a lot tougher than I look, believe you me."

"Oh, I do," Malcolm said. "You wouldn't believe how well I know."

The Other Malcolm started backing away, his fist with the keys up. It was so gentle a threat that Malcolm actually felt a little glimmer of humour. But there was nothing humorous in the boy's face. He backed up and up, before finally turning from Malcolm and starting to stomp away.

313

"There's a boy who could love you," Malcolm called after him. "A boy *you* could love."

The Other Malcolm stopped, but didn't turn around.

"He's called Nelson," Malcolm said. "I think he needs your help."

"Imagine that," Agent Dernovich said. "A world with dragons in it, just flying around like birds. Of course, being who we are, we built up an entire scenario should one ever cross the boundary between universes."

"Was that the only scenario?" Darlene asked.

Agent Dernovich looked somewhat abashed. "We have ninety-four in total. An incursion by a real, fire-breathing dragon isn't actually the most alarming possibility."

"Oh, my." Darlene sat down on her chair.

"Okay," said Agent Dernovich. "An exchange of information. Your turn."

Sarah and Kazimir exchanged a look. "Shall you or shall I?" he said.

"You should," Sarah said. "And you know where you should start."

Kazimir sighed heavily. "Fine," he said. "We both come from one of your other universes. One where I am a dragon."

There was a silence in the room, as even the little girl looked up in surprise.

"You don't really look like one," Agent Dernovich said.

"I was what was known in our world as a Russian blue. Smaller than the red you saw destroy your town, but perfectly capable of doing so should I choose. Which, I hasten to add,"

314

he said to their looks of alarm, "I never would. And neither would any other dragon in our world. We have lived in peaceful if somewhat uneasy coexistence for centuries."

"You're a dragon," Darlene said, clearly not believing him.

"In sheep's clothing," Agent Dernovich said.

"That is apt," said Kazimir. "I changed shape as I came into this world. You can imagine my surprise."

"Are you who Kelby meant by a 'teenage assassin'?" Dernovich asked.

"No," Sarah said, "that's someone else who you don't need to worry about."

"I beg your pardon–"

"But Kazimir's telling the truth," Sarah said. "I knew him, *know* him as a dragon. My father hired him to work on the farm. He saved my life from our world's version of your Sheriff Kelby."

"He was just a Deputy in our world," Kazimir said. "Clearly *some* universes had the good sense not to promote him."

"Was?" Agent Dernovich said.

"I ate him," Kazimir said, "after he tried to murder this young woman and the Japanese boy."

Another silence at this.

"But perhaps we are getting off-track," Kazimir said. "Let me tell you about our Goddess."

"There are more worlds than this one," Malcolm said. "And I come from one where I made a *huge* mistake."

The Other Malcolm was watching him again, but warily, like he might jump at any second.

315

"Nelson helped me." Malcolm felt his voice choking. "He was tender to me. I can remember the smell of him. The touch of his skin."

The Other Malcolm's eyes grew wider. "You can't talk like this. You can't talk like a queer here."

"It's what happened," Malcolm said. "I feel like I loved him in the short time we spent together. And then I brought him into danger."

"How?"

Malcolm swallowed and met the Other Malcolm's eyes. "That's for me to find the solution to. But here, Nelson may be in trouble. From his family. They'll throw him out when they find out what he is."

"So would my family. So would most people's."

Malcolm frowned. "Not where I come from. Parts of it anyway. The world changes. It keeps on changing. It'll change here, too."

"Those are just words."

"Maybe, but Nelson is real. And he could love you. You could love *him*. But whatever happens, he deserves better than being thrown out into the world alone."

"Then why don't *you* go to him?"

"Because I have my own Nelson to save."

"Your what?" Agent Dernovich said.

"Goddess," Kazimir repeated. He paused, obviously reluctant. "It is forbidden to tell this part to humans. More than forbidden. A taboo so strong it is almost physically difficult to break it."

He closed his eyes, took a breath, and said, "She created us. Before memory. She brought us into our world and probably many others. But not this one." He looked at Agent Dernovich. "Not yet."

"Oh," Agent Dernovich said, his ease and smile disappearing for the first time. "Oh, dear."

"It is an old story, the oldest," Kazimir said. "Assumed by most of my kind to be fable, assumed by *me* for most of my very short life."

"How old *are* you?" Sarah asked.

"Just under two hundred," he said. "A mere babe. And rare for our world. A stripling like me comes along once a century, perhaps. But I was taught the story of she who created us all. Who burst through the walls between the universes and channelled the magic that brought dragons into our world. She saw a place where dragons would rule, because she is what all gods and goddesses are. Creator and Destroyer. She set out to annihilate humans, and very nearly succeeded."

"There's nothing I learned in history about this," Sarah said. "Even in *archaeology*."

"The archaeology of it is ... yet to be fully discovered, let us say. There is probably awkwardness coming to the dragon/human relationship when you start finding things out, I imagine."

"Not any more," Sarah said. "There'll be war now. She'll get what she wanted."

Kazimir looked very troubled. "Yes. Destruction of man. Which in the wilful blindness of a Goddess, she refused to see would be the end of dragons, too."

"How?" Agent Dernovich asked.

"That, I will not tell you, but rest assured, all mass destruction is eventually mutual. We knew we had to stop her."

"How did you convince her?"

Kazimir laughed. "Convince? Good grief, no. One does not *convince* a Goddess. A Goddess takes no advice. She does not change her mind unless she chooses to, and she has no interest in what her Creation might think of her. No, there would be no convincing. She had to be defeated."

"And she clearly wasn't," Agent Dernovich said.

"I beg your pardon, she clearly *was*," Kazimir said. "Or you and I would not be having this conversation. She would have found your world considerably sooner than yesterday, and trust me when I say, it would be a very different place. You cannot kill a Goddess. If you think dragons are immortal–"

"You are?" Agent Dernovich asked, surprised.

"Then you can imagine how very much *more* immortal the dragon Goddess would be."

"So what did you do?"

"Again, I personally did nothing. This was thousands of years before I was even born, and most dragons regard this story as–"

"Myth, yes, you've said," Agent Dernovich urged. "I'm rushing you, Kazimir, because whatever was done once, can be done again. What did the dragons do? And can we repeat it?"

Kazimir looked wary. "As I told Sarah, what the dragons did – or what our legends *tell* us – was to trap her. In a human body. We took a spur from her so that she would remain forever incomplete, then we confined her to life as one of you."

"How?" Agent Dernovich asked.

318

Kazimir gave a little shrug. "The problem with myths, Agent, is that they tend to be light on science. The only explanation that has survived is ... magic."

"Magic," Agent Dernovich said, flatly.

"Yes."

"Magic isn't going to be helpful here," Agent Dernovich said. "Our universe is conspicuously lacking in it."

"Not any more," Darlene said. "We've got a great big dragon flying around now. I'd say that was magic."

"Not a word of this can be real," the Other Malcolm said. "This is some ugly, horrible joke."

"It isn't," Malcolm said. "How could I look so much like you? Not similar, *identical*."

"A twin, maybe. Something my mother–"

"Even if that were true," Malcolm said, starting to unbutton his shirt, "are these a part of your world?"

He exposed his chest, the tattoos that covered every inch. The Other Malcolm's eyes opened very wide. He stepped forward slowly, looking. "They're *dragons*."

"Which is what attacked the town you read about in your newspaper."

The Other Malcolm scoffed. "Yeah, right. Tattoos don't prove anything. There are tattooed men in the circus–"

Malcolm grabbed a fistful of the Other Malcolm's shirt, pulled him suddenly close, and kissed him on the lips. The Other Malcolm, clearly surprised, resisted only for a second, before making a grunt of further shock as Malcolm let the kiss end. The Other Malcolm put a hand up to his lips. "You...

My God, you taste exactly *like* me. How do I even *know* that?"

"I *am* you. And you are me. From different worlds a sliver apart."

The Other Malcolm kept his fingers to his lips. "You're the first man I've ever kissed." He frowned. "That's kinky."

"Do you want to love? Answer me that. Because I didn't know until I met Nelson."

The Other Malcolm lowered his hand. "I've always wanted to love." He looked down. "I never thought I was allowed."

"Then at least let me tell you you are. That you *can*. That you will."

The Other Malcolm looked around, not seemingly because he was checking for anything but just to keep his gaze away from the intensity of Malcolm's. He even turned a full circle, and when he came back round, Malcolm saw that his eyes were wet.

"My name is Hugh," he said.

"It's nice to meet you, Hugh."

"You can't imagine how lonely I've been."

"Yes. I actually can."

Hugh blinked a few times, until his eyes cleared. "Where did you say this Nelson was?"

"She is right," Kazimir said. "There was not magic in this world – hence my appearance – but there is now. I can feel it. And it is growing."

"She'll create more dragons?" Agent Dernovich said.

"She will lay eggs, yes. She will have young."

"How?" Sarah said.

"She is a Creator. It is what they do."

"Wait, wait, wait," Darlene said. "You're saying she's been a human for thousands of years, but she only found a way to get revenge now?"

"That is where the myth gets tricky," Kazimir answered. "They trapped her in the body of a human, and then the myth says, they made her forget who she was."

"But gods leak," Agent Dernovich said. "You said you could never convince a Goddess. You could probably never truly take one's memory either."

"No," Kazimir said. "Nor can you properly kill one. Her human form dies and the loose magic is born in another, again and again. This is what our theologians believe. *Blue* theologians, for we seem to be the only ones who care."

"You're a theologian?" Agent Dernovich asked.

"When you are made of magic, Agent, it is not a surprising choice."

"So what happened to the dragon-woman?" Darlene asked.

Kazimir looked sheepish.

"You lost her," Agent Dernovich said. "You lost track of her."

"Decades passed. Millennia did. We found our peace with humans. No Goddess came to destroy us. We forgot she ever existed. And then the Believers came."

"The Believers?"

"A religion."

"A cult," Sarah said.

"Nomenclature," Kazimir said, "but who do you think founded it? A woman. Two hundred years ago. Their leaders are always women, a strong one, followed by a weaker one, followed by a stronger one."

"Your Goddess," Darlene guessed. "She'd lead them till she died, then take over again when she got old enough."

"Yes. She did not fully remember who she was, as that was part of the prison, but the Goddess was, as you say, leaking. She was driven to dragon worship with such intensity an entire belief rose up around her. Then something must have broken through for her, if not complete self-awareness, then a vision, a plan, one she may have pursued without knowing entirely why. Because fifty-five years ago, we discovered that the Believers – two Mitera Theas ago and beyond all possibility – knew about a prophecy, one we had kept deeply secret, stating that an end was coming, fomented by the Goddess herself, but stopped– " he looked at Sarah– "by a human girl."

"Fifty-five years ago," Sarah said.

"Yes," Kazimir said.

"What's so special about fifty-five years ago?" Agent Dernovich asked.

"That's when dragons stopped talking to people," Sarah said.

"*She* will want to talk to us," Kazimir said. "She could be back any time. It will be worse once she realizes."

"Realizes what?"

Kazimir grew frustrated. "Realizes who she is. When she knows her full power, believe me, we will *all* know." He held up the Spur. "When especially she knows what is lacking to access that full power."

Another silence. Agent Dernovich looked worried for the briefest of moments, then smiled to his daughter. "Well, this is exciting, isn't it?" he said to her.

"Way more exciting than Grandma's," the little girl said.

"Yesiree, it is that," her father said. Then he turned back to face Sarah and Kazimir, and said, "Would it help if I got you an army?"

24

The dragon woke.

And knew who she was.

She left her clutch of eggs on the mountaintop. It was morning; she didn't know how long she'd slept, but it didn't matter.

It mattered less than anything had ever mattered.

They trapped me, she thought. *For thousands of years, they robbed me of who I was.*

Because they were afraid.

As she flew up through the thinning winter clouds, she had only one thought in her mind.

They will pay.

She flew north and west, her nose guiding her towards the highest concentration of human smell. Once she was away from the mountains and the forests began to thin, she saw how they infested the land. Long strips of road for their belching cars, vast empty swathes of pitifully weak houses, even down to the great water that dipped into the landscape, where boats spilled oil into the world.

Rage filled her, familiar but now given a fuel she could never have imagined. She had been one of them. She had been forced to live as one of *them*. For century upon century. Her own creation had done this, she remembered now, but she would not make the same mistakes twice. Her new brood would wake to a world where humans were already on the run. The broods after that might wake to a planet where humans had never been.

Look at them here. Humans were vermin, a disease.

She hated them with her whole raging, fiery heart.

It was time they learned their place.

She considered the first large town she flew over, a stinking cesspit with factories and refineries all along the waterfront. But even from this height, the smell was almost choking. She flew on, north, over the strip of concrete she remembered in her old world, one she had driven in a car like the thousands down there, trapped, earthbound, propelled by a fire she never fully understood, until now, until this very morning. The thrill of her new knowledge, the *fury* of it, rose in her gut again and she couldn't stop herself from swooping down to freeway level, just over the roofs of the cars, taking a deep breath and—

Oh, the release. The fire – no, fire was wrong, fire had always been wrong, this was more than just flame, this was annihilation, *erasure*.

Half a dozen cars in front of her disintegrated. Others drove right off the road, smashing into trees and one another at the sight of the destruction, at the sight of *her*. She blazed the lanes travelling in the same direction as her, then veered into oncoming traffic, already colliding and breaking into itself as they watched her bear down on them, as they watched their end uncurl from the mouth of this impossible beast. She could hear their screams. She could smell the roasting of their skin, the boiling of their fat.

She was their rightful end, coming from the sky.

Seattle approached. As a human, she had visited New York once. She had been overwhelmed by the skyscrapers there, buildings so tall, you had to lean back to even see the top, buildings that gave you vertigo just standing next to them. Seattle had, as yet, no similar heights, which made her angrier still. She'd have liked to knock one over. Ah, well, a conflagration would have to do. She aimed her head to the sky and soared straight up.

From high above, the city was more or less a north/south strip, a massive lake one side, the saltwater Sound on the other. It rose and fell over a number of sharp hills, all thoughts of it bent to the water.

There would be less room to flee.

A buzz sounded on the edge of her hearing. She spotted two small planes, heading towards her. Silvery husks with rounded noses. She remembered some of the information she'd gathered in her undercover role in the government. The planes were F-86s. The fastest ones the military had.

So they knew she was here.

Good.

She whirled about. She flew slower than an aeroplane – so she assumed, but that was a hypothesis worth testing one day soon – but manoeuvrability was no contest. She flew down in the simplest of loops, and by the time she'd turned once more, she was on an intercept path with the planes from below.

She inhaled a long breath, but then changed her mind, simply *slamming* into the planes with her anger. She was winded, but both aircraft crumpled into pieces with a thrilling ease. She watched those pieces fall, fall, fall, a mile out of the sky.

She finished her loop high above the city and let herself fall, too, wings outspread, breath intaken, the buildings growing closer and closer, so close she could see people on the streets screaming, hear a siren starting to wail, the terror beginning to spread.

"I AM YOUR END!" she said, as she let go her breath.

The first building exploded, her fire blasting out the entire ground floor and bringing down the eight floors above it in an almost slow-motion tumble. She breathed in again, held it, felt the temperature rise and rise, before blowing it on an even taller building. The entire front half nearly evaporated before the rest of it toppled backwards like it had been shot with a gun.

The people were running, screaming now, going in all directions. She spread her wings and flew this way and that, killing swathes of them by altering her mouth so the spray of fire became exactly as wide as the street. Up they went. Their pointless little lives over in one breath.

She flew over two police cars, parked, with officers outside, their guns aimed at her, bullets flying. She felt them as so much sand on the wind.

They had no idea how to face a dragon. No idea at all.

"I AM FIRE!" she roared over them, her voice, her words, causing more screams and people to stop and stare up at her in wonder. "I CANNOT BE CONSUMED!"

She flew down into the crowd, grabbing two clawfuls of humans with her back feet, flying high into the air, and flinging them away.

One was a woman in a long skirt. A skirt like she herself used to wear when she was Agent Woolf. She watched the woman fall, her arms flailing as if that could stop her plummet, and the look on her face, her eyes up at the thing that had grabbed her, had dropped her to her death, the look, the eyes—

She found herself flying down, racing to catch the woman. She let the others fall and die, but this one she snatched out of the air before she hit the pavement. The woman was not this world's version of Veronica Woolf, but she was close enough. A woman like she herself had been. She landed, the woman looking back at her in terror, in a kind of, what was the word? Submission. The woman was entirely at the dragon's mercy. As it should be. As it always should be.

And yet.

She set the woman down, releasing her. The woman staggered back, stumbling, clearly injured in the grab and the fall, but still trying to get away.

"You'll have to be stronger than that," the dragon said. The woman froze, just for an instant, long enough for the dragon who had formerly been Agent Woolf to say, "You'll have to be much stronger than that."

The woman ran, fast as she could, limping but running through it, disappearing around a corner and not looking back. The dragon, the *Goddess*, stood on the pavement for a moment, watching the space where the woman had disappeared.

Why had she saved her? When the woman would almost certainly die in the waste the dragon was planning to lay to the rest of the city? It was not as if she mattered, one flea among millions.

"Not even when I have been a flea myself," she said out loud.

She had saved that woman nonetheless.

She shook her head, shook the troubling thoughts from it. She roared. It echoed through the buildings, above the screams of the humans, above the sirens that wailed now, above the distant roar of more military planes converging on her. She roared again. And again.

She took to the air and destroyed a city.

A few hours later, she stood on the rubble of a burning hill. Nothing was left of this particular neighbourhood: no house, no human, no trace of life at all, not even a tree or flower. On the hills beyond her, every tall building burned, and not lightly, but in infernos so strong they seemed to make mini-tornadoes of smoke that dotted the skyline.

Smoke rose from the water, too, where she had knocked a dozen more military planes, but there would be no help coming as every dock also burned. She had likewise destroyed the bridges into and out of town, so the humans who were still alive had resorted to trying to swim in the frigid waters. She could watch them drown from here.

She hadn't seen the woman again. She could only assume she had died along with so many others. So very many others.

She had conquered. One single dragon had taken down a major American city in the matter of a morning. She was barely even fatigued, though a rest would be welcome, now that she thought of it.

And when her babies were born...

She would give them back the world that had been taken from her.

She wondered again what had happened to the woman in the skirt.

No. She must not forget what today was. Today was the first real strike against this world. That little town had only been a flexing of the muscles, a stretch before the real activity.

She had levelled a city. She would level more.

Their reality would now change to accommodate her.

For what else was a Goddess for?

25

"Yes, sir," Agent Dernovich said into the phone. "I understand, sir."

Unlike Gareth Dewhurst in the last world, Darlene had a television set. There was not a lot to see in detail, no camera crew had made it into Seattle, but the shots from far away – from Bellevue across Lake Washington, from some of the islands in Puget Sound – were more than enough.

"There seems to be almost nothing left of the city of Seattle," the national news anchorman said, unable to keep a startled horror out of his voice. "Half a million people live there, and I'm told half a million again add to the population on a workday like today. We have no word yet on survivors, though the little we've seen suggests casualties will be catastrophic–"

"There it is again!" his fellow news anchor interrupted, as the silhouette of the dragon rose above the dozens of smoke funnels peppered over the former city. Both anchors fell silent.

The dragon spread its wings, showing all its unambiguous glory, before it disappeared into the clouds and was gone.

"I stress to you, these are, uh, live pictures," the first anchorman stumbled. "We still have no information about what exactly has happened or what this ... creature–"

"Could be an aircraft," the other anchorman said. "Something Soviet. This could be an act of war."

"There's no doubt it's that," the first anchorman said, still staring at the footage, even though by now it was just burning rubble. "But that didn't look like an aircraft to me, Ted. I don't think it did to anyone watching."

"Remarkable," Kazimir said.

"What is?" Sarah asked.

"He is seeing what is really there. Not what he expects to be there, like the other man. A rare talent among humans."

"I understand, sir," Agent Dernovich said into the phone. "All *I'm* saying is that I have very strong reason to believe that the ... object will be coming my way very soon, and it would be in the strongest national security interest to have more to meet it than just me and my pistol."

"We can't stop her," Sarah said, quietly.

"She will come anyway," Kazimir said. "And the prophecy says you will be in the right place at the right time to thwart her."

"We're just going to keep ignoring the fact the prophecy was dead wrong about that in the last world?"

Kazimir squirmed. "Prophecies... Sometimes you have to improvise with them as circumstances arise."

"How on earth is that supposed to be a comfort?"

Agent Dernovich said, "Thank you, sir," and hung up the phone. He looked at Kazimir and Sarah. "We've got an army."

* * *

Hugh had a car, one he had paid for himself out of after-school jobs. It was extremely long and a spotless light blue, even in the bad weather. He took exquisite care of it; Malcolm had watched him run a finger over a single mote of dust before they'd got inside and headed north.

They made bewilderingly fast progress. They'd already crossed the border, which had given Malcolm panic, but they had literally been waved through without stopping. The address Malcolm remembered from Nelson was a further forty-five minutes away. It had all gone so quickly.

"So have you...?" Hugh blushed so hard Malcolm could see it on his neck. "Have you done more than kiss a man?"

"Yes," Malcolm replied.

"And you weren't ashamed after?"

Malcolm's forehead creased. "Not at all. Why would I be?"

"Because it's, you know, it's ... an abomination."

"Against who?"

Hugh swallowed. "God, I guess. People hate it. They hate people like me."

"They're wrong."

Hugh turned to look at him at that.

"They *are*," Malcolm said. "There are people who believe that in my world, but I was told it was their weakness. Not mine."

"So you're not ashamed at all?"

"I'm plenty ashamed at things I've done, but I'm not ashamed of holding Nelson close to me. Feeling his skin on mine. Taking him into my body."

335

"Oh, my God."

"None of that shames me. None of the tenderness, none of the carnality, none of the intimacy. None of it." Malcolm felt his eyes filling. "It was love. And I threw it away."

Hugh looked over from the driver's side. "Tell me again why we aren't taking *you* to see him?"

"Because my Nelson needs me," Malcolm said. "And this one needs you."

"Well, according to the map," Hugh said, "we're nearly there."

They had come to a poor section of the outskirts of Vancouver. The houses were smaller than the ones they'd been passing, but were clean and well tended. "What was the number again?" Hugh asked.

"Two two one."

221 was mid-block, quiet like the others. After a bit of quibbling, Malcolm was the one who went to knock. No one was home. He went back to the car.

"Maybe he got held up at school," Hugh said, then gave a little laugh. "Gosh, I'm actually disappointed. I've never even played truant before. I had some stupid fantasy we'd drive up and I'd meet this dream man and ... I don't know. Live happily ever after?"

"I never promised that," Malcolm said. "No one can ever promise that. Believe me."

"Will he even know me?"

"No."

Hugh frowned. "Then what am I supposed to say?"

"Ask him if he needs a place to be safe. Ask him..." Malcolm thought. "Ask him about his grandfather's truck."

"Why?"

"It's his only escape route."

"And then what?"

"And then I don't know, Hugh. All I can tell you is that I saw him, and he saw me, and there was ... an understanding. One deeper than should happen just by accident."

Hugh started jiggling his leg up and down, but then he smiled. "I wish I had a recording of everything you've said."

Malcolm laughed, along with his other self. It was, he thought, one of the nicest things that had ever happened to him.

"Holy moly," Hugh said, the leg stopping. A young man was walking down the street towards them. "Is that him?"

They watched Nelson – for oh, yes, it was him – as he came down the pavement, head low, his posture hunched and closed.

"He looks unhappy," Malcolm said, and it took everything in him, all his training, not to get out of the car right then and take Nelson in his arms.

He had no idea what he expected of or for Hugh, really. No idea what future either of them could forge. They lived in two countries, for one thing; they were both teenagers in a world that didn't give teenagers much freedom. Was there even a chance for them?

Yes. There had to be. He had to at least *give* them that chance. If nothing else, they would both know there were chances to be had, even in this world.

Nelson never fully looked up as he turned into his walkway, took out a key, and entered his house.

"Your turn to go knock," Malcolm said.

337

"What am I supposed to say?" Hugh looked panicked. "This is crazy. This is completely crazy." He put his hands back on the wheel. "I'm not doing this. This is a dream that's now come to an end–"

Malcolm put his hand over Hugh's. The heat of Hugh's skin was surprising, almost shocking in this cold. Malcolm took Hugh's hand gently off the wheel and brought it up, pressing his face into it, letting Hugh feel his skin in return. Hugh let out a little gasp.

"For us," Malcolm said. "For him, but also for us."

"What do I–?"

"Just knock. Pretend you've made a mistake if it doesn't seem right. I swear to you, this isn't a trick. You can feel my flesh. You can feel that it's yours. I have to save you."

"Why?"

"Because no one saved me."

Malcolm released his hand, and without another word, Hugh got out of the car, closing the door behind him. Malcolm watched him gather his courage, heard him mutter, "This is crazy," but he crossed the street.

Malcolm found he couldn't watch Hugh knock, couldn't face seeing Nelson answer. Hugh had left the car running, so Malcolm clicked on the radio, anything to distract from the ache of Nelson being so close but so impossibly far.

"–estimated deaths could be in the hundreds of thousands," the radio said. Malcolm listened for a few minutes more. He glanced at Nelson's house, saw Hugh speaking, though Hugh stood in a way that was blocking Nelson from sight.

Which was for the best, Malcolm thought, as he slipped

quietly out the passenger's side and headed stealthily for the main road and hopefully a ride that would take him back south as fast as humanly possible.

"I'm just saying you guys should probably leave," Sarah said.

"My dad isn't going anywhere," Jason said, from the driver's seat. "You know how hard he worked for this farm?"

"I do."

"Do you? You're not the Sarah I knew. I don't know *what* you know about me."

They were sitting in Jason's dad's truck. The sun had gone down, but there was still no dragon in Frome. It had flown to Seattle instead, leaving it little more than smoking heaps on its seven hills. Estimates at the number of dead were still going up, and the best warplanes in the US military hadn't even made a dent in the dragon, according to Agent Dernovich, which didn't bode well for the army on its way here.

So what chance did she and Kazimir stand?

A prophecy. One stupid prophecy.

But it was at least a prophecy that had brought her here.

"My Jason lived with his dad, too," she said. "His mom died in an internment camp in Idaho during the War. I know how hard his dad worked for his farm. My Jason's dad was the one who suggested we hire Kazimir in the first place, so in a way, he started this whole thing."

"Kazimir," Jason said. "The one who's supposed to be a dragon on the inside."

Sarah shrugged. "I don't understand any of this either, but maybe we don't have to. There's a problem out there. Maybe we can fix it. And maybe..." She looked into his eyes. It was too dark to see the colour, but she knew the exact shade of brown they were, knew the small chickenpox scar just to the side of his nose (this Jason had it, too, she'd seen it in her mother's kitchen), saw the familiar way his jaw set when he was trying to figure something out. "Maybe we shouldn't question second chances when we get them."

"My mom died over there, too?" he said, quietly. "There's a second chance I'd have liked."

He tapped his hands on the steering wheel. That was a new habit, a different one for this Jason. So strange how the similarities could be as exact as a chickenpox scar, but as different as Sarah's mom being alive here.

"And now, a dragon," Jason said.

"We had plenty of those over there. A dragon isn't news to me."

"It sure is news here. Bad news."

"Which is why you should leave."

"Is that why you walked all the way out here?" he asked. "To warn us? About something we already knew?"

"Yes," she said. "Maybe. I don't know."

They sat in silence for a moment, then he said, "So that's why I was with you."

"What?"

"In your world. I was with you when the big attack happened. The one where, if I understand correctly, a woman shot me dead before she turned into the dragon that just destroyed Seattle."

"It was actually the Sheriff that shot you. Not that that helps."

340

"This is so crazy," Jason said, quietly. "All of it." He looked at her now, then looked away again. "Like I said, I did think about it." *Tap, tap, tap,* with his fingers. "About you."

"You really did?"

"Of course." He looked at her again. "But you died."

"There's a lot of that going around."

"Don't be funny. It was horrible. And it wasn't you. It's not like you've come back to life. A girl called Sarah still died."

Sarah nodded slowly. "So did a boy called Jason."

He tapped his hands on the steering wheel again. "Second chances," he whispered in the dark.

"It was almost over, though," she said. "You and me."

"What do you mean?"

"The school in Minnesota your dad is sending you to."

"What? My dad's not sending me to any school."

She opened her mouth to respond but the words didn't come immediately. She finally just said, stupidly, "He's not?"

"No," Jason said, laughing ruefully. "No way he trusts the world to treat me properly when he's not there to protect me. I'll go to college, but no farther than University of Washington." He frowned. "Which isn't there any more, is it?"

"I guess not."

"Well, don't give him any ideas about *Minnesota.*"

She laughed. "I won't."

He nodded, thinking. "Which means I'm staying around." He turned to her. "Are you?"

She felt that ache for him again, but this time it wasn't so hopeless, so heavy. It was almost pleasurable. She had lost him so completely, refound him so suddenly, and if it wasn't exactly the same, who knew what the future might hold?

"If we all get through this," she said, "I'm not sure what I'll do."

He nodded, seriously. "If we all get through this."

"I need to get back home," Sarah said. "My mom... *Darlene* wants me there in case the dragon comes. She won't leave either."

"Do you want me to be with you when it does?"

She could see his smile in the faint light. "Don't get cocky," she said, but she was smiling, too. "I want you as far away as absolutely possible."

She leaned over and kissed his cheek as she left, his delighted surprise following her back home.

"There you are," Darlene said, opening the back door before Sarah had even walked up the first porch step.

"I told you, I went to Jason's–"

"Yes, yes, come inside." Darlene practically dragged Sarah through the door.

"What's going on?" Sarah asked.

But Darlene was already turning and saying, "Here she is."

Gareth Dewhurst stood motionless in the middle of the kitchen. He held a hat down at his side in his left hand. When he saw Sarah, it tumbled right out of his fingers.

"My God," he whispered. "Darlene, what is this?"

"It's... Well, it's not quite our daughter, but..."

His voice sharpened. "You told me the farm was in danger from the thing that attacked Seattle–"

"And it is, Gareth–"

"Who the hell is this?"

"Language in my house," Darlene said, sharp.

"*Our* house. I'm still on the mortgage, remember? What the hell is going on here? Who *is* this?"

Sarah couldn't help herself. She knew she shouldn't, but she had waited as long as she could and then there was just nothing more but to move across the floor of the kitchen and grab her father around the chest in an embrace. His arms didn't move up to hug her back at first, but he didn't push her away. She held on and on.

Then she heard the breath, the telltale breath of her father about to say something.

"Her smell," he said, so quietly she might have been the only person in the room to hear him. "My God, she smells just like her."

"I think you could explain it to me a hundred times," Gareth Dewhurst said a little later, his face ashen, his eyes red with unsuccessfully withheld tears, "and I still wouldn't believe you."

"Gareth," Darlene started. "Don't you think I felt the same?"

"I don't know what you feel, Darlene," Gareth said. "I haven't for a long time."

"And you were Mister Understanding and Sympathy? Sarah died and you were out planting the next morning."

Her father raised his voice. "Yes, well, it was like two people died for me. My daughter and the walking corpse my wife turned into."

Darlene's face became a storm. "I didn't lose the same?"

"Darlene–"

"My dad planted the day after my mom died," Sarah said. They both turned to look at her. "I think he just had to do *something*, and that was the job that was there. I wish he'd... Well, I mean, I always wished he'd come in and hold me some in the days after, but I knew he still loved me. He planted so the farm would keep going, so we'd have a future. He kept trying. He taught me how to drive. He stood up for me when I needed it. He taught me how to deal with dragons." She was crying in full flow now. "He made mistakes, sure, and there were times I wished I had a father who was softer." She wiped her cheeks. "But I never wished for a father who was kinder. Sometimes you need something to lean against. Something holding you up so regular and strong you forget it's even there."

Her father – or not her father, but so close – crossed his arms slowly. "That's all very pretty," he said, "but it doesn't change anything."

"*Look* at her, you stubborn old fool," Darlene said. "You said yourself she smelled like our daughter."

"I'm *not* your daughter," Sarah said.

"See?" Gareth said.

"But I'm the daughter of Gareth and Darlene Dewhurst. I go to Frome High School with Jason Inagawa, son of Hisao Inagawa. I had three pigs called Bess, Mamie, and Eleanor. I'm good at math and English, but a bit slow in history. I hate onions, but you both forced me to eat them because they were from the vegetable patch. I can't sing, even when I try. I fall asleep sitting up in church sometimes..."

She trailed off. They were both staring at her hard now, their eyes wide.

"I'm not her," she said again, "but I'm a version of her. A version who didn't die. Just like you are to me."

Darlene let out a long sigh. She looked at Gareth. "You see why I asked you to come?"

He lowered his head. "Yeah. Yeah, I do."

"So what are we going to do about it?" Darlene asked.

He didn't answer. A long silence fell.

"Right now," Kazimir finally said, stepping in from the living room where he'd obviously been eavesdropping, "we are going to plan for the end of the world."

"By midnight," Agent Dernovich said, "soldiers and tanks will be coming down these roads. We're not even sure if they'll be in time." He glanced at Kazimir. "After the Seattle attack, we're not even one hundred per cent sure this is where the dragon is coming next."

"It is," Kazimir said. "She is waking up to herself, and she will know she is incomplete. She will come for the Spur, and if she gets it, this whole world is lost."

Sarah shook her head. "I still don't see how it can actually be hers if Malcolm only just chopped off her finger–?"

"Recurrence," Kazimir said. "Everything always happening, again and again. Maybe this Spur literally belongs to a world before, and the finger of the woman we saw will be the Spur in a world to come. All I can tell you, it is close enough. She will be after it." He grinned, weakly. "We have seen its power, have we not? What it can do to even a satellite?"

Agent Dernovich coughed. "What do you mean by that?"

"She blew up a Russian satellite," Sarah said. "Which

pretty much starts a war that will end all wars, but between men and men, not men and dragons."

"Which it turns out is what she wanted all along."

"I'm sorry," Agent Dernovich said, "you're saying, this person who turned into a dragon, she had a weapon that could destroy a *satellite*?"

Kazimir waved the Spur. "It is much more impressive when it lights up."

"And this satellite was enough to make her declare war on the entire world?"

"As a pretext," said Kazimir, "but yes."

Agent Dernovich stroked his chin. He glanced over at his daughter, asleep beneath a blanket on Darlene's couch. Or at least seeming so. He wouldn't put it past her to have been listening for the past several hours.

"What is it, Agent?" Darlene asked.

"We launched a satellite last month," he said. "We know the Russians are planning on launching their first later this year. We had to beat them to it. No one knows this. It's top secret."

Kazimir looked deeply thoughtful, concentrating so hard you could almost *see* him think. "My dear Agent Dernovich," he said at last. "I think we might now have a plan that could actually work."

26

She flew above the clouds after destroying the city, out of sight of any eyes that might follow her. She needed time to think.

Maybe she *could* conquer the world on her own. Maybe they'd come to her with an offer of surrender. They'd seen her might. Perhaps she could tell them about the dragon brood currently waiting to hatch. Maybe they'd roll right over and she'd never have to breathe another flicker of fire.

Unbidden, she thought of the woman in the skirt again. Of the way she fell. The way she screamed.

The way the dragon formerly known as Agent Woolf had caught her and set her free. Well, not free exactly as she was running into almost certain death, but moving from certain to almost certain was still an act of unexpected mercy, wasn't it? Possibly the most a dragon could give to a human.

She still couldn't find the thought in herself that had triggered the saving, though. The woman obviously looked a bit like she had done all those years, and for all those lifetimes before, trapped in the body of the enemy, memories that now came rolling back to her from generation upon generation.

No, she must not forget herself. Humanity had been forced upon her like a cattle brand. She was not human. She had simply worn their skin. For a time.

For a long, long time.

She flew through the winter sky. She couldn't even smell planes in the distance, not military nor passenger. They had clearly emptied the air when they realized what else was flying up here.

She guided herself by smell, knew exactly where her brood lay, ready to hatch. She could smell other things, too, could in fact smell nearly *everything*, it was almost overwhelming. The soup of humans and their bodies and their industries, masking but not entirely drowning the scents of the lands and the forests and the animals within them and the contents of those animals' stomachs and the blood that pulsed in their veins and the pheromones they gave off for one another and the sap in the trees they·ran by and the needles on those trees and the chipmunks that hibernated there and–

She shook her head. All right. There would be a period of adjustment. She was obviously getting all of herself back now. Who knew what power she might end up with? She could feel it thrumming in her, almost as if even this great body wouldn't be enough to contain her. How had that human-sized one ever done so?

She aimed a direct course for her brood.

* * *

They were even closer to hatching than she expected. Her instinct had told her days, but now she was thinking one day, maybe less. She could feel herself running hot with magic. Of course it would translate to her offspring.

Very well. She had destroyed one city, all on her own. With her brood, she would do the same again – she could smell Vancouver farther north and Portland to the south – and then she would move on to somewhere truly major. Los Angeles, maybe, so spread out she would need her children.

She would do it until they surrendered. Then she would take their surrender and throw it in their faces as she destroyed New York, London, Paris, Moscow, destroyed so thoroughly they would lose their names, their history, anyone who ever remembered them.

Their world had already fallen. They just didn't know it yet.

There was one last thing to get. She'd felt it as she destroyed Seattle. That on top of all her strength–

There was yet more.

When she was complete.

She was incomplete. Missing a claw, one that, in the recurring way dragon magic worked, had somehow followed her into this world.

For her to conquer, for her brood to thrive, for all the broods after that to proliferate, she instinctively knew she would have to be whole, knew it with the same clarity she knew she was a Goddess.

She had been foolish to fly straight to safety when she'd entered this world, but she had been disoriented, her body changing with an excruciating violence, her mind suddenly teeming with everything she had been forced to forget. A crime had been committed upon her, and it was no wonder there was a process to go through to uncreate it.

She knew where it was, though. Could smell it even from this distance. It was nearly inert here, but once it was part of her again, dragon magic would start flowing into this world properly.

She would rest. She would, if they kept up at this rate, maybe even see her babies born. Perhaps she would take them all down to reclaim what was hers. Yes, maybe that was actually the next step. They had seen what one dragon could do. They would cower before her and her children.

She hoped this world slept well tonight. It was the last good night they would ever have.

She woke the next morning with a start. At first, she was sure the eggs were hatching, but there they all sat, incipient but not quite there just yet.

There was a new scent in the air.

She took to her wings and flew.

27

Kazimir pulled the Spur of the Goddess across his hand. A thickness of black blood filled his palm. The Spur started to glow, still only a little but more than before. Kazimir said the Goddess was awakening to herself, bringing more dragon magic into the world every moment. It was the only plan they had. If she hadn't come to them by dawn, they would try to give her an invitation she couldn't resist.

"It's weird your blood didn't change," Sarah said to him now.

"Yes," he said. "I have enough magic to save that much of myself, but it would be a problem in this world if I ailed, would it not? A doctor here might have strong opinions." He smiled at her. "Then again, if this does not work, ailing will be the least of my worries."

Sarah looked across the fields of her farm and the Inagawas'. The sun was just coming up, the clouds thinning enough for them to actually see it behind Mount Rainier, which had also put in an appearance. But she wasn't looking at the mountain.

She was looking at the army, not two hundred yards away.

The tanks had started arriving at midnight, on the back of flatbed trucks. Troop trucks followed, and in the space of a few predawn hours, several thousand soldiers were bivouacked around her home.

They all held weapons. Rifles and pistols, but also bazookas and Gatling guns and flamethrowers ("Ridiculous," Kazimir had said), all to back up the tanks. Agent Dernovich had said missile-carrying planes would be on their way, too.

"What kind of missiles?" Gareth Dewhurst had asked.

Agent Dernovich had not answered.

"They will bomb us with nuclear weapons if this does not work, you know," Kazimir said, holding the still-glowing Spur up to the breeze.

"At least they evacuated the town," Sarah said.

"It was for show. If this plan fails, they will bomb this entire county into oblivion, just to be sure."

She gave him a look. "How do you know that?"

"Do you honestly think the agent would keep his daughter at his side if he thought there was safety elsewhere?"

"Is the dragon coming, Daddy?" Grace asked.

Her father lowered his binoculars. "Not yet, sweetie."

"But she will."

"I think she will, yes."

They were behind the front line, well back at the Dewhurst farm, watching out from the hayloft doors on the second floor of the barn. Darlene and Gareth were there, too, and Hisao Inagawa, though not Jason, as Hisao had forced his son to evacuate with the others, an evacuation that, yes, Agent Dernovich knew was just for show. General Kraft had made his orders quite clear if the plan of the strange-eyed dragon boy and the girl from another world failed. Who knew? Maybe the tanks and the troops would do the job on their own.

They probably wouldn't.

He stroked his daughter's hair. The bombs they would drop weren't the bombs used on Hiroshima and Nagasaki, as terrible as they were. In the nearly twelve years since then, nuclear weapons had grown exponentially more powerful. What they dropped on this county would evaporate everything within twenty miles, burn everything to death sixty miles beyond that, and poison everyone with a fast-killing cancer in at least a two-hundred-mile radius. And still they didn't know for sure if it was enough to kill the dragon.

If this went wrong, there was genuinely no way to save his precious Grace. He would not have that happen to her alone and frightened. She would be in his arms, knowing at least someone was trying to protect her.

He would just have to do everything in his power to ensure it didn't go wrong.

"Will she come here to the barn?" Grace said, and he noticed how they all had slipped into the *she* of Kazimir and the girl.

"She'll be stopped by what they've got planned. If she's not, that's what the army is for. Trust me, sweetheart, everyone here is *very* motivated to stop that dragon."

"Or Russian contraption," Gareth Dewhurst grumbled. "I still can't believe it's an actual *dragon*."

"You wouldn't believe God Himself if He came to our front door handing out loaves and fishes," Darlene grumbled back.

"What would God Himself be doing in Frome?" Hisao added. "I wouldn't believe Him either."

Agent Dernovich could see how close the Dewhursts were standing together, how Gareth's left arm draped across Darlene, how she leaned ever closer to his side.

"Is everything going to be okay?" Grace asked. He saw she had tucked her book into her little waistband. Somewhere along the way, it had become the security blanket he'd made her give up when she was five. If they got out of this, she could carry that book for the rest of her life, for all he minded now.

He lifted his binoculars again. "Absolutely, sweetheart."

He hoped he was right. With all his being, he hoped he was right.

Malcolm raced down the middle of the road on foot, between the logjam of oncoming traffic on either side. Cars honked at one another, at him, at their sheer frustration at not moving. A woman leaned her head out of her passenger window. "Where you going, kid?" she shouted as he ran past. "We gotta evacuate!"

He ignored her, as he had the previous five people who'd shouted, as he'd ignored the police officer who'd actually tried to block his way. Malcolm was sorry for it, but that police officer was currently nursing a broken elbow for his efforts.

What had happened in Seattle was unthinkable. It was the greatest fear in his own world, the outcome both sides had spent their entire histories trying to avoid, and she had done it in an afternoon. One dragon, an entire city, maybe a million dead, and that would be only the beginning. He had to get back.

Which had proved exceedingly difficult. There was no longer a freeway south, because several major bridges of it had been taken out by a dragon. This left the other roads packed with cars fleeing the area around the city. Hardly anyone had wanted to go towards it, and he'd had a devil of a time getting *around* it, finally stealing a running car from a lady who only that morning had bought him breakfast out of the kindness of her heart.

Again, he was sorry, he was sorry for so very, very much, but he had to get back. If he did, maybe he could help set things right, maybe he could start making up for everything he had done.

"The Russians are coming!" a man yelled out his window.

"They really aren't," Malcolm said, under his breath.

He wasn't going to get there, not on foot. He'd had to abandon the car he'd stolen miles out of town as both lanes of every road he found were crowded with people fleeing. He stopped in the middle of the tarmac, eyeing the cars around him. He'd have to steal one again, drive it on the embankment or over fields or *something*. A frightened family looked out the windows of a station wagon on one side of him; another frightened family looked out of a pre-War Ford on the other.

Could he strand an entire family?

"I'm sorry," he said, turning to the family in the station wagon.

"Assassin guy?" he heard.

He spun around. Three cars down on the left, Jason Inagawa leaned out the driver's side window of his dad's truck, waving frantically. Malcolm ran towards him.

"What are you doing *here*?" Jason asked as he arrived.

"I need your truck," Malcolm said.

"Well, hop in," Jason said, unlocking the passenger door.

"No," Malcolm said, still standing on the driver's side. "It's too dangerous. I have to go alone."

"And stick me on the roadside? I don't think so."

"I'm sorry but–"

"Do you know the back roads well enough to get farther than half a mile?"

Malcolm hesitated. Perhaps there was Providence after all, even if it didn't come from the Mitera Thea.

He ran around, got in the truck, and said, "We have to hurry."

Jason started the tortuous process of getting out of the gridlock and up onto the embankment. "Why so fast?" he asked, spinning the wheel.

"She's coming," Malcolm said. "I can feel it."

Malcolm looked out the back window, as if he could see her.

He paused.

"What do you have in the back of your truck?"

"Kazimir," Sarah said, her wide eyes looking at the Spur in his hand.

It was glowing brighter. And brighter.

"She's coming," Kazimir said.

* * *

She flew towards the scent of dragon blood. She had smelled it before, smelled the weakness in it, the blue was truly inferior, but this time there was a scent of something else, something in the air like a living razor. The clouds were still thick heading north, away from her brood, but the twin smells rang like a clarion bell.

She knew what it was. She knew everything now. It had all come back to her.

Dragon blood and dragon magic.

She would greet them with fire. She would greet them with death. And when she had the Spur, there was nothing – not one single thing in this wretched dragon-free world – that could stop her.

She pumped her wings faster. The clouds broke open.

"Now," Kazimir said, quietly, as the distant dragon appeared.

"Now?" Sarah asked.

He looked at her, incredulous at being questioned at this of all moments, and she ran to the side of the field, towards the fence that marked the beginning of the Inagawas' land. They weren't stupid; they were pretty sure the dragon would come in flaming, but Kazimir thought he could stop her before that.

Only thought, though, so Sarah was to run the instant they spotted her and hope she went for Kazimir first. *And not the girl prophesied to defeat her,* Sarah thought, leaping over the low wooden fence and hiding. *This plan makes perfect sense.*

Here came the dragon.

"Here she comes," Agent Dernovich said, still looking through his binoculars.

"Holy God," Hisao whispered.

"Where's Sarah?" Gareth asked.

"She's moved as planned," Agent Dernovich said.

"For all the good it will do her," Darlene muttered, but she put her arm through her ex-husband's. He held it tightly back.

Agent Dernovich felt a little tug at his own elbow. Grace, eyes on the dragon flying towards the field, had reached up, asking to take his hand. He gave it to her with gratitude, using the other to hold his binoculars.

There was nothing they could do but watch.

She saw him, the dragon now dressed as a man, alone in a field. She smelled the girl from the other world, hiding behind a fence off to one side. She saw the tanks and troops arrayed behind them, and she laughed to herself, actually laughed.

This would be so easy. So very, very easy.

The ground flew past as she lowered herself towards it, slowing but staying in the air. She got close enough to see his face.

"Goddess!" she heard him yell. "I wish to speak with you!"

She opened her mouth and buried him in flame.

Sarah screamed as the fire geysered down from the great dragon's mouth. In all her life, she had only seen dragons flame for farm work. That was impressive enough: the disintegration of fields, the casual way Kazimir himself would vaporize stumps and debris.

It was *nothing* like this.

She could feel her face burning even from this distance and had to turn away. The air seemed to boil. She struggled to breathe, falling face down into the snow which was already turning to steam around her. The flannel of her shirt grew so hot she thought it would burst into flames.

She was sure she was dying.

"Oh, dear God," Darlene said, her hand to her mouth. "That poor boy."

"We should have run," Hisao said. "Why didn't we run?"

"Because there's nowhere to run to," Grace said, calmly, too calmly. Agent Dernovich put an arm around her, pulling her close.

"Let this play out," he said, having to look away from the binoculars because the dragonfire was so bright.

"*Play out?*" Gareth shouted. "That thing just killed that—"

"Wait," Darlene said, grasping his arm.

"Are you finished?" Kazimir asked, as the smoke cleared.

The dragon formerly known as Agent Veronica Woolf was so surprised she dropped to the ground in front of him.

He was now standing in a crater of bare earth, all grass

and snow burnt away, the soil beneath blackened into charcoal. All his clothes had been annihilated from his body, but he stood there quite whole, if completely naked, the hair on his head barely ruffled. His eye scarf was gone, but the stitching still held his eye shut.

"I am dragon," he said to her. "Dragonfire does not harm dragon."

"You wear their shape," she said. "Dragonfire may not harm you, but claws and teeth surely will."

She took a step towards him.

"We can solve this," he said.

She took another step. And another.

"This does not have to end this way."

She picked up speed, smiling now.

He sighed, and said, "They know how to find where you hide."

This stopped her cold. "What did you say?"

"You destroyed the satellite in the other world," he said. "You were driven to do it. Perhaps not even knowing why. But you forgot to ensure this world did not have one either."

She raised her head. "You're bluffing. I've not seen nor smelled anything–"

"You did not look enough. Because of you, the satellite now knows how to find the heat signature of a dragon. Not an issue in a world teeming with dragons, but in a world where they only need to find one? You do know a direct hit from one of their nuclear weapons would probably destroy even you, Goddess."

"They would not dare."

"You killed a million people. They would dare." He

clenched his hand; more black blood came out. "I used to laugh at them, just as you do. At their *society*. Their lack of honour. Their lies." He took the Spur into his bloody hand. "When you get to know them as a dragon, though, they can still be quite wondrous."

"I lived as one for thousands of years. You have nothing new to tell me about them. I know their cowardice, their avarice, their hate. They proliferate like a disease. I am superior to them in every conceivable fashion." She was smiling now. "And when my brood hatches—"

There was a silent flash of light on the horizon, so far away no sound was heard yet. They all turned at the brightness of it, a ring of light rising into the sky, evaporating the clouds above it.

Then the sound came. A rumble like an earthquake, rolling and rolling and rolling.

"Your brood," Kazimir said, "will not hatch."

"What the hell was that?" Gareth Dewhurst asked.

"The General dropped a quarter-strength nuke on the crater of Mount St Helens," Agent Dernovich said, his voice disbelieving.

"Why?" Darlene asked.

"It was supposed to be just a threat," Dernovich said. Kazimir had told them what the Goddess would almost certainly be doing and where might be good places for a satellite to look. But it was meant to be a bargaining chip to drive her back to her own world or, failing that, at least a ceasefire to ensure other cities didn't burn. Exile or treaty was their only hope, but the General had clearly been unable to resist the nest, not when it was unguarded by the mother.

A mother who would now be enraged.

"You kill my children?" she screamed. "This is supposed to convince me to bow to you?"

"They were not supposed to bomb them," Kazimir said, visibly shocked.

"And this is the species you trust, blue?" she sneered.

"I never said I trusted them." He looked her in the eye. "But you know, even you, deep down, know that we need them."

Her fury went from hot to cold, which was in no way an improvement. She lowered her head so that she was level with Kazimir. "I am a Goddess. I am a Creator. I will birth another brood. They will still not stop me."

"Perhaps not," Kazimir said, "but she will."

He held up his hand, the signal for Sarah to come out from behind the fence.

Sarah nearly missed it. She had been consciously looking away from Kazimir's nakedness – again, this had been such a weird week – when fire wasn't being breathed or mountaintops being nuked. But now he was waving urgently (for him). Ignoring the mind-warping terror that told her to run the other way, she jumped back over the fence. The ground gave off waves of heat that bent the air like tarmac on a hot summer day. She stumbled a couple times, but kept going towards his outstretched hand.

Towards the giant red dragon, watching Sarah like fury itself.

Darlene gripped Gareth's arm tighter. "There she goes."

"This is madness," he whispered. "Oh, please be safe."

"You said she wasn't our daughter," Darlene said, but gently.

"Close enough," Gareth said.

"And what exactly will she do?" the Goddess said, watching Sarah stop next to Kazimir. "She will not survive my flames so easily."

"She will stop you," Kazimir said. "The prophecies say so."

The dragon billowed out her wings, and Sarah remembered the pose from Kazimir on the night they hired him in the gas station parking lot. She was making herself look her most threatening, as if Sarah wasn't terrified enough–

Then she realized the dragon was frightened of *her*.

It took all of Sarah's courage not to back away as she came nearer. And nearer. She felt Kazimir take her hand, the other still holding the Spur of the Goddess, sticky with his own blood.

The dragon brought two great nostrils up to Sarah and inhaled hugely, again reminding her of that night by the gas station.

"There is no magic in her," the dragon said, watching Sarah from less than a foot away. "She is human, through and through. She is nothing special."

"She never has been," Kazimir said.

"Then what am I doing here?" Sarah squeaked, unable to not watch the Goddess.

"The prophecy said you would be in the right place at the right time," Kazimir said. "And so you are."

He leapt forward and, just like Malcolm had done to him in another world, he slashed at the dragon's neck with her own Spur.

"He's made his move," Agent Dernovich said, still watching through the binoculars.

He felt Grace pressed against him and held her tight. He saw Darlene and Gareth do the same, Darlene taking Hisao's hand, too.

The world rested in the balance.

The dragon flinched, a winged claw flying to her neck to feel the wound. She roared, but then she laughed.

"A scratch," she said, leaning back down towards Kazimir. "That was your plan? Have the girl distract me, while you tried to kill me with my own claw? I shall chew you both alive, then spit out your screaming bones."

"I was not trying to kill you," Kazimir said. "My blood alone was not enough."

"Enough for what?" the dragon said.

Intoning the words, invoking the magic through her blood, Kazimir activated the Spur of the Goddess and shot her with the same spiral of light that had so recently destroyed a satellite.

* * *

The blast was even stronger than Kazimir had warned. It had been enough to take down a massive hunk of metal from space, he'd told Agent Dernovich, it should be enough to take down a dragon without anyone else having to die.

But it needed dragon blood for that. A more potent, purer kind than Kazimir's changed body could offer.

Well, he'd got that, Agent Dernovich thought, having to look away from the binoculars for a second time as the light blazed. He'd got the blood of a Goddess.

"Please work," Darlene said next to him. "Oh, please work."

"Daddy?" Grace said by his side.

"Hide your eyes, sweetheart," he said.

"Daddy, it's not working."

He shielded his eyes with his hand and looked back out into the field of battle.

It wasn't working.

It wasn't working. The light was hitting her, just as it had the radio tower, just as it had the satellite, but it was like she was being sprayed with a strong fire hose. It knocked her back, but didn't seem to be doing her any harm. It was as ineffective as dragonfire.

Kazimir finally lowered the Spur as she rose into the air.

"Shit," Kazimir said, then he turned to Sarah. "Run!"

They ran. The dragon wheeled in the air, a roar of pure fury coming out of her now, as she turned on them.

"No," Sarah said, sprinting for the fence, as if those three feet of wood planks were going to protect her. "Please."

Kazimir was looking behind as they went, firing the Spur at the dragon again and again, trying desperately to keep her at bay. "It did not work!" he shouted.

"No kidding!"

"But the prophecy!"

He fired again, but she was on them, above them. They could even see the cold air turning to steam as it roared down her throat, ready to incinerate them.

The army opened fire.

Grace screamed wordlessly as the barrage began. The tanks all fired, the big guns throwing out their charges, the soldiers firing their guns.

"Sarah!" Darlene yelled, turning to Agent Dernovich, who barely heard her over the roar of firepower. "They'll kill her!"

Agent Dernovich shook his head. "There's nothing we can do."

"What do you mean?" Gareth said, but then he saw how Agent Dernovich picked up his daughter, how he held her close against his chest, closed his eyes and softly kissed her on the head.

It was then that Gareth Dewhurst began to pray.

The first tank mortars hit her on the neck, knocking her to one side. They exploded against her skin, and they *hurt*.

But they did not kill her.

She flapped her great wings harder as the small explosions continued against her chest and wings and legs. Still she rose. The bullets were as nothing. The charges from the bigger guns hurt like pellets, but did no damage. She could endure the mortars. She could certainly endure them long enough to melt the tanks where they stood.

Sarah screamed against the sound of the artillery. It was so loud, she thought she'd go mad. She felt a weight against her back and only slowly realized it was Kazimir, trying to shield her from any stray bullet or shrapnel that came their way. They were in an insanely dangerous place, but running would have been suicide.

She turned her head up to his.

"It's over," she said. "Isn't it?"

He nodded slowly, and she knew it really was. They had failed to stop the dragon, failed to even hurt her much. There was no option left but to drop the biggest bomb the army had on top of her and hope it did the trick.

Everything was lost. Her family there. Her family here. Both Jasons. And soon all hope. Kazimir's arms were around her neck, and in the cataclysm of the barrage, she took them in her hands and held him tight back.

It was the end. They would face it together.

"You were remarkable," he said into her ear.

"You, too," she said.

They huddled against the ground and waited for the world to end.

They would all die. All of them.

She flew straight into the barrage, carving a line of gathered forces with as hot a fire as she could create. Soldiers didn't even have time to scream as they were atomized. Tanks exploded, melting into vapour as they flew through the air.

They would die. They would pay for killing her brood. They would pay for not bowing to her. They would pay for the lives she'd had to lead as one of them for too long.

She remembered who she was.

She was a Goddess.

She destroyed another row of tanks, another row of soldiers, flying fast along the front line, pulling up to circle around for another pass. She knew they would try to bomb her. She knew it must be coming any moment, but she would knock the planes from the sky.

There'd be nothing to stop her.

Mortar and tank fire followed her. One blast punched a small hole in her wing. She cried out in pain, wheeled to one side and found herself flying straight for a barn.

The dragon shifted suddenly in the air, and in a split second, was heading right for them. Agent Dernovich vaguely heard the Dewhursts and Mr Inagawa cry out.

He held Grace away from what was coming. He would face the dragon. He would face it so his daughter wouldn't have to.

* * *

There was a man still standing on the open second floor of the barn. Others were trying to escape, but this man stood his ground as she steadied herself in the air with the hole in her wing. It was difficult, but it was doable.

The man's face...

His smell...

She knew it.

He held a little girl in his arms, but it was him she knew.

She flapped her great wings to slow herself, landing in a muddy part of the drive.

"You," she said.

The man stared back at her, eyes wide.

"Dernovich," she said. The mortars were still firing, loud and heavy, but the barn seemed just slightly out of range. That would change soon, of course, they would be on their way, as would the planes.

"You know me?" the man shouted, astonished but still not fleeing. "How do you know me?"

She didn't answer. As Veronica Woolf, she had regretted shooting Agent Dernovich, even though in her mind it had been required. He had been an oaf and an overbearing partner, but he had treated her expertise seriously, which was more than most men at the Bureau did. And he was dedicated to his job, dedicated – if he'd only known – to stopping her. So she had killed him.

But here he stood.

The feeling was the same as when she saw the woman. The one who fell. The one she caught. The one she freed.

Recognition. A pause. Could she burn this man? She had shot him once before.

But he had no children in the other world. Had regretted it bitterly. And here he obviously had a daughter, they smelled so similar. Could she so consciously kill his little–

His little girl.

No.

No.

A girl with no special powers, a girl simply in the right place at the right time, a girl who would be responsible for dooming her–

She had paused too long.

As she took in her breath to destroy them, Jason Inagawa, unheard under the artillery, drove a truck directly into her belly, his family's steel plough attached to the hood.

She cried out. Instead of a blast of pure fire, a rush of acid spilled from her mouth. She fell forward, over the truck as she felt something break inside her, something terrible, something final.

"No," she said, her great voice gurgling as she collapsed, unable to even flash her claws at the two boys running out from either side. Her head hit the ground. She was unable to raise it as the great engine of fire inside her burst its banks, ravaging her organs, burning them, melting them.

She looked up to the last face she expected to see. The last face she ever would see. "My son," she said, in agony, in shock. "You killed me, my son."

"Goodbye, Mitera Thea," was all Malcolm said.

A pulse of magic flew out of her in a great circle, unleashed from her body, all that had ever bound her together and allowed her to live, to be, to destroy, exploded from her. It blew out the windows of the farmhouse and knocked Malcolm and Jason back as it shot into the great world beyond.

The dragon who had been Agent Veronica Woolf was dead.

28

"One blow?" Agent Dernovich said, as they stood over her corpse later, after he had called off the nukes, after emergency services were flown in to tend the wounded, after Malcolm had made an effort to explain who he was. "All that, and it only took one blow to kill her?"

"You have to know exactly where." Malcolm glanced up to Agent Dernovich, who was surprised to see tears in his eyes. "It's a rare chance, almost a folk legend. And exceptionally difficult to pull off."

"No kidding," Agent Dernovich said. He was still holding Grace. She hadn't let him put her down, even when he was making his phone calls, and to be fair, he hadn't put up much of a fight.

Malcolm kept watching her.

* * *

So did Kazimir and Sarah. "It wasn't me, after all," Sarah said. "I wasn't the girl."

"Without you," Kazimir said, "I would have never got the Goddess's blood. Which would have never put her in the right place to *see* the other girl. Not that I had any idea what was happening at the time, to be honest, but there it is. Prophecy." He shrugged, back in the clothes of Gareth Dewhurst, another bandanna tied around his lost eye. "You were crucial."

"My father died in the other world for my crucialness," she said. "And Jason."

"But billions here were saved." He gently put an arm around her. "It feels like a terrible exchange. And it is. But she is defeated, which she would not be if you were not you."

"Me, the girl who wasn't special."

He sighed. "You saved a world. I would take your brand of non-special any day."

There was a crowd outside the farmhouse. Soldiers guarding what was now a kind of crime scene around the corpse of the dragon. General Kraft wanted Kazimir and Sarah for questioning, but Agent Dernovich had given them his sworn promise that they would be free to go after that, as much as General Kraft wanted to learn more about the dragon hiding under Kazimir's skin.

"I told the General you wouldn't take kindly to that," Agent Dernovich had said to them. "So we're just going to call you an Ambassador, which has a special status."

"That convinced him, did it?" Kazimir had said in return.

"I hate to say it," the agent said, "but if you stay here, you're going to need an ally. I'll be that ally, if you allow me.

I saw what you did here. I won't forget it."

"So are you?" Sarah asked Kazimir now.

"Am I what?"

"Staying here? In this world?"

"Give up my dragon form?" He looked at the bandage on his hand, where the blood stained black. "Or face another world war in the one we came from and perhaps give up any form forever?" He looked at her. "Not my favourite choice. What about you?"

Sarah saw her parents – well, she saw Darlene and Gareth Dewhurst standing together, really *together*. They'd not left each other's side. Darlene had offered her her old room back if she wanted it.

"I've got nothing to go back to," she told Kazimir.

He squeezed her shoulders. "It will be nice to have a friend here."

"Does that mean you'll never be a dragon again?"

"I will *always* be a dragon, Sarah Dewhurst, no matter how I look." He turned to the corpse of the Goddess, massive still, terrifying still, a hill all on its own on this little farm, tucked away in this little corner of the state. "Besides, you saw it when she died. We all saw it."

"That pulse?"

"That pulse. A Goddess can never truly be killed. Her magic is all over the world now. *Dragon* magic."

"Which means?"

He looked concerned. "It means this world may have some adjusting to do."

* * *

Sheriff Kelby got to his feet in his office. He hadn't evacuated with everyone else and was still fuming that he hadn't been allowed to take part in the army manoeuvres against the monster. In his own town! He was brooding over ways to make that agent pay for the slight when a kind of pulse had come through the wall, throwing him off his feet, banging his head against his desk, and knocking him out cold.

He was awake now. He assumed at first it had been the shock wave from another bomb, closer this time, but if that were true, how could he still be breathing?

He shifted his arm, which still hurt in his cast.

He felt weird. He felt...

Strong.

"Better not be radiation," he said, putting his free hand to the back of his head, feeling the wound there from the desk, still wet.

He drew back his hand to look at the blood.

His eyes widened when he saw it was black.

"But I feel strong," Kazimir said. "Stronger than I have felt since I got here. The magic rises. Who knows where it will stop? Perhaps I will be able to change shapes at will."

"That's a terrifying thought."

"An exciting one." He turned and smirked as he backed away towards the approaching General. "Especially if you are the Ambassador."

* * *

While Kazimir walked towards the General's temporary tent – Agent Dernovich and daughter by his side – Sarah found Jason with Malcolm, looking at the wreckage of the truck.

"How's your dad taking it?" she asked him.

"Pretty well," Jason said, "what with me being alive and the dragon being dead and all." He smiled in that shy way she'd known so well from the Jason in her world. "Still think he's kinda mad, though. The plough was the most valuable thing we owned and it melted in the belly of a dragon."

"He'll get over it," she said. "Everyone likes a hero for a son."

Jason nodded towards Malcolm. "He's the hero. His idea. He's the one who insisted we drive through that war zone with explosions all over the place. We could have died."

She saw that his hands were shaking a little. She reached over and took one. He let her hold it.

"But you didn't," she said.

He smiled that shy smile again. Malcolm approached them. "The General's taken Kazimir into his tent," he said to Sarah. "I think now's the time."

"Are you sure?" she asked him.

"Absolutely," he said.

Kazimir barely engaged with the General's questions, listening and answering with only part of his mind. He talked about the Goddess, how she had created dragons, how they had all come to be in his world, but sorry, the Spur of the Goddess had been destroyed in the battle so there would be no more going back and forth. This was a lie, but not one that required his full attention.

With the rest of his brain, he considered the future, now that there was one. The Goddess would find a way to return, if not completely as herself, then as the vast wave of magic he still felt rippling through this world. There might even be dragons born today, and not from her brood. If not now, then probably soon, and it was another reason for him to stay that he had not told Sarah, nor quite yet the General, who would be heavily discomfited.

Because that was the great secret. The greatest of them all. The Goddess hatched dragons, of course, as the Creator across worlds, but that was only the smallest part of the dragon population, a dozen here, a dozen there, over millennia. It was not, however, where most dragons had come from, *still* came from.

Most dragons started as human.

And so did the Goddess herself.

She'd been the first to find an accidental hole in the world, one that she reached into with a hand and pulled out of with the Spur. She was a woman so impressive, so powerful, this untamed magic had not killed her. It had changed her instead. She became the Goddess in an explosion that tore the skins from certain men and women across many worlds, those too fiery, too prickly with yearning, too *much* – good and bad – for the normal world. A whole society was born, one that, in its arrogance, immediately set about erasing all knowledge of its origins. The Goddess even made herself forget she was human become myth.

Because this was the other secret. There *was* no dragon magic. There was only human magic. All they wished for, all they yearned for, all their unfulfilled *reach* that shone out of them like the sun. It burned from them every day, boiling just out of sight between worlds. The simple fact was, if there were not humans around to create it, the unreality of dragons would cease to be.

All annihilation was mutual in the end.

"I still feel if I'd had any of this information earlier," the General was saying, somewhere distant to Kazimir's thoughts, "Seattle could have been saved."

"How many people died when you bombed a mountain you promised not to, General?" Kazimir replied, still barely paying attention.

The blues were guardians of this secret human/dragon knowledge, and they had gone to great lengths across many worlds to ensure the survival of both species. Which was really only one species and its personified (dragonified?) aspirations. Every human would be a dragon if they could. Why else were there people like the Believers? Kazimir himself was proof. He was born human, but had an exceedingly powerful drive that would have driven him mad had he not accidentally found his way to the Russian Wastes two hundred years ago. They had granted him his true form and begun to teach him the ways of dragons, thinking him the best vessel to counteract the prophecies to come.

In that, they had been wrong. He had not been enough to stop the destruction of the last world. It angered him, all this loss. Dragons regretted very little, but he knew he would never shed this failure.

On the other hand, as he had tried to explain to Sarah, perhaps this *was* the version that saved the most. Or perhaps in the next world, the next *Kazimir* would find a way to save absolutely everyone. As he'd said, he would never know for sure, and that was hard, especially for a scholar.

Either way, he felt it in his dragon bones, his dragon *blood*: the explosion of magic that had created dragons in all the other worlds was finally about to happen in this one.

"And that will be something to see," he said.

The General looked irritated. "Are you even listening to me, dragon?"

"Forgotten my name so quickly?" Kazimir replied, with a smile that clearly irritated the General even more. Kazimir glanced over at Dernovich and his daughter. The man had kept his promise, had been an ally in both the parameters of this interview and the interview itself, stopping the General from being too rude or too threatening. A good man, with a good daughter.

Allies, he thought. *I have allies here. And a friend, a* human *friend, in the really quite special Sarah Dewhurst.*

It was a pity they were going to lose Malcolm, who Kazimir found quite handsome. For a human. This world would need good men and women in the days to come.

Kazimir made a decision.

"Let me tell you about your future, General."

Epilogue

They walked out behind the barn, away from the farmhouse, away from the hustle and bustle of the soldiers. Malcolm had agreed to an interview later. Kazimir was in his. Sarah had gladly agreed to be next. No one expected or could have known what they were about to do.

Sarah and Malcolm – and Jason, who'd come along out of curiosity – walked past Bess, Mamie, and Eleanor, oinking happily as they saw Sarah. The three humans went behind the barn, and Malcolm took the Spur out of his pocket.

"They're going to be really mad when they find out it wasn't actually destroyed, just stolen," Jason said.

"Do you trust a weapon this powerful with someone who'd nuke a mountaintop?" Malcolm said. "I don't even trust *myself* with it."

"You realize what you're going back to," Sarah said. "A world where you might see more than a mountaintop nuked. They might already be dropping bombs there."

"Doesn't matter," he said. "I have to find him."

"It's been days," Sarah said. "He could be anywhere."

"Wherever he is, I left him in a pile of trouble. I have to get him out of it." He met her eyes, as he so rarely had in this world. "I'm sorry," he said. "I'm sorry for everything that led to this. I'm sorry for coming to kill you."

"You failed, though," Sarah said, with a slight smile, "so that turned out okay."

"Everything I was ever taught was a lie." He looked at the Spur in his hand. "But it still led to the right place."

He was surprised when he felt a sudden pressure of arms around him. Sarah was hugging him. He slowly put one hand on her back to return it. He would probably never see her again. This unknown girl who had played the largest part in shaping his life and who he had only actually known for the briefest few days.

She let him go. "I'll ask you one last time," Sarah said. "Are you *sure*?"

"I have to," Malcolm said. "I love him."

"Love him?" Jason said, looking confused. "Like a brother?"

Sarah stepped away, bringing Jason with her. Malcolm took a deep breath. There was magic in this world now. Too much. It would cause trouble. But it also was enough to make the Spur of the Goddess work again.

He touched it into the ground and said the words. An aura started to glow.

He would find Nelson, one way or another. If Nelson was in jail, he would break him out. If he was on the run, Malcolm would get him to safety. He would offer his love, offer an apology and amends, offer, at the very least, to take him away from a world at war. But he would find him. And he would offer him his hand. He could only hope Nelson would take it.

The aura opened, smaller this time, less out of control. It was all he needed. Malcolm took one last look at Sarah and Jason, who were holding hands again. He nodded to them, then – grabbing the Spur as he went – he stepped out of this world and into the next, intent on finding his love.

Enjoyed *Burn*?
We'd love to hear your thoughts.

🐦

#PatrickNessBurn
@WalkerBooksUK
@WalkerBooksYA

📷

@WalkerBooksYA
@patricknessbooks